"It's not proper for us to be in a bedroom together, Will,"

Cassie said in a harsh whisper.

He grinned. "We've been sleepin' together for better than two weeks already. Unless you want to go down there and tell my ma that we're not the married couple she thinks we are, we're stuck with this until I can figure something out."

"Once we sleep in this room together, we're stuck with the story, no matter how you slice it," she hissed at him.

"Well, I can't come up with any better idea," Will said softly. "I'm afraid your reputation is about shot, Cass. And it's my fault. Do you want me to go downstairs and tell my mother we've traipsed clear from Texas without being married?"

She shook her head. "I don't know what I want. I just know I don't want to ~~sleep in the bed with~~ you tonight!"

Dear Reader,

It's June, so start thinking about your summer reading! Whether you're going to the beach or simply going to relax on the porch, don't forget to bring along a Harlequin Historical® novel. This month we are delighted with the return of the immensely popular Carolyn Davidson. Carolyn is a self-described writer of "farm love" whose stories feature hardworking, masculine heroes and strong family ties. Never is this more obvious than in *Runaway*, the story of a young woman who, hours after her mother's death, fatally wounds her stepfather in self-defense and is rescued by a kind cowboy, who takes her back to his parents' Missouri home as his "wife."

Widow Woman, by long-time Silhouette author Patricia McLinn, is a compelling Western about a beautiful rancher who must win back the heart of her ex-foreman—the man she once refused to marry and the unknowing father of her child. Laurel Ames returns with *Infamous*, in which a dashing nobleman and spy, having put up with a very silly and snobbish mother and sister all his life, finally meets a woman he feels is worth pursuing—much to his family's chagrin!

Rounding out the month is *Midsummer's Knight* by award-winning author Tori Phillips. Here, a confirmed bachelor and a reluctant widow betrothed against their will switch identities with their friends to spy on the other, and fall in love in the process!

Whatever your tastes in reading, you'll be sure to find a romantic journey back to the past between the covers of a Harlequin Historical® novel.

Sincerely,

Tracy Farrell
Senior Editor

Carolyn Davidson

Runaway

ISBN 0-373-29016-0

RUNAWAY

Copyright © 1994 by Carolyn Davidson

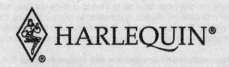

HARLEQUIN®

TORONTO • NEW YORK • LONDON
AMSTERDAM • PARIS • SYDNEY • HAMBURG
STOCKHOLM • ATHENS • TOKYO • MILAN • MADRID
PRAGUE • WARSAW • BUDAPEST • AUCKLAND

ISBN 0-373-29016-0

RUNAWAY

Books by Carolyn Davidson

Harlequin Historicals

Gerrity's Bride #298
Loving Katherine #325
The Forever Man #385
Runaway #416

CAROLYN DAVIDSON

Writing about small towns, ranches and farms comes naturally to Carolyn Davidson, who hails from a long line of farmers on her mother's side. From her father's side of the family, a strain of Gypsy blood lent flights of fancy to the mix, creating a child with a wild imagination. In her early years she made up stories to tell her nieces and nephews; as a teenager she wrote them in notebooks.

Then came marriage to her high school sweetheart, a union that thrives today and has produced six children. Only when the nest was empty did she try her hand at serious writing. Serious, as in love and marriage. Romance, in a word. After selling seven novels during the past few years, she has decided that writing is far and away the most exciting venture she has embarked upon.

Be sure to look for Carolyn's next book, *The Wedding Promise,* available in October 1998. Readers' comments are more than welcome in her mailbox, P.O. Box 60626, North Charleston, S.C. 29419-0626.

To old friends, who only improve with age.
To childhood memories and growing-up years. To those
who have shared my life and enriched it—but especially
to cousins Shirley and Kate, my first friends, who have
wonderful staying power. And, as always—to Mr. Ed,
who loves me.

Prologue

North Texas, 1894

His hands curved, fingers spread, as if ripe peaches waited to be grasped and held against his palms. But the avid, greedy heat of his gaze focused not on a tempting display of fruit, but on the gently rounded breasts of the young woman across the room from where he stood.

"Your mama would have wanted me to look after you, Cassie." Thin and rasping, his voice grated on her ears, and the girl backed another step closer to the doorway.

"I'll take good care of you, girl." He'd begun to wheedle now, and she recognized the direction of his thoughts. She'd seen him, heard him distract her mother with his coaxing, whining small tributes to her fading beauty, until he could reach out and grab the woman he'd sorely misused for three years.

One more step and she would be within sight of freedom. One small glide to the right, the careful easing of her foot past his rumpled pile of clothing, and she would flee. She could outrun him, once she made the doorway. He'd had enough to drink, waiting for Cleta's last breath to sigh past her ashen lips, to make him clumsy, to make his voice slur as he spoke.

"Your mama's barely cold. We need to see to her buryin', you and me." He lifted his grimy hand to swipe beneath his nose, and Cassie's flesh crawled, as if hundreds of small worms moved beneath her skin.

She slid her foot a few inches, brought the other to meet it and caught sight of filtered sunlight, patterned across the floor of the next room. Her hands flattening on the wall behind her, she groped for the curved molding marking the doorway.

"Don't be thinkin' you'll run off, girl. We got things to settle here. Your mama told me you'd need lookin' after, and who better than your pa to tend to you." The same hand he'd smeared beneath his nose extended toward her, the ragged fingernails rough against her arm, and she bolted.

Shuddering at his touch, she rounded the doorway, blinking at the sunlight, her eyes accustomed to the dark bedroom. She'd huddled next to the lumpy mattress for hours, tending the woman who'd lost almost all resemblance to the mother she remembered.

"Come back here, young'un!" Remus Chandler plunged after her, his lips drawn back, his tobacco-stained teeth bared in a grim travesty of a smile. His curved fingers snagged the fringe of her shawl and he tugged sharply.

It was a simple choice, and Cassie made it without a second thought. Releasing the hold she'd maintained during the night hours, when the shawl had been a matter of warmth, she relinquished it into his keeping. She scampered across the outer room, past the rough table that held the remnants of Remus Chandler's breakfast, along with the dirty plate from his meal last night.

Was it only yesterday when she'd found her mother

curled on the bed, breath rasping as if she must conserve each small measure of air? Cleta had mumbled words of instruction against Cassie's cheek. Words that warned of the evil inherent in the man she had married, both mother and daughter long since ruing the day.

"Run, child. Get away…Remus…hide, Cassie." Cleta's frail voice had moaned the broken phrases and Cassie had brushed countless kisses against her mother's brow, whispering words of assurance in reply.

"I'll be fine, Mama. Rest easy now." She'd cried her tears in the months gone by, and now her eyes were dry, burning from the sleepless night. Hours without rest had left her body weary, but her mind and senses were sharpened, honed by the fear instilled in her by her mother. Remus Chandler was cruel, rotten to the core, and her legal stepfather. Only the needs of the frail woman who'd borne her had served to keep Cassie within the man's clutches.

Now his groping hand tugged at her dress, sharp fingernails digging at the flesh beneath, and Cassie cried out at the indignity of it. She reached back to snatch the cloth from his grasp and met the bony grip, his fingers wrapping around her wrist.

"Let go of me, you filthy bastard!" As if it were familiar to her lips, the curse was spit in his direction, and he met it with a snarl.

"I'll teach you to talk to your pa thataway, girl!" His other hand reached for her and he shoved her to the wall, slamming her head against the logs.

Pitching her slight weight against him, she retaliated, and caught him off balance. Together, looking like a tipsy pair of dancers in a barroom, they slid across the floor, Remus tottering, Cassie shoving him in a desperate attempt to free herself from his grasping hands.

The table was against his back and his whiskey-laden

breath was foul in her nostrils when he pulled her flush against his scrawny body. She reached to balance herself on the table, and her fingers met the sharp side of the knife he'd used to saw at his stringy beef last night.

She grasped at it, unaware of the slice she inflicted across her palm. Allowing the knife to slide within her clasp, she gripped the bone handle with a fierceness that radiated to her very soul.

Lifting the weapon, she plunged it to the hilt. It entered his back just next to his shoulder blade, the tip exploring the very center of his heart.

Chapter One

It looked like a bundle of clothing, tossed by the side of the stream, until he caught sight of a bare foot emerging from the froth of undergarments.

If Will had had his druthers, he'd have finished watering his horse and gone on his way without a second glance. But the upbringing he'd received at his mother's knee, way back when, would not allow such a thing to happen.

Looking into the face of death would be disruptive to his morning, but over the years he'd managed to inure himself to the sight. So it was with a sigh of resignation that he nudged the toe of his boot beneath the middle of the shabby bundle of clothing and lifted the slight form buried within.

The body rolled, the foot being joined by a second as it slid even farther from the protective folds of fabric surrounding it. Two rounded calves, pale against the grassy slope, caught his eye. Then a slender arm that had covered her face fell beneath her, exposing a length of dark hair, a bare shoulder and the profile of a young girl.

"I'll be damned!" Whether he was relieved by the flutter of eyelashes that bespoke life or aggravated by the responsibility he'd taken upon himself with his investigation was a moot question. Will was on his way to parts north, and

being attached in any way to a female—and especially one
as young as this—was not a part of his plan.

He squatted, reaching with one finger to nudge at the
bare shoulder. "Hey there, missy! Let's take a look at
you."

The eyelids ceased fluttering, the nostrils flared and the
mouth opened.

The finger he'd poked her with joined the other three just
in time to curve across her mouth, stifling the scream he'd
figured would be greeting him. What he hadn't figured on
was the set of even white teeth that nipped sharply at him,
just as the creature within the bundle of female clothing
rolled from his touch.

Already too close to the bank of the stream for any degree of safety, she plunged with amazing speed into the
gently rippling water. Within seconds, the flurry of movement spurred Will into action. Kneeling in the spot the girl
had occupied, he reached one hand to grasp at an arm that
was groping from the surface of the water.

She was small, slim and supple, but weighed down by
the dress and petticoats she wore, and his muscles bunched
and flexed as he hauled her from the water. Hoisting himself to his feet, he dragged her up the creek bank, both
hands full of wet clothing, then held her before him.

Her dark hair hung in wet strings across her face, and
her eyes squinted shut against the water. Coughing and gag-
ging, she clung to his arms, sagging as if her legs would
not hold her erect. The blue dress was torn, exposing her
right arm and shoulder and the very top of a lush, curving
breast.

Hell's bells! This was no kid, no youngster in need of
rescue. He'd just managed to get himself tangled up with
a woman, full grown from the looks of it. And of all the

things in this world Will Tolliver didn't need, a stray female topped the list.

She'd coughed her way out of choking to death at least, and her legs seemed better able to hold her upright. He eased his grip on her shoulders, noting idly the texture of her skin as his fingers slid over the wet surface.

And then she looked at him. Opening her eyes, blinking several times at the sunlight, she gaped at him.

Eyes like the forget-me-nots his mother had growing by the outhouse took his measure. Blue as the summer sky, edged with a darker rim and surrounded by a fringe of black lashes that clumped together with a residue of water from the stream, those eyes made a journey from the top of his head to the middle of his chest and then back.

"Who are you?"

It was a woman's voice, sure enough, he decided. Low pitched, holding only the faintest tremor, it issued from a soft mouth that trembled and then stilled its giveaway movement as she clamped her lips together.

The shivers racking her body were another matter altogether. Only a warm fire and dry clothing would solve that particular problem, and with a sigh of aggravation, Will set about bringing it to pass.

"My name's Tolliver," he grunted. "And takin' care of a half-drowned female is a far sight from what I had planned for today."

Her eyes widened at his words, and she planted her feet more firmly against the creek bank. "Then take your hands off me, mister, and make tracks. Nobody asked you to wake me up and shove me into the stream."

Will plopped her down where she stood, only too aware of the clinging fabric of her dress and undergarments, resisting the urge to tug the wet material into place over the rise of her bosom.

Bad enough to be needing a woman's touch for longer than he could remember. Even worse was standing here eyeing this female's form, bosom half exposed to view, and him randy as a barnyard rooster.

His sigh of resignation was deep and heartfelt. "Sit right there and don't move. I'm gonna build a fire and find you something to put on." He turned from the sodden lump she'd become with his urging, her arms winding around her knees, bent almost double to better warm herself.

"Yes, all right," she said grudgingly, her eyes wary as she watched him head for his horse and pack mule. Within moments he'd stripped the mule of a bulky, canvas-wrapped bundle and begun rooting around in its depths. With a grunt that appeared to signify success, he pulled out a nondescript shirt, slinging it over his shoulder. It was wrinkled, but looked to be fairly clean. A pair of heavy stockings came next, joining the shirt, and then a pair of trousers.

"Tolliver?" Her voice had lost its tremor, but not the low, sultry sound he'd noted right off.

"Yeah?" He looked back at her over his shoulder. She was too young to sound so damn womanly, he decided. Her face was sunburned across her nose and forehead, freckles dotting her cheeks and joining across the bridge of her narrow nose. The dark hair was long, hanging almost to the ground as she crouched before him.

"Thank you for pulling me out of the water. I can't swim." The words were grudging, but issued in a polite form that suggested she had just remembered her manners. Blowing ineffectively at a lock of hair that hung just in front of her right eye, she looked up at him.

"You wouldn't have been in the water if I hadn't scared you into jerking away from me," he told her after a moment. Fair was fair, and the girl was trying to be decent.

She was probably scared to death of him, too much so to get up and run, lest he be after her.

"Were you serious about building a fire?" Shivering as she spoke, she hugged herself even tighter as she rocked in place.

"Soon's I find you enough warm clothes to put on." He searched another moment, then cast her a glance. "You'll have to do without underwear. I seem to be scrapin' the bottom here."

A faint flush crept up her cheeks, joining the sunburn. "I'm sure anything will do, as long as it's dry and big enough."

His laughter was short and harsh. "This shirt will wrap around you a couple of times, if my eyes serve me right. Don't know about the pants. You'll have to find that out the hard way, I suspect."

Stuffing the clothing into a compact bundle, he headed back to where she sat. "I'll gather up some firewood and get it going while you get those wet things off." He waved his hand at a nearby thicket, where bushes and undergrowth vied for space near the stream.

The girl rose quickly, with a sinuous grace, her arms wrapped around herself, as if she would hold against her skin whatever small amount of warmth she had garnered. One hand reached for the proffered bundle, snatching it from him quickly, her eyes barely meeting his before she headed for the shelter he'd suggested.

Her clothing clung, draping her in a wet, dingy array, another tear exposing one shoulder blade, the hem of her dress trailing a torn portion in the dirt as she walked. And walk she did…her hips moving, that wet dress emphasizing the curve of her bottom.

A bruise caught his eye, the discoloration dark against her skin, showing through the torn part of her dress on her

back. Either she'd been in one dickens of a fuss with someone, or she'd fallen and gotten herself scraped up somehow.
Whichever, she was shivering and about at the end of her
tether, so far as he could tell.

If he had his directions right, he was about ten miles or
so from either the small settlement of Loco Junction or the
town of St. Catherines. And which one this woman had
come from was a moot question. Certainly, she'd not
walked more than ten miles, unless she had shoes hidden
on her person or tossed aside beneath the trees before she'd
made her bed by the water.

His gaze traveled again to encompass the form that was
even now disappearing behind the bushes, and he grunted,
a low, negative sound that echoed his mood. Nowhere
beneath that clinging mass of clothing was there hiding
anything so cumbersome as a pair of shoes. Indeed, the
arrangement of the girl's body was a pure line from head
to toe, unblemished by any bulge or lump other than those
she'd come by through the process of just being a woman.
And every one of those were in fine shape, her bottom
being a prime piece of work if he'd ever seen one.

His fire was ablaze, the dry leaves and kindling he'd set
to burning well covered by larger pieces of dead wood, by
the time she reappeared. She'd buttoned the shirt partway
and was clutching the waistline of his spare pants just beneath the fourth shirt button. His stockings were barely in
sight beneath the multiple folds of pant legs, and she took
mincing steps as if she feared dislodging the clothing before
she reached him.

"Need some help there?" Will offered, crouched next to
the fire, his eyes peering from beneath the brim of his hat.

"Do you have a piece of rope or a belt, maybe?" Her
hair hung down her back, making wet stains on the gray

shirt he'd loaned her, and the sleeves were folded several times.

He'd solved one problem. She was more than covered from his view.

"I should have a spare belt." The bundle of clothing was at hand and he dipped into it once more, coming up with a braided leather length from its depths. "This oughta work. Come here."

She halted, her eyes wary as she considered his words. "Toss it to me. I'll figure it out myself." One hand reached toward him and he shrugged, rolling the leather before he cast it in her direction, across the fire.

She caught it deftly and fed it through the belt loops, tying it in an awkward knot at her middle. One final tug at her handiwork seemed to satisfy her, and she lifted her head to look at him again.

"Do you have any extra food? I'm afraid I can't pay you any money, but I'll write you a due note. As soon as I'm able, I'll make it right with you." Her tongue touched her top lip and she tilted her head, fussing with the remaining buttons on her shirt. "I'd rather not go back toward Loco Junction, if you don't mind. Any place north of here will do nicely."

His eyes narrowed, his mouth twisting briefly. "A man never turns down a stranger's need for food out here, honey. Hard to say when I might be in the same boat. I'll share what I have."

She nodded, accepting his offer, then hunkered down by the fire. As if the beckoning heat gathered all of her energy, she slumped where she sat, her head drooping, her arms wrapped about her knees, her eyes closing.

Setting to work with a measure of reluctance, Will put together a meal of sorts, unwrapping biscuits he'd made early in the day by another campfire. He settled a frying pan over the glowing coals, filling it with thick slices of bacon from his pack. As the bacon fried he added chunks of cooked potatoes, left from last night's supper. He'd baked several in the coals, saving two for today. From the looks of the girl, she'd be more than able to eat her share.

The scent of bacon and the coffee he'd put to boil roused her after a few minutes and she raised her head, sniffing and blinking, her mouth rosy as she warmed finally from her chill. Her hair had begun to dry, curling around her face, and she gathered it together, her slender fingers twisting in its length to braid it quickly.

"Do you have a piece of string I could use?"

"You can leave it hang, honey. I don't mind seein' the curls." His gaze moved from stilled fingers, still holding the end of her hastily fashioned braid, to meet her own, wary and dark with apprehension.

With a short oath, born of aggravation but heartfelt nonetheless, he reached into the depths of his pack once more. His fingers snatched at a short length of twine, filched from the seemingly bottomless bundle of supplies he was raiding for her benefit, and handed it to her.

She wrapped it in a familiar gesture around the end of her braid and tossed the braid over her shoulder, letting it hang down her back.

"When was the last time you ate?" He glanced at her as he spoke, making a quick survey, taking in the weariness she took pains to conceal. The sleep she'd snatched beside the stream had done little to freshen her, if the circles beneath her eyes were anything to go by.

"Yesterday." She eyed him defensively as he pursed his lips. "Maybe the day before," she added grudgingly, leaning once more toward the warmth of the fire.

He dished up a plateful from his skillet and held it out in her direction. Her eagerness stifled by good manners, she took it from him and snatched up a piece of bacon dangling from the edge of the metal dish. Delicately she bit off a mouthful, her eyes closing as she chewed.

"I reckon you were hungry, all right," he said, scraping the rest of the food onto another plate. Handing her a fork, he watched as she set to with a will, almost neglecting his own meal as he watched her. And then he ate slowly, lest she'd make her way through the food he'd allotted her and still be looking for more. It went against his grain to see a woman go hungry.

The last bite disappeared past her lips and she sighed, savoring the flavor. "Thanks, Tolliver. That was good." She straightened, her blue eyes focusing on him. "Do you have an extra cup? That coffee smells wonderful."

He nodded. "Yeah. Dig one outta that bundle." Motioning with his thumb, he sent her in the direction of his mule, where another pack lay open on the ground, having yielded cooking utensils and matches for the fire.

She rose gingerly, as if various aches and pains had made themselves known, and stepped to where his supplies were stashed. Squatting, she sorted carefully through his belongings, as if she would touch only what he had given permission for. A metal cup filled her hand and she turned back to where he sat. He'd filled his own cup to the brim and waited, coffeepot in hand, for her return.

"Thanks." She lowered herself to the ground, watching carefully lest she spill the steaming brew, as if unwilling to waste a drop of it. Her hands curled around the cup, shifting from the heat as she sipped, then she placed it on the ground beside her.

"Where'd you come from?" He'd leaned back, tilting his hat forward a bit, his eyes in shadow.

"Does it matter?" she asked, her lashes fluttering as she lowered her gaze to the fire.

"Nope, I reckon not." Sipping once more at his coffee, he narrowed his eyes, silently assessing her appearance. She was young, probably not yet twenty.

Her clothing had been well made, but the dress had undergone a heap of wear and tear. And then there was the matter of a lack of shoes. Her feet were dirty and bruised up a bit, now that he took a good look at them. Maybe she had walked barefoot after all. At least ten miles, if he had it figured right.

"Loco Junction." She cast him a sidelong glance as she offered the information. "But I'm not going back there."

"Your choice." His shrug signified his uninterest. And then his next words belied the gesture. "Looks to me like you're on the run, honey."

"Maybe." She glanced up at him, catching his sardonic grin, and she flushed, her chin tilting defensively. "I'm on the run."

"Want to tell me about it?"

She shook her head. "I don't think so. It doesn't matter, anyway. I'm not going back."

"Somebody after you?"

She looked up quickly, peering to see his eyes beneath the wide brim of his hat. "I hope not. But I wouldn't be a bit surprised."

"You steal anything?" Withdrawing a narrow-bladed knife from its sheath inside his boot, he inspected his fingernails, then cleaned them as she watched.

"I've never stolen anything in my life." She lifted her cup and drank the dregs of coffee, savoring the last drops.

"You in bad trouble?" Glancing up, he caught the quickly indrawn breath, the telltale flaring of her nostrils as she searched for an answer to his query.

"You can just go on and leave me here if you want to.

I'll be fine.'' Her mouth was set in a thin line, her jaw firm, her eyes trained on his left shoulder.

His laugh was rasping as he considered her chances, adrift in this country. Northern Texas was raw, rough territory, not fit for a woman alone.

''You got any idea how long you'd last out here by yourself?'' he asked, his long, elegant fingers precise as he slid the knife back inside his boot. He looked up quickly, hoping to catch a stray emotion, perhaps a sign of indecision on that sunburned face. She'd tightened her lips, hiding behind a sullen countenance.

''What are my choices?''

''How old are you, girl?'' She made him feel a hundred and one, this child masquerading in a woman's body. She'd offered no payment for his protection, asked no favors but for the food she'd eaten, leaving herself wide open to the perils inherent to the situation she was in. That he could have had any answers he wanted with a few probing questions, or a threatening movement in her direction, was a fact, he figured.

''What's your name?'' He threw the question in, then felt a twinge of compassion as she frowned at him. The arrogance had not suited her; the indecision did. She'd not lived long enough to build a protective shield, not played poker with men like Will Tolliver.

''Cassie. My name's Cassie Phillips.'' She'd decided to trust him with that much, the indecision fading from her eyes. Her mouth pouted for just a few seconds, and then she told him what he wanted to know. ''I'm eighteen…almost.''

''Damn! You're just a kid. Who turned you loose out here? He needs to be hung by his—'' He tugged his hat from his head, his strong fingers plowing through his hair, furrowing the dark, straight length of it.

"I'm not a child. I don't need anyone." She delivered the ultimatum in a terse undertone, her teeth gritting on the final words, and he was unwillingly touched by the stalwart strength of her.

"Well, I'm headin' north." He'd made her an offer. If she took it, so be it. If she wanted to dillydally around in this godforsaken spot between two hellholes, he'd—

"Are you saying you'll take me along?"

"Yeah, I guess I am. I'll take you along till we can find a place for you to stay. Maybe some preacher and his wife somewhere along the way will give you a home, let you work for your keep." He latched on to the thought. It sounded respectable, plausible even.

She considered it, her eyes calculating, and once more he was amused by the transparency of her features. "I'm not overly fond of preachers."

"One of 'em chase you out of town?"

Her flush was indignant. "Hardly. Loco Junction didn't welcome decent ministers. The only one I've seen lately was the one who came knocking on our door late one night, hoping to find my mother home alone." Her mouth tightened and she closed her eyes, as if that particular memory still rankled.

He nodded. "All right. We'll figure something else out. Maybe a farmer. Maybe you could work in a store." Cassie looked doubtful, and Will shook his head. He'd about run out of ideas, and the ones he'd proposed hadn't been much to speak of. But he added, "Since we'll be traveling together, you'd better call me Will."

She sure was a piece of work, with that long hair and curvy backside. His mouth drew down as he forced that thought from his head. Clearly the girl was an innocent, yet he was hard put to rid his mind of the memory of a softly rounded breast and long slender legs, wrapped in a sopping wet dress.

She was a temptation, all right. But one he had no business dwelling on, if he planned to carry her with him. And it looked as if he was about to do that very thing.

Chapter Two

She'd awakened twice during the night from the same nightmare, her heart pounding, her eyes searching the dark- ness. He'd been there both times, his hands firm as they pressed against her shoulders, his voice ragged but soothing as he murmured phrases of comfort.

Cassie's eyes filled with tears and she blinked them from existence. Crying was a luxury she hadn't allowed herself in a long time. She wasn't about to allow the hands and voice of a stranger to reduce her to childish behavior.

For just a moment she remembered the warmth of those long fingers as they'd clasped her, their gentle strength pen- etrating the worn cotton of the shirt she wore. He'd shaken her, just enough to get her attention, to pull her mind from the enveloping horror of the dream. And she'd reached for him.

Her face hot with shame, she remembered groping in the dark, grasping the front of his shirt, burying her face against his masculine form. He'd held her there, one hand cupping the back of her head, the other across her shoulders. Just for a moment, until she'd realized where she was, that the bosom she rested against bore no resemblance to that of her mother.

She'd pulled away then, and he'd let her go. He'd delivered one final grunt of instruction as he rose to his feet, a growling admonition to go back to sleep, and then he'd stretched out on his blanket and turned his back.

Men were cunning creatures, she'd decided just months after her mother had married Remus Chandler. He'd been all sweetness and light until the first time her mother had not done his bidding to his exact standards. His hands had been weapons, used often, and Cassie had been safe from him only because of her mother.

Will seemed to be a different sort, gruff and not given to gentle behavior, though she couldn't fault his actions in the middle of the night. That she'd been held in his arms was a wonder. That she'd tolerated his touch was almost a miracle, given her dread of most men.

They'd traveled for several hours yesterday, she perched on the broad back of his stallion, clinging to the leather of his saddle. He'd lifted her in place and hoisted himself into the saddle with care, with only a cursory glance at her stocking feet and a muttered curse as his horse danced in place, protesting the double load.

She'd been almost asleep, her head nodding against his broad back, when he'd stopped for the night. Grateful for the blanket he'd handed her, she'd slumped to the ground without a murmur.

She blinked, the call of a bird shrill in her ears. It was the piercing, territorial warning of a blue jay, and she scrunched her eyes against the brilliant hues of sunrise. Her gaze flew to the blanket on the other side of the clearing, the empty space where Will Tolliver had spent the night.

And then she heard him, heard the same gruff tones he'd used against her ear, speaking morning greetings to his animals. She sat up, the better to locate his direction, and

found that he was behind her, not more than twenty feet
distant. Twisting around, she met his gaze.

"Morning." His nod accompanied the brief greeting, and
she responded in kind.

Her body rebelled as she arose, her legs and feet aching
a protest. The walking she'd done had been off the beaten
path—her instincts had told her to stay clear of the trail—
and her feet had borne the brunt of it. Unable to stand with
any degree of comfort, she lowered herself to the ground
once more, gingerly rolling her borrowed stockings down
to uncover her toes, bending to inspect them. She frowned
as her fingers traced the bruising from multiple scrapes
she'd managed to inflict.

"Think if you washed them they'd look a little better?"

Her eyes narrowed as she heard the dry humor behind
his suggestion. "Not a whole lot," she allowed, rising with
a muffled groan, stepping gingerly as she passed him by.

"There's a pond just beyond those trees," he told her,
pointing the way. "It won't hurt to dangle your feet in the
water a bit. Might make them feel better."

"Thanks." She limped past, following his direction.
Leaving her shoes behind had been a mistake of major pro-
portions, one she'd regretted more than once during the
hike she'd undertaken. And then there was another regret.
Her conscience had been sorely pierced by the memory of
her mother's body, and her not seeing to a decent burial.
Although the best she could have done was barely fit to
mention.

Besides, Mama's soul was surely in heaven, far removed
from the man who'd made her life a torment.

Lastly, there was the small matter of Remus Chandler.
Her landing in jail if she'd hung around was almost a certainty. Whether or not she was being pursued by the law
was the thing she needed to consider.

Cassie sat on the bank of the shallow pond, gingerly breaking the surface of the water with her toes. Chilly, but not icy, she decided, scooting forward until her feet were covered by the water.

"Want some soap?"

He'd come up behind her, and she jerked in response to his query. "You could let a body know you're prowling around," she said sharply. His boots moved beside her and he squatted inches away, his hand holding the narrow piece of hard soap.

She took it, glancing up into dark eyes that pierced her with silent reproach. Their hands brushed, her fingers curling around his offering, and then she relented.

"Thanks for waking me up during the night. I don't usually have bad dreams." It was a gruff acknowledgment of his kindness, about the best she could come up with.

He rocked on the balls of his feet, balancing beside her. "We all take a turn with nightmares sometime in our lives, Cassie. I've had my share." He dropped a dingy towel into her lap, rising to his feet. "I'll take a look at your feet after you clean 'em up a little. Breakfast will be ready shortly."

"Thank you." She'd dreaded seeing him in the daylight, but he'd made it easy on her. Of course, she still hadn't actually faced him, other than that one glance. She bent over, lifted one foot and set to work. Maybe the soap would help. Maybe there was more dirt than bruises.

"Damn, you sure beat up these poor feet of yours. You're not used to goin' barefoot, are you?" Will lifted her foot for his appraisal and shook his head at the sight. She'd suffered numerous small cuts from stones, and what skin wasn't scratched up by the rough ground was nicked by bushes she'd tramped through. Already healing, her feet had responded well to the soap and water.

Now he added the benefit of alcohol to the treatment he'd prescribed. His bottle of whiskey, wrapped in another shirt, had been at the bottom of his saddlebag and he'd poured out a small measure into his cup.

"That burns!" she cried, curling her fingers into fists, drawing her shoulders high, watching as he scrubbed at each scratch with a whiskey-soaked cloth.

"It'll burn worse if these start to fester up." He held one foot high, her heel resting in his palm. "I'm usin' my good whiskey on you, girl. Don't give me any grief."

She bit her lip, holding back the remark she'd been about to make. As far as she was concerned, whiskey wasn't good for much, other than washing out wounds and making hot toddies. It certainly hadn't improved Remus Chandler's disposition any. Rotgut was what her mother had called it, that vile stuff Remus had swigged down with great regularity. Cassie shuddered at the memory.

"Cold?" Will Tolliver asked. "You'd better toughen up. It's still pretty chilly up north."

Cassie lifted her foot from his grasp, placing it cautiously on the blanket where she sat. She eyed it carefully. Another day of healing and it would be fit to walk on, she figured. "I'm not cold, just took a chill." She met his gaze. "Are you going home? That where you're from?"

"Not lately. Not since I was just a kid, settin' out to see the country."

"Did you? See the country, I mean?" She leaned forward and took the stockings from him, then carefully covered her feet with them. One more thing she'd be owing him for.

"Saw Texas and parts west," he told her, shifting to one knee. "'Course, I don't think anybody's ever seen all of Texas. It just goes on beyond what most folks consider civilization, right down to the border."

"Now you're going home?" She tugged the stockings up, then covered them with the rolled-up cuffs of his trousers. His eyes had been on her movements, and she flushed as she recognized his interest in the pale flesh of her calves and ankles. His fingers had been gentle on her feet, their touch sending slivers of fire on a race through her that had little to do with the whiskey's potency. It seemed she was not immune to his style of doctoring, nor the gruff tenderness he dispensed.

"Yeah, I'm headed home."

"You don't sound very happy about it," she said quietly, squinting against the sun's rays as she looked up at him.

His smile was a grimace. "I've been happier, like when I faced a whippin' from my pa, or had to split a cord of firewood before breakfast." He rose quickly, offering her his hand. "Come on, we're wastin' time talkin' and the day's half-gone."

"Half-gone?" She eyed the sun, barely visible through the trees. "It can't be more than eight o'clock or so."

"I'm saddlin' up, Cassie. If you're ridin' along, you'd best be ready to go."

She looked around the clearing, trees on three sides, beyond them the trail leading back to Loco Junction, now at least thirty miles away.

Crouched beside his belongings, Will delved deeply into the pack holding his personal things, muttering beneath his breath as he sorted through the miscellany of his scant supplies. A grunt signified success and he hoisted himself to his feet, a brown-paper-wrapped package in one hand.

"Here." He tossed it in her direction as he glared at her, his lowered eyebrows adding a menace to his look. "Bought those for my sister, back down the trail. They oughta fit you. She won't mind if you borrow them till we can find somethin' better for you to wear."

Cassie's fingers trembled as she unwrapped the soft bundle. A gift was to be enjoyed, even if it was just on loan. A pair of moccasins tumbled into her lap and she touched the supple leather with one finger, then lifted them to her nose to inhale the distinctive scent. He'd picked out pretty ones, beaded and sewn with careful stitches, and for a moment she envied the sister who merited such tender regard.

"Well, go ahead. Try 'em on." His tone was impatient and she cast him a glance of apology as she slid her stockinged feet within the soft leather protection of the shoes.

"They fit just fine." It was all she could manage, her throat filling with a strange tightness she could suppress only with a rapid blinking of her eyes. "Thank you." Her teeth pressed against her bottom lip as she stuck one foot out before her, displaying the beauty of his purchase to his view.

"They'll do."

Gruff and abrupt, his approval pleased her nonetheless, and she tucked away her pleasure at his thoughtfulness.

She watched him as he packed his gear, loading the mule in a systematic fashion, balancing his packs, one on either side, tugging and testing the ropes.

"Fold up that blanket and bring it here," Will called impatiently from the other side of his horse.

Cassie folded the rough fabric quickly and limped to where he worked at the cinch, watching as he pulled the stirrup into place. His hands reached for the blanket, and he arranged it behind his saddle, then lifted her with an ease that left her breathless, settling her as he had yesterday, astride the horse's back.

The animal shifted beneath her and she held the back of his saddle, balancing herself as the blanket slid in place.

"Whoa, there," he ordered sternly, approaching with the mule's lead line in hand. He wrapped it around the saddle horn twice, then eased his way up, his foot and leg coming perilously close as he seated himself in front of Cassie. Looking back at her over his shoulder, he scowled. "Hangin' on all right?"

She nodded. "Yes, I'm fine." Fine or not, it beat walking, and she'd be a fool to complain.

The noon meal was a godsend, as far as Cassie was concerned. Will had caught sight of a fat rabbit just ahead, and his gun had brought down the small game with one shot.

"My pa said you should never turn down a meal when it's offered," he said, lifting Cassie from behind his saddle. He pressed the blanket into her hands and led the animals to be tied to a nearby tree.

She spread the blanket and watched as he prepared the rabbit for their meal, his movements quick and knowledgeable. "Looks like you're an old hand at that," she said as he readied a fire, lighting the small pieces of kindling with a match from his pack.

His shoulders rose in a shrug. "Yeah, I guess. I was in charge of hunting game back home. If I didn't bring home a rabbit or squirrel—or better yet, a deer—once in a while, we didn't eat much meat those first couple of years on the farm. Ma said she wasn't wastin' her chickens on the dinner table. The eggs were worth more in town than the hens were, cookin' in a stew pot. We ate up the roosters, soon as they were big enough to fry, then it was back to the wild game."

"How many of you were there?" Cassie asked, crosslegged on the blanket, feeling useless in the face of his dinner preparations.

"Ma and Pa had four of us. My sister, Josie, and two other boys." Spitting the rabbit, he settled it over the fire, then mixed cornmeal with water from his metal flask. A small pan from his pack held the mixture, and he placed it on a rock at the edge of the coals.

"Will it cook like that?" She'd baked corn pone in an oven, but trail cooking was beyond her.

"The rock's pickin' up heat from the fire." He tossed a thick flannel pad her way. "Turn the pan once in a while. It oughta be done about the time the rabbit is."

She nodded agreeably. Will Tolliver was turning out to be the best thing that had happened to her in a long while. Whether he tired of her company in day or so, or if he took her as far north as he was heading, anything was better than her stepfather's shack in Loco Junction.

It had been a long slide downhill the past three years. Her flesh crawled as she thought again of the man her mother had married. She shivered, remembering the feel of the knife in her hand, shuddered as she recalled the flow of blood that had stained her fingers, pooling beneath Remus as he slumped to the floor.

I killed him. Cassie's eyes closed, then flew open as she beheld the vision of death she'd left behind. Lips pressed together tightly, she breathed the fresh air, the scent of meat roasting over the fire, the clean smell of freedom.

"We've got company." Will stood, a casual gesture, stepping a few feet from where she sat to stand next to his rifle, which was snugged against his pack.

Cassie felt the hair rise on the back of her neck, and turned her head to view the approaching horseman. Tall, rugged and riding as if he were a part of the animal he straddled, the man neared. His hat shielding his face, both hands visible on the reins, he rode in from the south, as if he had followed their trail.

"Howdy there, folks." He was within hailing distance and he slowed his horse to a walk. The animal nickered, and Will's big stallion responded, a shrill challenge, jerking on the reins that held him fast to a tree.

"Behave yourself, horse," Will growled, impatience tingeing his words, then he thumbed his hat back, calling out to the approaching horseman, "Hello yourself, stranger. You lost your way?"

The horse halted several yards away and the visitor lifted a hand to push aside his coat, revealing a silver star pinned to his shirt. "Nope, just takin' a look around." His gaze swept the area, a wide open space, only a few trees for shade and a sparsely grassed field. "You folks from hereabouts?"

"No, sir," Will answered, casting a quick glance at Cassie—a warning glance, if she was any judge.

"This your missus?" The lawman nodded at her, and Cassie dredged up a smile as his deep-set eyes scanned her from top to bottom.

"Yeah, this is Sarah Jane. I'm Will Tolliver, Sheriff."

Cassie caught her breath. In one short sentence she'd had her name changed and been tagged a married woman. Her smile trembled as she brought up one hand to shade her eyes.

"Haven't seen a young woman hereabouts, have you?" the lawman asked, his gaze still fixed on Cassie's borrowed clothing.

"A young woman?" Will looked perplexed, then glanced at his female companion. "We haven't noticed anyone around about, have we, honey?" His grin appeared then, his demeanor transformed as he kicked at a small stone with the toe of his boot. "Of course, we've been kinda…"

His pause was lengthy and he cleared his throat. "Well, we haven't been married too long, Sheriff, and we don't pay a whole lot of attention to anybody but ourselves, to tell the truth.''

''Is that so?'' The horse sidestepped and the lawman tightened up on his reins. ''Well, if you should come across a young gal, you might want to keep an eye out. She's wanted back in Loco Junction. The sheriff wants to talk to her.''

''Sorry to hear that,'' Will said, frowning and shaking his head. ''She considered dangerous?''

The sheriff nodded. ''Maybe so, under the right circumstances. She's pretty young. I'd hate to think of her bein' alone, out on her own.''

Cassie inhaled sharply and closed her eyes.

''I believe you've upset my wife, Sheriff. She's a quiet sort, my Sarah Jane.''

Cassie opened her eyes, forcing her mouth to curve in what she hoped looked like a shy smile, befitting Sarah Jane Tolliver. Her heart was thumping with an irregular beat, and she felt stifled by the weight of guilt pressing on her chest. Will Tolliver had lied for her. He'd put himself on the line.

''We'll sure keep our eyes open, Sheriff,'' Will said, easing back to the fire, turning the spit, even as he cast a look of warning at Cassie.

She returned it with a bland smile, wary of matching wits with the lawman, her eyes trained on the man who'd just claimed to be her husband. She watched as Will's fist uncurled, focused on the lean, strong fingers, the muscled forearm where his shirtsleeve was rolled almost to his elbow.

Her gaze swept higher and found his eyes intent upon her. From the brown depths he watched her, and she quailed beneath that look. As if he saw within her very soul, as if he could pierce her thoughts, discern the knowledge she held, his watchful eye penetrated her guise of calm control.

She'd managed to arrange her features in such a way that the sheriff had gone on his way, apparently not associating the shy young bride, Sarah Jane, with the woman who had wielded a knife in the town of Loco Junction. She'd managed to smile, hiding the thundering heartbeat, the clammy palms and the mouth that twitched alarmingly unless she held it firmly in place with the force of her will.

And the man before her had seen beyond all that. The unblinking look was less than an accusation; it held a question whose content she could only surmise.

"You never answered me, did you?" His tone was harsh. "I asked if you were in bad trouble, yesterday. And you offered me an easy out. You told me to go ahead and leave you there." He cast one last glance at the figure of the lawman, heading south on his horse at an easy canter, then bent to turn the spit once more.

Cassie cleared her throat. It was time to face the truth, as much as she was able. She'd accepted his help, allowed him to put his honor on the line for her. She'd trespassed on that honor in an unforgivable manner, and now she struggled, wishing she could make it right. Wondering if there was any way to apologize to a man for forcing him to lie outright to the law, placing him in a hazardous position.

"I didn't lie to you yesterday," she said, rising to stand before him. Somehow she felt more secure on her feet, as if she were better able to run, should it become necessary. Though thinking she could escape Will Tolliver was a foolish thought indeed.

"You didn't lie?" He repeated her words, his tone mocking, prompting her reply.

She shook her head. "I didn't lie. I just didn't tell you

the truth." Her mouth twisted and her hands fisted at her sides. "I ran off from my stepfather. He's a cruel man and I was afraid of him. That sheriff was probably looking for me. At least, the description fit."

His gaze narrowed on her. "You think so? He said he was looking for a young gal. Could be any one of a hundred women hereabouts." As if he reconsidered, he looked around him at the vast horizon, unmarred by human habitation. "Well, maybe twenty or so, anyway." His eyes softened, the darkness fading from his somber gaze.

"Sit back down, Cassie. I think it's time you told me what happened."

She obeyed, more because her legs were trembling beneath her than for any urge to oblige him. "Remus Chandler was...is my stepfather. I think maybe for a long time he wanted to..." She looked up, knowing her eyes were filling with tears, and choking back the need to cry.

Stripping the bandanna from his throat, Will handed it to her.

"Thank you." Cassie blew once and wiped her nose. "He'd been married to my mother for three years or so, and all that time he was mean to her, hateful sometimes, with his name-calling and pushing her around."

His eyes measured her, a bleak emotion darkening their depths. "Did he hurt you, Cassie?"

She shook her head. "No, not really. It was like he knew my mother would do what he wanted, to keep his hands from me. Anyway, she was sickly, really bad off for the past few weeks, like she was too tired to live anymore. She had a pain in her stomach, and she couldn't eat much. Not at all, there at the end. Remus wouldn't go for the doctor, and she told me not to cross him. He just kept watching me." Her voice trailed off and she gulped, swallowing the grief that had been postponed for too long.

''What happened then, Cassie?''

She drew in a deep breath, following his urging. ''Mama was bad all night long, hardly breathing. She told me to run, to leave, get away from Remus. And I promised her I would. I think she was afraid for me to be there with him, once she was gone.''

''How did your dress get torn?'' Will asked quietly.

Cassie's fingers ached from the squeezing, her fists clenching so tightly, she could barely release them. And then Will squatted before her.

''After she died, what did you do then?'' He clasped her cold fingers within his own, sharing the heat of his palms, giving warmth to the chilled flesh he cradled within his long, strong fingers.

''I was going to leave, but Remus wouldn't let me. He said I had to stay, that we had to tend to Mama's burying. When I tried to get away, he grabbed my shawl, then my dress. And he pushed me against the wall, cracked my head on the logs. I pushed him back but he kept grabbing at me, pulling me across the room, till he was smack up against the table. The knife he'd used for supper the night before was there and I grabbed it. See?''

She moved her fingers within his and spread her hand wide. The slash was shallow but swooped across her palm, scabbed over now. ''I heal fast,'' she said, her head down, her gaze on the wound.

''Maybe he would have left me alone if I'd gone to the sheriff in town...or someone.'' She shook her head. ''But I don't think so. He'd been after me for too long already. He couldn't even wait till Mama was in the ground. And I couldn't just stay there and let him hurt me...that way. I threatened him with the knife and he let go of me.''

A shudder racked her body, as if the telling of such a great lie had released the quaking within. Most of it was

the truth, all but the last part. And that she could not bring
herself to confide.

"He didn't chase you?" The thought of her peril sharpened his voice and she flinched from him, shaking her head.

"I don't know…maybe. I just ran." The lie came hard,
and she lowered her head.

"And you just walked out of town? Why didn't you wear
your shoes?"

"I couldn't go back once I'd left that place. My shoes
were in the bedroom with Mama, and I'd have had to get
past Remus to get them. I was afraid to try."

"Did you recognize that lawman, Cassie? Was he the
sheriff from Loco Junction?"

She looked up, her eyes welling, and shook her head. "I
don't know, Will. I've never seen the sheriff. It could be,
I suppose."

"Well, it doesn't matter now," he told her firmly. "If
we meet anyone else, you're Sarah Jane Tolliver. You're
my wife, Cassie. Can you do that? Until we get north into
Missouri, anyway?"

"You're going to take me with you?" She'd thought he
would find a place to leave her, somewhere safe that would
salve his conscience. Most any man would have either
taken advantage of her or dumped her at the first chance.

Obviously, Will Tolliver wasn't cut from the same cloth
as most other men. He was taking her home with him, if
she'd read him right. With his horse and pack mule, his
hands that knew how to heal and comfort, and his conscience that had to be churning away at the lie he'd told
for her benefit, he was heading north, and taking her along.

He'd placed his honor on the line for her and told a
whopper that could land him in a peck of trouble.

If ever there was a man in the world Cassie Phillips could respect, Will Tolliver was his name. And that fact alone was enough to keep her riding along in his wake, for now at least.

Chapter Three

"I think we've found a place to buy you a horse," Will announced, drawing his stallion to a halt. Cassie peered over his shoulder to where a ranch nestled in the shallow valley just ahead. In pole corrals, horses milled about, men in wide-brimmed hats and dust-laden clothing apparently directing the general flow.

"What are they doing?" Her chin brushing his shirt, Cassie watched the activity ahead.

"Looks like they're sortin' them out, branding, maybe." Will's hands were firm on the reins as his horse shifted beneath them, snorting as the scents from the corral reached the stallion's nose.

"I didn't know you were planning on buying another horse. Won't that be pretty expensive?"

"Beats ridin' double for the next week." As if he'd made up his mind, Will loosened the reins and nudged his mount into movement. "Stay still, Cassie. I'd as soon they didn't pay you too much attention."

Their arrival had little noticeable effect on the men at work, their ropes circling and snagging one or another of the herd of horses they worked with. The chosen animals were taken to a gate and led outside the enclosure, then inspected by a tall man who watched the proceedings, clearly in charge.

Circling the side of the corral, Will rode slowly up to the man, then slid from his saddle, his grip shortening the reins until his mount was left with no leeway to move.

"Those horses for sale, mister? I need a mare or a gelding." Halting several feet away, Will met the gaze of the older man as an Indian led another horse past him.

"There's some of each here, son." Lifting his hand, the man tilted his hat back, angling his head to enclose Cassie in his line of vision. "Don't know if the lady could handle one or not. They're green broke. Goin' to the army."

"Got any tack to sell? I'd need an extra saddle and bridle." Will waited while the man looked over another specimen, the horse jerking impatiently at the rope holding him. Then he nodded, waving the horse and the man leading it on their way.

"Probably some spare stuff in the barn," he told Will, his attention on another cowboy, approaching with a dusty brown mare from the pen. "Bring her closer," he told the rider. Then, reaching out a hand, he grasped the rope, drawing the horse before him. The animal's eyes rolled, the whites showing as she whinnied her distress.

"Kinda shy, are you?" It was a different voice he used now. Cassie listened as he murmured softly in rusty tones to the horse, his other hand untangling her mane, then patting with rough affection against her jaw. "Was she easy to lead?" he asked the cowboy, squinting up at him.

"Yeah, she followed along like a tame puppy."

As if to deny the claim, the mare snorted, tossing her head. Cassie laughed, the pure rebellion of the gesture pleasing her.

"Can I saddle her up, see how she rides?" Will asked. The big man shrugged. "She's gonna be sold today, either to you or the army. Makes me no never mind who gets her. She may dump you, now," he warned with a grin. "She looks kinda feisty to me."

"I reckon I can handle her."

It was no idle claim. During the next half hour Cassie watched from beneath the overhanging eaves of the barn as Will saddled the horse, catching her breath as he fought the animal for several seconds before the mare accepted the bit he offered.

And then she watched as he gained the saddle with a fluid movement that made her blink in surprise. The horse moved uneasily beneath the man on her back, snorting and laying her ears back, then sidestepping a bit. Will's hands were firm on the reins, his words gentle as he coaxed the horse to his bidding. Releasing the tight grip he held, he set her into motion, and she circled the area before the barn doors, her neck bowed, head tossing against the stricture of the bit. Her tail swished, waving high, her feet stepping in double time as she kept to the pace Will dictated.

"She's beautiful," Cassie breathed, her eyes wide as she watched the mare perform to Will's command. "But I don't think I can make her behave the way you do."

Turning the mare with the pressure of reins across her neck, Will drew closer. "You ride much, Cassie?"

She nodded. "A little. But not a horse this wild."

Will's mouth twitched. "You call this wild, honey? She's downright tame. 'Specially for a green-broke animal."

"Maybe I could ride your stallion?" Her words sounded doubtful, and Will's frown was a silent deterrent to that idea.

"The mare will follow along, I think, once you get your seat," he told her. "I'll lead her from here, till we're away from the rest of the horses, then you can try her on your own."

"You're going to buy her for me?" That Will would fork over his own money for the benefit of a virtual stranger was beyond Cassie's comprehension.

"No, I'm gonna buy her for me. I'll just let you ride her," he corrected her. "You stay right here while I talk to the man."

Cassie nodded, willing to be removed from the flurry of activity at the corral. She stepped to a bale of hay and sat, conscious of the pants she wore and the occasional looks of speculation drifting her way from one or another of the cowhands. There was an air about some of them, a hint of furtive searching of her person that reminded her of Remus Chandler, and she shivered at the memory.

From within the barn she heard the shuffling of feet, a murmur of voices, and then in the doorway beside her a man appeared, the strong odor of perspiration announcing his presence. Cassie glanced over her shoulder, her gaze colliding with narrowed eyes that slid over her slender form.

"Hey, there, missy. Want to step in here a minute?" His voice was low, almost guttural, and Cassie's eyes widened as another man appeared just behind the first.

She shook her head. "No, I sure don't, mister." A quick look toward Will, who stood near the corral, prompted her to speech and she opened her mouth to call his name. A grimy hand whipped through the air to cover her mouth, and she was hauled with harsh hands into the yawning mouth of the barn.

"No need to be shy, honey," her captor whined, releasing her mouth, turning her to face him. "I'll warrant I can cut you a better deal than the one you got from that fella you rode in with."

"Let go of me!" Cassie struggled against the grimy hands holding her.

"I'm not hurtin' you, honey. Just want to give you the taste of a real man."

The second assailant chuckled behind her and Cassie turned her head to shoot a vengeful glare in his direction. "I'm not interested," she said, her stomach rolling as she turned her head aside, avoiding his seeking mouth.

"The lady already has a man." From the shadows a third figure stepped into view and Cassie's eyes pinned him with the terror she made no attempt to hide.

"Outta here, half-breed." Snarled from the mouth she'd been trying so desperately to avoid, the words carried the stench of cigarettes. She gagged, turning from the fetid breath of the man holding her.

The Indian stepped closer, his lithe body tense as he surveyed the two cowhands. "Let her go." It was the bravest display Cassie had seen in a month of Sundays, this dark-skinned horseman confronting two white cowhands.

Gasping for breath, wiggling against the grimy hands that held her, Cassie flung herself in desperation toward the ground. Her legs collapsed beneath her and the man holding her lost his grip for a moment.

She inhaled and shrieked for Will, attempting to crawl toward the open barn door. The second man lurched toward her, grasping her ankle. She kicked out at him. His yelp of surprise spurred Will into a loping run, catching the attention of several other cowhands.

"Damn stinkin' Indian! Get movin'."

The two men had their hands full tussling with the Indian, who had blocked their exit, and Cassie scrambled to sit against the barn wall as Will burst through the doorway.

Cassie's bronze-skinned defender staggered into the shadow of a stall, reeling from a blow. Will ignored him, his hands fisting as he considered the two cowhands facing him. Barely pausing, he drew back to deliver a telling blow to the nearest of the pair.

The cowhand's head lolled to one side as he slumped to the floor. Without pause, Will swung to size up the second man. Cassie's eyes widened in dismay as her assailant's hand reached for his holster, drawing a gun even as he backed from the brief battle before him.

Dropping to the floor and rolling in automatic reflex, Will ducked as the bullet hit the wall behind him. He came to his feet smoothly, his hand flashing with the knife he had drawn from his boot. In one shimmering, underhand movement, the blade flew to lodge in the cowhand's shoulder. With a clatter, his gun fell to the barn floor.

"What the hell's goin' on in here?" The man from the corral stood in the doorway, his keen gaze focused on Will, then sweeping over the two cowhands and finally coming to rest on Cassie.

"You hurt, girl?" he asked bluntly.

"No, sir." She shook her head, pressing back against the wall, brushing distractedly at her clothing.

"You particularly attached to these men?" Will asked harshly.

"What did you have in mind?"

"I'm bleedin' bad," the wounded man whined, and then, at Will's vengeful glance, subsided.

"I'll pull out my knife, but that's all the help you'll get from me," Will told him, fury alive in each word. "If I had my way, you'd be on your way to a hangin' tree."

"She was askin' for it." He twisted his head to inspect his injury, then yelped as Will's hand grasped the handle of the knife and pulled it from the wound in a swift movement.

With contempt, Will wiped the blood from the blade

against the victim's pant leg, then slid it into the sheath inside his own boot. "You'd do well to shut up while you're still able to talk, mister, or the next thing she'll be askin' for is your head on a platter," Will said with deceptive mildness.

The cowhand stifled his muttering and appealed with an uplifted hand to his employer.

"I'll give you a rag to wrap your shoulder with, Hopkins, and then you'll be out of here. You'd be advised to make tracks before this gentleman changes his mind. From the way that knife stopped you dead, I'd say he's quite a hand in a fight."

Will turned to where Cassie sat against the wall, and dropped to one knee beside her. "Sure you're all right?" he asked. At her quick nod, he lifted her to her feet, steering her outside to sit atop a bale of hay.

"I'm sorry, Will," Cassie said softly. "I truly didn't say or do anything to give them leave to act that way."

"Just bein' here was enough of a nudge where men like those two are concerned." He tilted his hat back and surveyed her, his eyes still dark with the residue of anger. "You didn't do anything wrong, Cass. Just remember that."

With long strides he walked to where the older man stood. Gesturing toward the barn, he was sending several men on a mission, guaranteed to rid his operation of the pair of troublemakers. His look toward Will was apologetic, and his hand swept out in a gesture of respect.

Will grasped it firmly and shook it, then dipped his hand into his side pocket. Quickly he counted out cash, paying for the horse he'd chosen, and turned to where the mare was tied to the top pole of the corral.

Motioning Cassie to join him, he handed her the reins. "The fella's gonna write me up a bill of sale. We'll get some food from the house. Just have to tell the cook he sent us.'' Gathering up the reins of his stallion, Will started toward the house.

Breakfast had been scant—flat biscuits and some stringy, dried meat that required an enormous amount of chewing. Food freshly cooked would taste like manna from heaven, Cassie thought, trailing behind Will.

Tying the reins to a hitching rail near the back door of the big farmhouse, Will shot her a glance. ''Wait here. I'll only be a few minutes.''

Cassie nodded, then turned to the brown mare. She lifted one hand to touch the side of the animal's jaw, felt the flinch of alarm as the horse responded to the unaccustomed handling. ''It's all right, girl. It's all right,'' she murmured beneath her breath, feeling a measure of bravery as she increased the pressure of her stroking.

''You ride much, ma'am?'' From behind, the raspy voice startled her and Cassie jerked. The mare whinnied, tossing her head, and Cassie turned quickly.

The tall man from the corral had followed them, and now he eyed the young woman before him, her face flushed from the sun and no small amount of anger. ''She'll settle down,'' he said quietly. ''You married to that cowboy?''

Cassie swallowed, wary of the lie she must tell. Her chin tilted as she considered the man who watched her. ''Will Tolliver's my husband, yes,'' she said finally. ''I'm Sarah Jane Tolliver.''

''You're not in trouble, are you, Sarah Jane Tolliver?'' The eyes watching her narrowed a bit, taking on a speculative gleam as he awaited her reply.

Cassie stiffened, her gaze meeting his. ''No sir, mister. I'm not.''

''I've got a daughter about your age, girl. I'm not sure

I'd want her ridin' around the country dressed in a man's duds, drawin' the eye of every cowhand and stray Indian.''

Cassie's mouth firmed, her jaw tightening at his words. ''That Indian in the barn didn't hurt me.''

''You didn't answer me, girl. I asked if you do much ridin'.''

''Not much, lately. But Will says I can handle her all right.'' Cassie drew in a deep breath. ''Mister, that Indian in the barn was trying to help me.''

''He was part of the problem, miss. He's already on his way.''

She flinched at his words, but subsided, aware that nothing she said would make a difference.

His dark eyes gave her one more measuring look before he turned to the house. ''Here comes your husband now, ma'am. I told him to get some grub from the cook.'' His long fingers reached up to sweep the hat from his head and he nodded once in her direction. ''A pleasure to do business with you folks. I'm only sorry I had those roughnecks on my crew.''

''What did he say to you, Cassie?'' Will had helped her astride the saddle, adjusted the stirrups and snugged her moccasin-clad toes into them. Now he mounted his stallion, leading her horse behind him until the ranch was almost out of sight.

Cassie held fast to the saddle horn, riding the easy gait of the mare, aware of her swishing tail and the tossing of her head. ''I don't think he believed you, Will. He wanted to know if I was really your wife.''

''What did you tell him?''

''I lied, sort of.''

''I'll bet you blushed. Did he believe you?''

Cassie's mouth tightened and she unfastened the reins

he'd looped over the saddle horn, holding them firmly in her right hand. "I don't lie well," she admitted.

He turned to flash her a look of sober admiration. "I'm glad to hear that. My mama always said a man's word is his honor. If I have to start pickin' apart everything you tell me, we'll be in for a hard time together."

"My mama always said that lies multiply like flies. You have to tell another to hide the first, then another...." She caught her breath with a sob. "Let's not talk about mothers, all right?"

Will urged his stallion into a faster pace and cast a quick glance to check on Cassie. "You'd better leave those reins alone and let me lead your horse for now. We don't have time to talk about much of anything. We need to put some miles between us and Texas."

The darkness surrounding them drove Cassie close to the small campfire. She'd unrolled the blanket Will had assigned her and snuggled it around herself, her head resting on one corner of it. He'd chosen to sleep behind her instead of across the clearing, and her awareness of his presence was more than enough to keep her eyelids from closing. As were the mental images that insisted on floating through her mind. Memories of her mother, dying yet determined to keep her daughter free of the man who watched like a vulture from the corner of the room. Memories of blood, crimson against the pale flesh of her hands. The loneliness of her flight beneath the shadows of midnight, amid the night sounds. And now the image of the two men who had put their hands on her today.

"Cassie?" Raspy, his voice invaded her thoughts, a welcome invasion, she decided, given the turn they had taken.

She rolled to face him, finding herself tucked up neatly against his chest. Drawing in a breath of surprise, she scooted back a bit, only to be captured by a long arm that snagged her waist, holding her firmly in place.

"Don't move, Cassie. Just hold your little butt still." His voice was raw, as if he held some dark emotion under fragile control. His arm squeezed her gently, as though to soften the words.

"I didn't realize you were so close!" She blinked, fearful of the long length of him, his broad chest appearing to have expanded in size with its proximity. Her knees drew up in an instinctive gesture and she found herself nudging the V of his crotch.

Catching another breath of surprise, she attempted to straighten her legs, but he halted the movement, his hand sliding down from her waist to settle with a promise of hard strength against the backs of her thighs. She gasped at the intimacy of his touch and pushed at his chest.

"Hold still, girl," he said roughly, breathing harshly.

"I didn't mean...I just...I didn't know you were so tight behind me," she told him, her whisper turning to a wail of protest as she felt embarrassment and panic nudging her, warming her cheeks.

"Hush, Cassie. You're all right." His fingers eased their grip, his hand moving to rest against her back.

She stilled in her efforts to move away and relaxed the hold she'd managed to maintain on the blanket. Peering up at him, she found him unsmiling, his eyes shadowed, the dark outline of his whiskers hardening his visage. His gaze was intent as his arms enclosed her, one beneath her head, his hand buried in the length of her hair.

She watched in silence as his head tipped, lowering toward her, then held her breath. His mouth opened just a bit, and suddenly it seemed safer to shut her eyes. The touch of his lips against hers came as no surprise, yet at the same time filled her with amazement. No one but her mother had ever kissed her, and those sweet, loving caresses had in no way prepared her for the sensations that gripped her now.

His scent was masculine, a combination of leather and sweat, but his breath was clean, like a fresh breeze. Against her lips, his were warm, moist and moving. With a barely discernible rhythm they touched hers, soothing the tender flesh of her mouth, as if he were coaxing her to join him in this venture.

He nudged at her, his teeth touching her firmly closed lips, and she heard another muted groan as she backed from the contact.

"Did I frighten you, Cassie?" he whispered against her lips, a sardonic tinge accompanying the query.

She stiffened, indignant at the humor inherent in his tone. "I'm not afraid," she quavered, clearing her throat quickly. "I just think you're taking privileges I haven't offered."

"Ever been kissed, Cassie?"

He moved his lips against her once more, nibbling, like a rabbit in a patch of lettuce, and, stifling a giggle, she relaxed a bit.

"By my mother."

"That's not what I meant," he told her, glowering in the faint light shed by the campfire, his arms tightening around her.

Her giggle bubbled forth again and she bit at her lips, her breath catching in a half sob. "You laughin' at me?" He leaned back, the better to see her face.

"No, of course not," she denied, fearful of the tears that seemed to be hovering just behind her lids. Her words were shaky as she spoke on an indrawn breath. "I just...you just...you made my lips tickle when you bunny-kissed them."

"Bunny-kissed! What the hell's that supposed to mean?"

He rolled from her. Damn, he'd do well to keep his hands to himself and away from the bundle of innocence he'd managed to get himself tied up with. Horny as a bull in a pasture full of heifers, he fought the need that surged in his groin.

She was watching him, drawn up into a defensive ball, her lips tightly pressed together. He tucked his hands beneath his head, visibly relaxing, purposefully willing her to do the same, praying for the ache in his male parts to subside.

"Bunnies?" The single word of inquiry was a rasping whisper.

Her words were halting as she struggled to explain the game she'd played in years gone by with her mother, peering at him as if she would read his expression in the flickering firelight. "I've only ever been kissed by her," she confessed softly.

Will drew in a breath. Then, shifting, he rolled to his side and reached for her hand, clasping her fingers. "Don't let me set you to running, Cassie. I'll leave you alone." Much as the promise cost him, he vowed silently to bear it in mind. "You're probably one of the better things that's come my way since I left home," he told her quietly.

"Have a lot of good things happened to you?" she asked, wary of his nearness, given her own urge to nestle closer to his side.

"Yeah, I've had my share of good and bad, I guess. I took up with a sheriff down in San Antone and spent some time learnin' law and order. Then I worked on a couple of ranches, and got a real education. Found out more about horses than I'd ever expected to. And a few other things that opened my eyes, made me grow up in a hurry."

"Like what?" she asked, enamored of his remembrances, almost envious of the years he'd spent on his own, her apprehensions put to rest for a moment as he spoke.

Will's eyes darkened as if the memories were better left alone. "Most of it's the sort of stuff a young girl like you doesn't need to hear, Cassie." He rose to one elbow, leaning quickly to drop a quick kiss against the tip of her nose, unable to resist her nearness.

"Don't do that, Will," she said sharply, her heartbeat increasing as she shifted away.

It was quiet for a few minutes, Cassie pondering his words, considering the traveling he had done. "Men are lucky," she said finally, shifting to face him. "They can travel and meet folks and work where they want to, and a woman has to stay with her family till she's married. Or else be bait for gossip if she doesn't do what people expect of her."

"That's the way of the world, Cass." Sitting up, he wrapped his arms around one knee, shifting for comfort, and finding little to be had on the hard ground. He grimaced, wishing he'd kept his hands to himself.

"Are you going to find a place to leave me, Will?" She watched him, sensing his withdrawal. Perhaps he wasn't ready to get rid of her presence yet, if what he'd said was gospel truth. If he really thought she was good for him.

"I can't just dump you off somewhere, Cass. My ma would have my hide if she thought I'd rescued you just to leave you with strangers."

"Your ma? She doesn't even know about me," she said, frowning at his words.

"She will, once I get home. She'll get every livin' detail out of me, with her pickin' and yatterin' at me."

Cassie peered up at him. "And will you tell her everything?"

"Most everything, probably." Within reason, anyway. Some things a mother was better off not knowing.

"How come you're going home?" she asked, after a long moment.

"It sure as hell isn't my first choice," he said harshly. "But Pa's pretty bad off. Ma wrote me a letter, sent it to the last place I worked. I tried to keep Ma up on where I was, a couple of times a year, anyway. She said in the letter that Pa had taken a bad spell out in the field and just didn't get over it. His heart acts funny, fluttering and making him lose his breath sometimes."

"Did she ask you to come home?"

He nodded. "My brothers are both married now and have their own fields to work. Farmers can't be runnin' back and forth all the time to somebody else's place to lend a hand. And my sister ran off and married a scallywag a few years ago. My mother was pretty cut up about that."

"It sounds like you'll be a homebody for sure, once you get there." Her eyelids were getting heavy and the words she spoke were slurred. She yawned widely, covering her mouth with one hand, shifting to lie on her side.

Will looked down at her. "Homebody?" His laugh was harsh. "I'm not cut out to be a farmer."

Cassie's eyes flew open at his rasping tone. "Then why go? Why take me there?"

His hand silenced her anxious query. "I guess I owe it to my mother to lend a hand. She was always there for me when things got tough, with Pa on my tail all the time. You'll be all right. My mother'll take to you. There's always room for another hand, helpin' around the house and doin' chores." Cassie would probably be more welcome than he would, at that. There'd be hell to pay, with him and Pa in the same house.

Cassie looked up with sleepy eyes. "I doubt your mother

will be pleased to see me coming. Not after we've been traveling together.''

''I don't see that I have much choice right now,'' he muttered. ''You sure aren't capable of headin' out on your own.''

What he'd do with her once he got her home was another question, one he wasn't ready to examine too closely tonight. For one thing, he never should have kissed her. For all the good it had done him. She was about as innocent as they came, with her talk about rabbits. And then there was Pa. Ornery and miserable as the day was long. He'd give them both a hard time. The old resentment welled up within him, lending harshness to his voice. ''Go to sleep, Cassie. Between you and that damn mare and those two bas—'' He took a deep breath. ''Just go to sleep, hear?''

He turned from her, hauling the edge of the blanket over his shoulder.

Wide-eyed, Cassie repeated his words within her mind. *I don't see that I have much choice right now...you aren't capable...between you and that damn mare...* She bit at her lip, fearful of whimpering aloud as the words he'd spoken clamored in her head. Turning away, she stifled any sound she might make, burying her face in the blanket.

With a final look around the edges of the clearing he'd chosen for the night, Will settled down, his gun next to his head, his hat half covering it. Just as well she'd turned away. He shouldn't have been so short with her, he thought ruefully. His fingers itched to lose themselves in her tangled curls, and he shifted on the hard ground, his discomfort growing. As long as he could keep his randy hands to himself, they ought to get along for the next six days. Long enough to get them through Oklahoma and well into Missouri. Maybe he could hurry her along a little and make it in five.

*   *   *

The new mare dumped her twice on the second day. From her prone position, Cassie muttered words she'd only heard before, aware of a stone beneath her bottom, another lodged against her rib. Other than that, the ground was just rock hard all over, and her groan was heartfelt.

"Damn, girl!" Will was off the stallion and at her side, reins clutched in his hand. "At least she didn't run off like last time," he said, eyeing the mare. The brown creature stood just a few feet away, placid in her grazing. "You all right, Cassie?"

She sat up, rubbing at the bruised spot on her rib, her arm bending at an awkward angle to accomplish the task. "I don't think I broke any bones."

Will's hand brushed her fingers aside and he felt the spot carefully, a distracted look on his face as he traced the rib. "I don't feel a break, Cass." He squatted next to her, his fingers itching to brush the disheveled hair from her face, his mouth fighting a smile as he listened to her grumbling.

"Dratted horse just wanted to taste the grass," she mumbled. "Couldn't wait till we stopped for the night, could she?"

"Yeah, well, I think we're gonna ride on, Cass. I'd just as soon put some miles behind us tonight." His gaze traveled over Cassie's head, measuring the trail ahead to where it eased atop a shallow rise, disappearing over the crest of the hill. He'd come across the scant trail early this morning, passing through a small town at noontime, well into Oklahoma Territory.

They'd halted there just long enough to buy Cassie a pair of boots, more fit for a young boy than a woman, but suited to the trail.

Now she eyed the sturdy leather footwear as she sat on the ground, hoping the raw spot on her heel wasn't a blister, wishing for a moment for the soft comfort of the moccasins she'd given up for the protection of boot leather. "I can go farther," she told Will, lifting herself to her feet, limping a little as she took a few steps.

The mare lifted her head, her ears retreating to plaster themselves against her head, her eyes daring Cassie to disrupt her meal.

"Talk to her, Cass," Will said beneath his breath, rising and walking at an angle from the mare.

"What a pretty baby!" Crooned in a singsong voice, the words eased the mare's disquiet, her ears twitching a bit. "Why don't you just stand there and be a good girl?" Cassie smiled determinedly at the animal, aware of Will's stealthy, circuitous route as he led his stallion beyond the mare.

And then he had her. Catching the reins in one hand, the bridle in the other, he quieted the brown animal's snort, holding her firmly lest she bolt again.

"Think you can manage a few more hours, Cass?"

She nodded, wincing as she stepped up to the mare. "I'll be fine." Lifting her left foot to the stirrup, she hoisted herself atop the saddle, gritting her teeth as she settled within the leather cradle.

Chapter Four

The small cabin was a welcome sight. A ramshackle building, it was nestled beneath a willow tree next to a small stream. In Cassie's present state, it might well have been a palatial mansion.

The sky above promised nasty weather, and the smattering of cold raindrops she'd ridden through in the past few minutes had already managed to thoroughly wet Cassie's shirt. It was enough to dampen her spirits. More than enough.

She shivered, staggering toward the small log shack, just a few steps ahead of Will. One foot snagged on a root, half overgrown with grass and hidden from view, and she stumbled, falling to her knees.

Her head bent, she breathed deeply, then shoved herself to her feet, only to find Will's big hand clutching her elbow, propelling her forward. Her feet dragged, scuffing across the small porch, Will slowing his steps a bit to accommodate her slower pace. He followed her through the doorway, steering her with a decided lack of gallantry. One arm filled with saddlebags, the bundles from the mule across his shoulder, he edged past her into the dim interior, dropping his burdens just inside.

Cassie met his gaze, attempting a smile of reassurance, her lips trembling as a chill swept over her. "I'll be fine once I warm up a little," she said stoutly, rubbing her hands together, all too aware of cold skin and stiff fingers that resisted her attempts.

Will nodded, a flicker of doubt tracing his features as he brushed past her toward the doorway. "I'll take care of the animals. See if there's any wood for a fire, will you?" Ducking his head in an automatic motion, he headed back outside, his stride more energetic than Cassie could fathom. The man never seemed to run out of strength.

Riding throughout the night, she'd dozed off more than once, allowing her horse to slow to a walk, falling behind Will as he set a steady pace. His patience had been commendable, Cassie decided. He'd waited for her, neither hustling her along nor fussing at her when she slumped over the saddle horn, half-asleep.

Now she watched as he led the animals to where a pump promised water. A few vigorous movements of the long handle made that idea a vain hope, and Will reached for his water pouch, tilting it to drain the contents into the top of the pump. His mouth curved in a smile of satisfaction as the priming gained results. With a few swift up-and-down movements of the narrow handle, he had a steady stream pouring in abundance from the spout, into the wooden trough beneath.

Their noses bobbing in the water, the three animals drank deeply, then, blowing noisily, they sprayed, tossing their heads. Will stepped back to escape their antics, grinning at their good spirits.

"Are we going to spend the night here?" Cassie asked from the doorway.

"We don't have a lot of choice right now," Will answered. His hand lifted to gesture at the leaden sky. "Looks like we're in for it. The wind's comin' up pretty steady."

Cassie nodded. Getting caught in the rain would be miserably uncomfortable as far as she was concerned. Even this crude shelter was better than being out in the open at the mercy of a spring storm. Wrapping her arms around herself for warmth, she turned to where a fireplace yawned against the far wall of the small cabin. A scattering of wood promised the beginnings of a fire, but not much more. She dropped to her knees on the hearth, gathering the kindling and piling it loosely.

Will's bundle must surely hold more matches. Quickly she loosened the folds and searched for the small container she'd seen in his hands that first night. It held sulphur-tipped matches, safe from the damp, and she lit one carefully, holding it to the brittle kindling. It sparked, then caught, and a small flame sprang into being. Carefully she placed another fragile stick over the glowing wood, smiling as it caught fire. One piece at a time, she fed the flames until every scrap of wood from the floor surrounding her was piled inside the wide mouth of the fireplace.

Her fingers were finally warmed, and she rubbed them together, glorying in the heat. One hand lifted languidly to brush at her cheek, where wayward tendrils fell forward, her untended hair loosening from its braid. Then she sat back on her heels, gathering the warmth to herself, reluctant to leave the small haven of comfort.

It was there he found her, kneeling before the small blaze she tended, her unruly hair and smudged cheeks those of an urchin. And yet there was about her an allure he could not fathom. The soft line of her cheek, lashes shadowing the pale flesh, the profile of feminine curves as she lifted her hand to brush at a wisp of dark hair. Her arm lifting high pulled at the fabric of her shirt, its soft weave revealing the swell of her breast.

He inhaled sharply, pierced by his awareness of the woman kneeling before him. His eyes narrowed as his gaze slid up over the generous curve of her bottom to where her waist was cinched with the length of belt he'd given her.

Desire, hot and consuming, drenched him in its depths. The heat of his arousal was immediate, from the flaming ridge across his cheekbones to the throbbing warmth in his groin. His breath caught again, a rasping sound that drew her attention, and she turned, her eyes wide and startled, as if he'd drawn her from a dream.

As women went, she was far from the most seductive he'd ever seen. Hell, she wasn't much more than a child, all innocent and unknowing, her face smudged, her eyes anxious, her mouth soft and inviting as she opened it to speak.

"Will?" Hastily she rose, brushing her hands together, then wiping them against the sides of her denim pants. "I was about to go out and gather more firewood." She hesitated, uneasy as she searched his face, her fingers clenching into fists. Poised as if for flight, she looked away from him, to the doorway, then beyond, where the long branches of the willow beside the house swept the ground.

"The wind's coming up," she said in a wispy, small voice, sidling toward the open doorway. "I'd better look for wood before we get a downpour."

"Cassie." He spoke her name in a gruff exhalation of breath, his eyes closing for just a moment.

Her gaze skittered from the bleak vista beyond the doorway to clash with his as his lashes lifted. Allowing his mind to fill with her image—slender, bedraggled and all too tempting—he cast aside the caution he'd managed to gather.

"Come here." He spoke the words—softly uttered, but more than a request nonetheless—that would bring her to him. That she would not heed the implicit order never entered his head. Cassie had put herself under his care.

He watched as she turned reluctantly in his direction, his whole frame taut with the desire he fought to contain. Perhaps just holding her would suffice. He could gather that small body against himself, soothe his passion with the warmth of her soft, resilient flesh, surround himself for just a moment with the female scent that rose from her as an elusive, faint enticement.

"Will?" She stood before him, her eyes wide, her mouth soft, her bottom lip trembling. "What is it? Is something wrong?" Apprehension brought a frown to mar the smooth line of her forehead, and he lifted his hand, fingers smoothing at the lines.

"No." Abrupt, at odds with the gentle caress he bestowed upon her skin, his voice growled the single syllable.

She flinched beneath his touch and tilted her head to one side. "Will?" Her whisper was wavering, her nostrils flaring as if she scented a danger she could not comprehend.

She was more than he could resist, more than his self-control could deny. His hands met behind her waist in a smooth movement that caught her unaware. He tugged at her, catching her off balance, and she tumbled against him, lifting her hands in an automatic gesture to grip his shoulders. His head dipped, his jaw against her temple, his eyes closing as he deliberately blotted from his mind the gray skies outside the cabin, the dingy interior of the small room.

For this moment, for just these few seconds, he basked in the softness of the woman he held. His palms flat against her back, he urged her closer, forming her to his needy flesh. His heart pounded with a steady, harsh beat, radiating within his body like the sounding of a drum in his ears.

She stiffened for a moment, her breathing uneven, and he felt her tremble against him. Her face turned in the direction of his, tilting back until her mouth brushed against the line of his chin, opening so that he felt the moisture of her inner lips upon his skin. She kissed him there, rising on her tiptoes to whisper a string of soft words against his whiskered jaw.

"What is it, Will? Can I help? Is something wrong?" Her hands released their hold on his shoulders and slid to his nape, gripping tightly against his spine. She curled against him, forming her curves to the firm muscles of his chest, as if she would offer comfort, her fingers rubbing in a soothing rhythm.

A groan he could not stifle rose to his lips. Could she help? The one thing that would be guaranteed to solve his immediate problem was not an option, he admitted to himself ruefully. That this young woman would so innocently offer compassion, unknowing of his instinctive desire for her, was the crowning touch.

"Just let me hang on to you for a minute, Cassie." The words were muffled as he turned his mouth against her forehead.

She nodded, and his lips brushed her skin in an automatic caress. Probably the only clean spot on her face, he thought, his mouth twisting in an unwilling grin. And even that fact did not deter him. Beneath the smudges, the evidence of her hours on the trail, was the face of a girl...no, the face of a woman who had survived a hard night of riding without complaint. Whose small, compact body was pressed against his, whose lips were temptingly close.

He brushed his lips against her mouth and felt an eager trembling there as she responded, bringing to life a renewed surge of desire rising within him. Casting aside the good intentions he'd vowed to observe, he slid one hand up her back to hold her head in place for his kiss. She murmured beneath her breath, a soft, acquiescent whimper, and his jaw tightened, a sense of male triumph invading his very being.

Against her lower back his hand spread, fingers splayed widely, his palm pressing her firmly against his belly. His arousal met her there and he held her tightly in place, easing the tension of his needy flesh against her groin.

His mouth opening over hers, he delved deep, past the soft lips that parted for his entry, teasing the length of her tongue as it evaded his pursuit. She whimpered, almost a protest. Then, inhaling sharply through her nostrils, she joined the game he had begun. Their mouths met with seamless measure, hers opening to match the outline of his lips. Their tongues stroked, languidly touching, lavishly tasting.

Her flavor was like the fine wine he'd tasted once in a fancy place in San Antone, like bubbles and sweetness with a tartness overlaying the whole. He relished the flavor of her, inhaling the scent of her skin, his fingers twisting in her hair, his other hand almost brutal in his strength as he pressed her close. His body surged against her in a primitive motion, muscles taut, his need a barely controlled entity.

And then, with a shudder, he lifted his head, his eyelids heavy as he forced them open, anxious lest he find Cassie's face a frightened mask. That she had kissed him with fervor was a fact. That she would be fearful of her own actions was a possibility.

Her blue eyes were unfocused, as if she saw him with blurred vision, her cheeks flushed, her mouth open, lips shiny with the residue of their passion. She blinked, peering at him like a newborn baby he'd seen once in a hovel outside Amarillo. Such innocence was not to be believed.

Not from the woman who had just met his kiss with impassioned fervor.

"Will? Is kissing supposed to be like that?" Her voice filled with wonder, she blinked again, as if awakening from a particularly delightful dream.

And this was no dream, he decided. More like a nightmare, what with him coaxing her into a seduction he had no intention of pursuing. "It is if the right two people are doin' the kissin'," he said, inhaling deeply, tamping down the desire he had allowed full sway for these few moments.

"I feel…" She hesitated, her tongue touching her lips with a tentative gesture. "I'm sort of woozy," she said finally. "Maybe I'm just hungry."

"Yeah." Hungry was the word, all right. He grinned at that thought, easing his body from the contact it craved. He stretched his neck and stiffened his spine, his hands once more at her waist, lifting her to one side.

If the rising wind and the rain that was beginning to fall in earnest would tamp down his urges, he'd edge her from the doorway and do his own wood gathering. The only issue was getting past her without his randy hands taking hold of the temptation she offered.

"I'll be back directly. You stay inside," he said gruffly, bending to pick up his hat from the wooden floor. He who was so careful of the wide-brimmed hat that had perched atop his head for the past two years could not even remember it falling from its place.

Her face lit with a relief she made no attempt to hide. "I'll sort out something for supper," she offered.

He nodded, hunching his shoulders as he bent into the slanting raindrops. His steps were quick, his hands reaching for dead wood beneath the trees. It was barely dampened by the rain, protected by the trees towering overhead, and he found a double armful within minutes. Probably enough to last the night, if they were careful.

Beneath the small porch he caught a glimpse of more firewood, apparently gathered by an earlier occupant, and he welcomed the discovery with a satisfied grin. Dumping his heavy load just inside the door, he stepped back out to gather up the heavier chunks from under the porch. His shirt clung to his back, thoroughly soaked, and he thought longingly of the warm fire inside.

The small blaze welcomed him as he staggered through the doorway with his burden. Cassie knelt as closely as she dared to the fire, tending the small pot she'd placed in the coals.

"I opened a can of beans from your pack," she said, glancing at him over her shoulder. Her cheeks were flushed from the heat, her hair gleaming in the firelight.

This was not going to be an easy night, Will decided, carrying the heavy pieces of firewood closer. He bent, stacking them quickly next to the hearth, then squatted beside Cassie, his fingers working at the buttons of his shirt.

"Can you find me something dry to put on?" His hands were stiff, his movements slow, and he closed his eyes for a moment, soaking in the welcome warmth of the fire.

He heard her murmur of assent as she crossed the room to close the door against the rain. His every nerve attuned to her presence, he flinched at the click of her boot heels as they touched the wooden floor. The swollen wood of the door protested loudly as she dragged it across the uneven floorboards, and then she knelt by his saddlebag. The rustle of her movements had him gritting his teeth and closing his eyes, the better to visualize her as she handled his clothing, sorted through his belongings.

His hands tightened into fists, and he bent his head, aware only of her presence. Her clothing brushed the floor as she rose to her feet, and then he sensed her approach. His heartbeat slowed, his breathing deepened and once more he lifted his hands to undo his shirt buttons.

He stripped the shirt from his body, and unseen hands took it from him. Never had a fire felt so welcome. Grunting his thanks, he stretched out his hands to the crackling flames.

"Your undershirt is pretty well soaked, too," Cassie said from behind him.

He nodded agreement, his fingers once more working at buttons and buttonholes. He made quicker work of it this time and eased his way from the wet fabric. From behind him, Cassie enclosed his shoulders in the blanket from his pack and he basked in the warmth it captured from the flames as she draped it around his body.

She knelt next to him and reached to stir the beans. "They're almost hot," she offered. "We can put them on the biscuits left from breakfast if you want to."

"That's fine." He'd be willing to eat most anything she put in front of him right now, he decided. Between the sound of rain on the roof and the fire crackling in front of him, he was pretty near ready to doze off. If it weren't for the empty spot in his middle, he'd be content to drop his chin on his chest and spend the night where he sat.

"Here." Cassie's hand touched his and his fingers curled around the biscuit she held. Warm beans oozed from its depths and he licked one from his finger, then took a mouthful of the simple meal. He blinked, his eyes gritty with the need for sleep, and chewed slowly, savoring the flavor.

"I never knew beans could taste so good," Cassie said.

"Hmm." It was about as much conversation as he could manage. The night without sleep had caught up with him. It was hard telling what time it was, what with the early dark coming on, with the storm overhead. He suspected Cassie was about wiped out, too, even though she'd managed to doze in the saddle a few times throughout the night.

Will swallowed the last of the biscuit. "How many more of those you got?"

"Enough," she answered, her fingers deft as she split another, scooping on a generous helping of beans from the pot. She handed it to him and he muttered his thanks before he took a bite. Grasping the pot handle gingerly, she turned it toward him, handing him the spoon.

"Here, eat the rest. I've had enough." Settling her bottom on the floor, she folded her legs as she leaned toward the heat.

"You sure?" Will cast her a doubtful glance. She nodded, her gaze captured by the flames. "Here, have a bite," he offered, holding the spoon in front of her lips.

Her mouth opened obediently and he watched as her lips closed on the spoon. He eased it from her mouth and filled it again, feeding himself the next bite. There was about the small ritual a strange bonding, and he filled the spoon again, lifting it, watching as she ate from his hand. Scraping the last bite atop his final bit of biscuit, he popped it in his mouth, chewing slowly, savoring the flavor.

"Can we sleep now?" Cassie asked, not bothering to cover the yawn that accompanied her question.

Will cast a look around the small cabin. Against the far wall a rudely constructed bunk offered dubious comfort. "Seems to me we'd be just as well off right here by the fire," he said. "That bed doesn't look like much, and we'll be warmer here."

"I'll put some more wood on," Cassie said, rising. "Here's your shirt, Will." She dropped it into his lap, then found several chunks of wood to stack over the coals.

He watched as she worked, then, shedding the blanket,

he hastily pulled his shirt in place. The fire would dry his trousers, he figured. Taking them off would likely scare the bejabbers out of Cassie.

"Are you pretty well dried out?" he asked, pulling his pack closer, shoving the contents about as he sought a soft spot for his head.

She watched him, her eyes wary. "I'm all right. I'm warm, anyway." She tugged at her boots, placing them to one side of the wide fireplace. "These should dry out pretty well by tomorrow." As if she had done all she could to put off the inevitable, she turned to him.

"I'll roll up in the other blanket. You can sleep closer to the fire."

He shook his head. "No, we'll sleep together, right here." His hand motioned to the space they occupied and he stretched out, the blanket over his shoulders once more. "Bring the other blanket here," he told her, patting the floor in front of him.

She obeyed, moving silently on stocking feet as she gathered up the dark woolen square from his pack. Lowering herself to the floor, she spread the covering over them both, then settled down in the space he had indicated, just next to the hearth.

He moved to curl his body around her back, arranging the blankets to form a double layer over them as he slid his arm under her head, easing it from the floor. His other hand scooped her closely to his chest and she stiffened for a moment.

"Ease up, Cassie," he ordered in a rusty growl. "I need to get warm."

Getting warm wasn't the issue, Will thought, even as he muttered the words against the crown of her head. He was managing to generate enough inner heat to keep them both going all evening and half the night. He'd be better off if he kept his hands to himself and stayed six feet away from the bundle of temptation he held tucked so neatly against his needy body.

His sigh was deep. He was a glutton for punishment, sure enough. Here he was with a softly curving female in his grasp, his arm fitted around her waist and his thighs cradling her tight little rump. It was a damn good thing he was as tired as he was, or this would be a miserable night.

His arm tightened, eliciting a grumble of protest from the woman he held. "Don't wiggle, Cassie," he said, his voice muffled in her hair.

And then his eyes closed, the flames before him rising anew, bathing him with the comfort of their warmth.

Chapter Five

"What's wrong, Will?" Not for the first time, she asked the question, and once more he shrugged it off.

"Nothin' much, Cass. Just makin' sure we're on the right track. I've come through Oklahoma Territory before, but it's been a while." His grin was sudden and all the more welcome for its recent absence. "I wouldn't want to get us lost before we get to Missouri."

Cassie felt a great relief at his attempt to soothe her worries. That such a small thing as a smile from Will Tolliver would absorb her unease so readily was a wonder. That his touch, one finger against her cheek, would send a shiver of anticipation down her back was another marvel to behold.

His nearness at night was a comfort, and his tender regard for her well-being was a panacea for all the wounds of her soul. And yet, there was within her an aching, a dreadful need for more than Will had given thus far. *And that makes me foolish and greedy,* she thought with a twinge of conscience.

Will had already done so much in her behalf. The guilt that hung over her head like a lowering thundercloud plagued her as she considered his kindness. And how had she repaid him? Her deceit, the blatant lie she had told him, the blood she had shed...she bowed her head. And now she wanted what he had not offered, whatever that might be. How could she yearn for more, especially when she herself was not even sure what that more consisted of?

Now, on the third day out since they had stopped at that cabin, since Will had kissed her and held her with such a needy embrace, she found herself watching him closely. He'd been quiet, almost angry, as he'd ridden out last evening after setting up their camp.

He'd been narrow eyed and somber when he returned, evading her questions and soothing her concerns as they bedded down for the night. His hand had held his gun throughout the night. She'd peeked more than once, restlessly turning over on the hard ground, aware of his quiet watchfulness as she sought sleep.

Now she watched as he approached, her awareness of him heightened as he shot her a measuring look. His hand pulled at the brim of his hat, tugging it over his forehead as if he would anchor it there.

"Keep ridin', Cassie." He circled her, his stallion taking mincing steps as Will reined him tightly. "See that smoke on the horizon?" Will's hand swept up, his index finger pointing to the north and east. "I want you to head in that direction, hear me?"

Cassie nodded, perplexed once more by his somber look. He'd been quiet again this morning, and then, with no warning, issued his orders. "What's wrong, Will?" she asked, only to find herself talking to his back as his horse pivoted in place.

He handed her the lead rope for the mule and watched as she wound it around the saddle horn, nodding his approval. "Just do as I say, Cassie." His words gave her no choice, drifting back over his shoulder as he left her. Doubling back on their trail, he headed off to the south, even as she watched.

"Behave yourself, girl," she muttered beneath her breath, eyeing the twitching ears of the mount she rode. The mare was about as reluctant to keep moving as she was, Cassie decided. "He'll be back," she murmured. "Before you know it," she assured the animal, reaching one hand to pat at the horse's dark mane.

Easing back on the reins, she slowed the mare to an ambling walk, unwilling to ride at any great pace in the opposite direction from Will. The pack mule followed along, stretching the lead to its full length, but amiable nonetheless. Cassie settled into the saddle, lulled by the rhythmic vibration of her horse's hooves, which blended with the sounds of the animal's breathing.

Ahead, the blot on the horizon spread out before her eyes, taking form and substance, sunlight glittering on metal.

"It's a town!" On an indrawn breath, Cassie whispered aloud her discovery. Not much of a town, she admitted to herself, now that she was getting closer. Only a cluster of buildings, to be sure. But where there were townfolk, there must be a general store. And inside that store, if Will had the hard cash to lay on the counter, they might find something to go along with the biscuits and beans they'd been eating for the past two days.

To the north a farmhouse took form, a barn behind it, and smoke from the chimney wafted on the breeze. A dog barked sharply and Cassie squinted to seek its whereabouts. A dark smudge moved and the animal barked again.

"I'm not gonna bother you, pooch," she said, her words blending with a chuckle. Her hand tightened on the reins, halting her progress as she considered the distance ahead. It would take far less than a half hour to reach the settlement at the pace she was traveling, and she didn't relish riding into its midst alone.

Shifting in the saddle, she looked back at the horizon. Will had traveled fast once he headed out. Patches of brush and a few clumps of trees dotted the landscape, perhaps shielding him from her view. A line of trees gave mute evidence of water, over near the farm she'd taken note of, and as her eyes measured the boundary they formed, she was tempted to ride in that direction.

A place to water her horse and splash fresh water on her own face was a welcome thought. One best ignored if she planned on doing as Will had told her. She shifted restlessly, uneasy without him by her side.

And then she heard his whistle from behind her, like that of a hawk calling to his mate. She turned in the saddle again, shading her eyes as they swept the horizon to the south. With a quickening of her heartbeat she recognized him, there where his figure soaked up the sunlight, approaching at a hard gallop.

His lips were thinned, his nostrils flaring, and his dark eyes were hooded as he pulled his horse to a halt. The stallion's front hooves left the ground and he spun in a half circle as Will reined him tightly. He tossed his head, and white foam sprayed in the air.

"What's wrong?" Cassie asked, her eyes intent on man and horse, a bit uneasy at the stud's antics. Will's hard-edged profile gave her a start, a grimness she had only begun to associate with him altering his features. "What did you find back there?"

"We're being followed. Maybe by one of those bastards from that ranch where I bought the horse." His mouth tightened as he allowed his gaze to sweep over her. "I was afraid of this. Must be you were more temptation than I realized."

His frown deepened. "I didn't want to use my gun, but I reckon I'll have to face him down." He looked to where the small town huddled, less than a mile ahead. "We'll ride on and keep an eye out. My guess is that he'll circle around and pick up our trail later on."

It wasn't much of a town. On the outskirts was a blacksmith shop, where a muscular man in a leather apron plied his trade before a glowing forge. He'd allowed them a glance and gone back to his business as they passed by. Next, a white wooden church proclaimed the place to be Cooper's Crossing, and the church to be Methodist in its leanings.

A scattering of houses surrounded the middle of town, dogs and children playing behind picket fences. A bit farther on a small building boasted a sign designating it the bank, and beside it was the general store. Will tied their horses to the hitching rail as Cassie wearily slid to the ground.

"Don't buy out the place before I get in there," he told her, his words an attempt to tease.

Granting him a scant grin, she climbed the three steps leading to the door. It swung shut behind her, and Cassie inhaled the unique smell of the place. Her hungry eyes were eager as they devoured the merchandise lining the shelves. Canned goods and bags of flour and sugar lined up next to tins of tea and spices. Bits of lace and eyelet nestled within a glass case, and her eyes lingered there for a moment before she edged past.

The scent of leather drew her to a display of harnesses and halters hung on nails against the wall. A saddle sat on end, a pile of coarsely woven blankets next to it. Shoes were lined up on the end of one counter, and she was awed by the display. She'd only ever had one pair at a time in her life, and those, by necessity, had been sturdy and lacking in style.

When Will entered the store, his gaze softened as he watched her explore, her eyes wide as she eased her way down the length of the counter and past the barrels of salt pork and pickles. It looked to him as if the girl had lacked the chance to spend much time in a store lately, what with the ragtag clothing she'd possessed when he found her. Not to mention the awestruck look in her eyes now that she was faced with the splendor of plenty. He'd have to see to it she was outfitted with some new pants, farther down the road, before they reached the farm.

Quickly he pointed out the foodstuffs he'd decided on and watched as the storekeeper stowed them in a burlap bag. Will counted out the coins on the burnished counter and picked up his merchandise.

"You folks just passin' through?" the proprietor asked, sorting out the money into his cash drawer.

Will nodded. "We're headin' up to Missouri. My folks have a farm outside of Greenbush."

"Can't say I ever heard of it," the storekeeper said, one finger nudging his spectacles in place.

Will grinned. "Neither has much of anyone else. Reckon it's just a spot on the map. They were lookin' for the railroad to come through when I left. I figure that oughta lend some life to the place."

"Well, you're only a day or so from the state line, less'n you poke along. Ought to be home before it's time to plow."

Will shrugged. "I expect I'll remember how." He cast a glance at Cassie. "You about ready, Sarah Jane?"

She looked at him, her eyes widening at the salutation. And then she smiled, ducking her head, her shy, bridelike gesture a direct contrast to the sparkle in her eyes. "Yes,

Will,'' she said meekly. With a last, longing look at the merchandise surrounding her, she made her way to the door.

Will opened it, ushering her past, his load heavy, dragging the burlap bag almost to the floor. She walked ahead and his eyes fastened on the rounded bottom encased in boy's pants. There was definitely something to be said for Cassie in a pair of denims. He'd just better hope his ma didn't pitch a fit when he brought home a female in britches.

The pack animal well laden, they set out from the small community, Cassie looking back mournfully over her shoulder. ''That was a good-sized store for such a small town, wasn't it?''

''Probably the only place to trade for miles around,'' Will said. ''Farms are pretty scattered hereabouts. I doubt folks get to town more than once every couple of weeks.''

''Is Greenbush any bigger?'' she asked, nudging her horse into a quicker pace and pulling in beside Will.

Will shrugged. ''Could be by now, I reckon. I've been gone for a long time, Cassie. If the railroad came through, my guess is that Greenbush has grown by leaps and bounds.''

''Do you think I could get a job there?''

''Ma will probably put you to work on the farm, Cass. She'll be glad to get another woman to help out.''

Cassie shook her head in mute denial.

''You don't think you'd like it on the farm?'' Will asked, his eyes on her downcast face.

''I need to make a life of my own, Will,'' she told him firmly. ''I'm not going to be owing you for the rest of my life. I'm already in debt with no way of paying you back for what you've done for me.''

If she were a different sort of female, he'd be able to

come up with a solution to that problem in no time flat, Will thought idly, his thoughts never far from the needy condition he'd been dealing with for the past week or so. For such a mite of a girl, Cassie was about the nicest armful he'd ever managed to snuggle up against.

The campfire was small, but heat radiated from the rock wall behind her. Will's eagle eye had spied the site from the trail, and he'd managed to get the fire built and the animals tethered in no time. The sun slid beneath the horizon quickly, and Cassie spread their blankets between the small blaze and the curving rock wall that formed a shallow cave.

"You get enough to eat?" he asked, watching her deft movements as she made a pillow of sorts from his heavy coat.

She nodded, kneeling in the glow of the fire, her eyes not quite making contact with his, her teeth touching her lower lip in concentration. She'd been antsy since sunset, Will realized. Maybe since earlier this afternoon.

"What's wrong, Cassie?" He'd done his own share of worrying over the past few days, but now that they were settled for the night, and he'd done the best he could to make them safe and secure, he was ready to get some rest. There'd be no rest if Cassie was on edge.

"I feel like someone's watching me." Her mouth barely moved as she whispered the words, her hands busy with squaring up the heavy garment she planned to tuck beneath her head for the night.

"Yeah." There was someone out there somewhere. He'd be willing to bet on it. "I've got my gun, Cassie, but I don't think he's lookin' to have a shoot-out. He's had a couple of days to bushwhack us if that's what he was plannin' to do."

She moved her blanket back into the shelter of the rock overhang and sat on it, her eyes darting past Will to scan the darkness. The boots she'd worn all day were side by side nearer the fire, she'd tended to her business behind a cluster of trees at twilight, and now she cast one last searching look into the surrounding area.

"I'm going to try to sleep," she announced, her jaw set as she curled on her side, reaching back to pull the blanket over her shoulder. "Why don't you come sit on this side of the fire, Will?"

"Yeah, I reckon it's time for me to stretch out, too," he told her, hoisting himself to his feet. "I'll just be a minute, Cassie. I'm not goin' far."

He couldn't mistake the moment of panic that flashed across her face, the widening of her eyes as he backed from the small camp. There was no point in telling her an untruth. The watcher was very likely nearby. And yet Will had spoken the truth as he saw it. If the man meant them harm, he'd had every chance in the world to do his worst. Something about the whole situation failed to add up.

Noiselessly, each footstep measured and cautious, Will walked the perimeter of the area he'd chosen for their camp. And then, in the shadow of an oak tree, he glimpsed the silent figure who watched and waited.

Easing off to his left, Will moved in a wide arc, taking advantage of every bush and tree, willing the clouds that covered the moon and stars to stay in place, affording him a degree of concealment as he made his way behind the observer's chosen spot. Stealthily he eased behind the oak tree, his footsteps silent, his breathing measured and soundless. The man who watched and waited had not moved. Indeed, like a statue, he melted into the shadows, not a whisper of sound betraying his presence.

Will moved from behind the tree, one hand on the butt

of his pistol. "You plannin' on spendin' the night keepin' an eye on us?" His words were quiet, carrying only as far as the shaded area they shared beneath the tree.

The intruder moved, and Will was on him. Certainly it made sense to have this confrontation with him on top, he decided. Surprise was his advantage, and yet there was a lack of hostility in this short battle. With barely a struggle, the man lay beneath Will, his eyes glittering in the faint glow from the campfire.

"I'll be damned. You're the half-breed!" Will's gun barrel was poised mere inches from the man's head, and nudged closer with each word Will spoke. "Answer me, Indian."

He was well built, probably able to well defend himself if he so chose, Will decided, and yet there was about him an air of submission.

"My gun's with my horse." Except for lifting his hands in a show of surrender, the dark-skinned man lay quiet and acquiescent beneath his captor.

"Are you alone?" Will asked in the same almost silent tones. He looked toward the fire, where Cassie lay bundled against the rock wall. He doubted she could see him in the darkness, but he surely didn't want her frightened by their visitor.

The other man nodded his head. "I rode your trail. I come alone."

"Well, you've caught up with us now. Reckon you'd better speak your piece." Lifting himself from the ground, Will dragged his captive up with one fist buried in the man's shirt. His other hand shoved his gun back into its holster, then moved to rest against his thigh as Will relaxed his stance.

The Indian's gaze was open as he extended his hand in greeting. "They call me Many Fingers."

With a measure of surprise, Will accepted the gesture and completed the solemn handshake.

Common courtesy kept him from asking the obvious question, but his eyes scanned the Indian's hand as it parted company with his own.

"Not that hand, the other." Holding up his left hand, he allowed Will's scrutiny, spreading his fingers wide, the smaller appendage on the outside of his hand noticeable.

"Well, I'll be..." Will shook his head. "I've never seen the like of that before. Does it give you a better grip?"

Many Fingers shook his head. "No. My mother fought the rest of the women so I could keep it, but it ain't much good to me."

Will eyed him, in a quandary as he considered Cassie's reaction should he bring the visitor back to the campfire.

"Why are you followin' us?"

"Thought maybe I could talk you into letting me ride with you," the Indian replied.

Will's brow rose in surprise. "What on earth for? Where's your home? Got any family? Why didn't you stay on at the horse dealer's place?"

Many Fingers shook his head. "A half-breed's word doesn't mean much. The big man set to wondering if I was part of the problem with your woman." His shrug was slight. "Guess I don't belong anywhere, to tell the truth. My mother was a half-breed, born from a white man who never stuck around to pay her any mind. My father died before I was born, with a white man's sickness."

"Where you from?" Will asked.

"A settlement in the Territory. There's nothin' there for me." He waited, watching closely as Will considered the words he spoke. "I'm good at workin' with horses. And I read and write pretty well. Ma sent me to the white man's school when I was young."

Will's tension eased, his doubts held in abeyance as he made a decision. Perhaps another rider would add to their safekeeping. He'd leave it up to Cassie.

"Want some coffee?" He waved his hand in the direction of the camp.

The Indian nodded, glancing at Cassie's small form curled near the fire. "Will she want to shoot me?"

Will shook his head. "Doubt it. She's not much on blood and guts."

"I tried to step in, but things happened too fast back there." His footsteps silent as he walked next to Will, Many Fingers spoke in an undertone.

But it was enough to rouse Cassie from her near slumber. She sat erect, the blanket draped over her shoulders, peering through the darkness. "Will? Who's that with you?"

"Don't get all in an uproar, honey. We've got company. This here's Many Fingers, come to have coffee." Will spoke quickly, flashing her a smile of reassurance.

"Will!" Cassie rose to her knees, backing against the rock wall.

Many Fingers bowed his head, a gesture of apology, if Will had him pegged right. And then the Indian spoke. "I bring a gift to the wife of Brave One."

Will's head turned quickly, his look incredulous. "Who's Brave One?"

Many Fingers shrugged. "Any white man willing to go up against two men the way you did to claim his woman is about as brave as they come. I call you Brave One."

Cassie sat down, her legs curled beneath her, the blanket wrapped around her huddled form. "What gift are you talking about?" she asked, her eyes dubious as she watched the stranger approach.

From inside the neckline of his collarless shirt the man withdrew a necklace, a combination of silver and turquoise.

It glittered in the firelight and he dangled it from his index finger, holding it to catch the warmth and gleam of the blaze.

"For you, because you are wife to a warrior. This is made for a warrior's woman." Hesitantly he approached, hand outstretched.

Cassie's nostrils flared as she inhaled deeply, and Will sent her a silent message of encouragement. *Take it, Cass. Accept it nicely, honey.*

She nodded, holding out her right hand, palm cupped to accept the gift, and Will breathed a sigh of relief. "Thank you," Cassie whispered, clutching the gift to her breast.

She peered down at it, where the leather thong had fallen between her fingers, and then slowly relaxed the tight hold she had taken. The slender thong slid farther between her knuckles, and she grasped the turquoise beaded amulet that rested in her palm.

"It's lovely." A lilt of surprise touched the words and she looked up quickly, a small smile curling the corners of her mouth. "It really is lovely. Look, Will."

"Put it on, honey." It must be accepted properly, he knew. And obligingly, Cassie slipped it over her head, allowing the blanket to drop from her shoulders. She centered the amulet between her breasts, easing the thong beneath her collar, looking down at the beaded design that rested against her shirt.

"Thank you." Her look was wary, but she sent a glance at Will for guidance and he nodded at her. "I'm proud to be the wife of a warrior."

"Warrior's Woman," Many Fingers repeated. With fluid grace he dropped before the fire, crossing his legs and sitting erect.

"I offered our guest a cup of coffee," Will explained to

Cassie as he poured his own tin cup full of the strong brew that was still sitting by the fire.

Cassie nodded, no longer looking on the edge of sleep.

Will watched as Many Fingers drank his coffee, then, accepting the empty cup, he waved at the space near the gleaming coals. "You can share our fire, if you want."

Many Fingers shook his head. "I'll keep watch." He stood and moved away from the fire.

"Will?" Cassie's whisper met his ear as Will scooted his blanket closer to where she huddled. "Is it safe to have him here? Who's he going to watch for?"

He shook his head. "Don't know as there's anyone else around, Cass. But I sure don't think he's any danger to us. He stuck up for you when he didn't have to, back in that barn," he reminded her quietly. "Besides, he seems to have taken a shine to you, sweetheart."

"You're the one he called Brave One. I only got called the Warrior's Woman."

"That title is gonna keep you safe, ma'am." He chuckled as he brushed a kiss across the end of her nose.

"I'm probably fussing over nothing. And he did take my part, didn't he?"

"Go to sleep, Cassie," he muttered. "It's hard to say, but he may be gone by morning, anyway. In the meantime, we're as safe as we've ever been."

He heard her grumble beneath her breath and then her knees pulled up, rubbing against his spine as he stretched out full length between her slender form and the fire. With the rock wall behind her and the *Brave One* in front of her, he figured she was in pretty good shape for the night.

"I'm having second thoughts, Will. What will your mother think about you bringing an Indian home with you?'' Cassie's words were low, in deference to the man who rode fifty feet or so to the rear.

"I kinda like the man. It won't hurt to have someone else ridin' along with us, anyway."

"And your mother?"

Will shrugged diffidently. "Don't know as she'll have much to say. Now, Pa is a different matter. He could pitch a fit. He's never had much good to say about Indians. Calls them…well, never mind. You don't need to hear how ignorant my pa can sound sometimes."

"That's no way to talk, Will," Cassie scolded. "Maybe your pa would welcome some help on the farm, if he's laid up and all." She eased a glance at the spotted horse and its rider who had followed in their wake for the better part of a week. "Seems to me he's planning on looking after us, whether we like it or not."

"You know, I can't help but admire the man's way of handlin' the horses the way he does. You might be right. Pa may be able to put him to work. Last I knew, ten years ago, there were a few mares breedin' on the farm. Problem was, Pa wasn't much of a hand at trainin' them."

"Are you looking forward to seeing your father?" Cassie's query was cautious, as if she were feeling out the atmosphere. "I can't ever tell how you feel about him, Will. You always sound like you've missed your mother, but…"

"Me and Pa didn't get along much there at the end. By the time I left, he was hot on my tail all the time. Seemed like I couldn't do anything right."

"You left on bad terms?"

He nodded. "It was either leave or have it out with him, and I couldn't do that to my mother." He pointed ahead to where a long, low line of smoke lay across the horizon. "Unless I miss my guess, that's the railway ahead. If we follow it east and north, we should be in Greenbush in a couple of hours."

Chapter Six

Neglected. There was no other word to describe the assortment of buildings, beginning with the farmhouse and ending with the weather-beaten look of the barn. Not a smidgen of paint clung to any wooden surface that Cassie could see. It was about the most bedraggled-looking farm she'd ever laid eyes on.

But then, compared to some of the shacks she'd lived in with her mother and Remus Chandler over the past few years, it was pretty nearly an inviting sight.

She couldn't help but hurt for Will as they rode together down the lane from the road. They'd ridden through the town and Will had quietly pointed out the places he recalled from his youth. The railroad had made changes in Greenbush, with a new mill open right near the tracks and a small stockyard next to it.

A couple of people had given them a second look, but Will hadn't paid them any mind as far as Cassie could tell. Actually, Many Fingers drew more attention than either of them. The looks cast in his direction were far from friendly, although she didn't hear any disparaging remarks.

Indians were not popular in some of the places she'd lived, but after four days of traveling with Many Fingers in their wake, she'd come to accept his presence. If Will thought he was trustworthy, she wasn't going to argue the issue. And for some reason Will seemed to be quite taken with the man, sitting by the campfire the past two nights and talking about raising horses, as if they were friends of long standing.

Now there was only silence from the two men she rode with. From Will there emanated a sadness and reluctance she could only wonder at. He'd come home under duress, that was for sure. Perhaps his father would be happy to see him. Maybe…

The woman who came out the door and watched their approach was somber, her hair touched with streaks of gray. She wiped her hands on a colorless apron, twisting them in its depths long after they must surely be dried. Her hair was scooped into a knot atop her head and her dress covered every inch of her from neck to ankle, except for bare forearms, where her sleeves had been rolled almost to her elbows.

She took a slow step toward the porch railing, lifting one hand to her forehead to shade her eyes from the sunshine. She blinked, and leaned forward a bit. "Will? Is that you, Will?" As if she spoke seldom, her words were cautious, her tone rasping.

Beside Cassie, Will Tolliver cleared his throat and squared his shoulders. "Yeah, it's me, Ma."

Several feet from the porch he swung from his horse, sweeping his hat from his head and slapping it against his thigh. "I got your letter."

The woman's face crumpled. To Cassie's way of thinking, there was no other word to describe the transformation from stern and sober to undiluted hope. Two tears traveled the length of her cheeks and her mouth quivered as one hand lifted to cover the wavering smile that appeared.

"I didn't know if you'd come or not, Will. It's been so long since I wrote."

"You might have known I'd try to get here as soon as I could, Ma." He looked past her, peering at the screen door as if he could see past it. "Pa inside?"

His mother shook her head. "No. Your pa died two months ago. Just quit breathing one night. I found him dead the next morning."

In three quick strides Will was on the porch and his arms encircled his mother. Stiff and unyielding at first, she stood in his embrace and then, as if she dared to unbend, she leaned against him and pressed her forehead to his chest.

"How have you managed on your own?" he asked her quietly, his eyes bleak as he rubbed one hand absently against her shoulder.

"Eben comes over mornings to help with feeding and Samuel comes at night."

Will's mouth twisted in a smile. "Damn, it's been a long time, Ma. I still kept thinkin' of them both as tadpoles, and here they're full-grown men."

"They got places of their own, just down the road a ways," she answered, straightening and delving in her apron pocket for a handkerchief. She backed from Will's embrace and blew her nose, wiping at her eyes quickly, as if she would eliminate all trace of her lapse into sadness.

"Why didn't they stay here and help Pa? There's room in the house."

"They're both married, boy. Besides, there wasn't anybody could get along with your pa, once you left home, Will. He was about the crankiest man around, I reckon."

Cassie slid from her horse and Will turned, reaching out a hand toward her. "Cassie, come and meet my mother."

She stepped forward, conscious of Many Fingers taking the reins from her hand. Then Will grasped her wrist, his fingers warm and firm, tugging her to his side. She climbed the steps reluctantly, suddenly wary.

"Ma, this is Cassie." Will's fingers tightened against her flesh, then slid to enclose her hand.

Mrs. Tolliver looked past the couple to where Many Fingers waited, holding the reins of three horses. "Who's the Indian?"

"That's Many Fingers. He's been ridin' with us, Ma," Will said quietly.

"I'm glad to meet you, Mrs. Tolliver," Cassie ventured.

"You been totin' this gal around for long?" Will's mother asked bluntly, still taking wary measure of the Indian.

Many Fingers took a step forward. "She is Brave One's woman."

"And where's the brave one?" Mrs. Tolliver asked, swinging her attention back to her son.

"That's what he calls me," Will offered diffidently. "This is my mother, Cassie."

Confused was the best word Cassie could think of to describe the look on the woman's face as she finally took full notice of the young woman standing before her. Her gimlet eyes took in the dusty, bedraggled look of Cassie's clothing; her mouth pinched tightly as she measured the pants that formed to Cassie's slender legs, and the disapproving tone of her voice could not be mistaken.

"You didn't answer me, Will. How long has this gal been ridin' with you?"

Will's jaw set in a manner that had become familiar to Cassie over the past days. Her fingers tightening within his grip, she tugged at his hand.

His fleeting glance told her that his temper was about to erupt, his eyes darkening with a silent fury she could not fail to recognize. His mouth set in a mutinous line and he gathered Cassie closer to his side, ignoring her soundless efforts to gain his attention.

"Long enough," he grated. "We met in Texas, Ma. She was in a bind, and I figured since I was raised to be a gentleman, I'd give her a hand."

"Made her your woman, did you? Doesn't look good, a young girl traveling with two men," his mother said accusingly, her eyes assessing Cassie without mercy. "No matter how you slice it, her reputation's ruined."

"She is Warrior's Woman," Many Fingers said sternly, stepping forward to align himself with Will.

"You're claimin' her, too?" Her look incredulous, Will's mother faced the Indian.

He shook his head. "No. She belongs to Brave One. Your son."

"He's talking about you, Will?" As if her head were on a swivel, his mother's attention spun to him, and Will nodded agreeably.

"She is wife to your son," Many Fingers put in.

A look of relief swept her features as the older woman relaxed visibly. "Well, why in tarnation didn't somebody say so right off?" she asked smartly.

Will's mouth opened, ready to refute the words that marked him a married man, and then, with a quick glance at Cassie, thought better of it. This conversation needed to take place in private. Explanations to his mother might be long and loud, and this wasn't the time or place.

"I'm about to get supper started. Bring your things in and get those horses out to the barn." Turning her back to the trio, Will's mother went into the house, leaving Cassie openmouthed in her wake.

"Will!" It was a squeak of protest and as such Will felt the need to squelch it.

"I'll make everything clear to her after supper, Cassie,"

he said quietly, his mouth next to her ear. "Just go on in, and I'll bring our gear along in a few minutes."

He watched as she followed his mother into the kitchen, then turned to Many Fingers. "Let's get these animals fed and put up for the night."

The Indian nodded agreement, and together they headed for the barn. Will's mouth tightened as he noted the broken hinge on the big door, the musty smell of last year's hay and the clutter of tools and harness that littered the floor.

"Looks like my brothers haven't spent much time in keepin' things up," he said, bending to pick up a hammer.

Many Fingers nodded. "It takes a man full-time to work a farm." Dropping the reins of the horses he led, he hauled the pack mule past the wide doorway, tying the lead rope to a ring on the wall. "I'll unsaddle the horses. You can tend to your gear."

"I suspect you'll have to sleep in the barn," Will told him. "There's only three bedrooms in the house."

Many Fingers nodded. "I've slept in worse places. Don't think your ma would let me inside, anyway."

"You'll come in to eat," Will said bluntly.

Many Fingers' deft movements loosened the cinch and slid Will's saddle from the stallion. "I'll stay on here for a while and help out, if that's all right with you," he offered, carrying the saddle a few feet down the wide aisle, where he placed it over a sawhorse.

Will's survey was short as he cast a look down the walkway between stalls, noting the general disorder. "Looks like I'm gonna need all the help I can get. I won't turn you down."

"What are you doin' in my grandma's barn, mister?" a small voice piped from overhead.

Will tipped his head back, one hand snatching his hat from his head as he peered upward. A small face gazed down from the opening to the hayloft, dark braids hanging on either side.

"What are you doin' up there, young'un? Where'd you come from?"

The girl scooted closer to the ladder and, with a rolling movement exposing petticoats and stocking-clad legs, set her shoes on the crude ladder and began the trip down.

"I'm Maggie. Who are you? Is that a real Indian over there?" By the time her feet hit the floor, she had delivered her barrage of questions and was busily smoothing her skirts into place.

Many Fingers folded his arms, assuming a posture that would have done credit to Sitting Bull, if Will was any judge. Granted, his black hair and ruddy complexion were almost a guarantee of his heritage. But the tall moccasins he wore and the feather he'd stuck into his headband were classic touches Will suspected were hued with a bit of defiance.

"This is Many Fingers. I'm Will Tolliver, and who do you belong to?" Her narrow face looked somehow familiar, and yet there was no doubt he'd never seen the girl before. For a moment he wondered if a neighbor's child had wandered by, and then she spoke again.

"My grandma's name is Miz Tolliver and this is her barn. Do you know her?"

Will squatted, bringing him to eye level with the child. "Yeah. She's my mother, and I suspect you belong to one of my brothers, don't you?"

"Is Uncle Eben and Uncle Samuel your brothers?" she asked, reaching up to twist one of her braids around her fingers. Her small face was so earnest, her eyes so blindingly blue and familiar, she was almost like a carbon copy of...Josie. She had to be Josie's child.

"Who's your mother?" Will asked, reaching to brush a wisp of hay from her sleeve.

"My mother's not here," Maggie answered. "She had to go away."

"Is your mother named Josie?" Will asked, fighting the urge to draw her into his embrace. His hand slid to clasp hers within his grasp and his eyes were drawn to the sight of her plump fingers spread across his palm.

"My daddy calls her Josie and so does Grandma. I just call her Mama." Flexing her fingers against his callused skin, she eyed him warily. "Do you know my mama?"

"She's my sister, honey. That makes you my niece. What do you think of that?" His words were husky with an emotion he could not hide, and he cleared his throat noisily.

"Am I supposed to call you Uncle Will?" she asked dubiously. "And what do I call him?" She gestured at the watching man.

"You can call me Tall Horse," Many Fingers said, halting Will's reply.

"Tall Horse?" Spoken in unison, the words were a query in themselves.

"I never heard of anybody called that," Maggie announced.

"Me, neither," Will echoed. "How many names you got?"

Many Fingers shrugged. "Several. Tall Horse is what the tribe called me."

From outside the barn a loud clanging drowned out Will's reply, and Maggie squeezed his index finger with her pudgy fist. She urged him toward the doorway.

"That means that supper is about ready. Grandma wants me to wash my hands before I eat."

Will freed himself from her grip. "I'll unload my mule

and bring the pack inside. You go on ahead, Maggie. We'll be right behind you.''

The child nodded and ran off, her pigtails bobbing. Will watched in wonder. She sure was the picture of Josie. At least, the Josie he'd last seen ten years ago. And that would make her about twenty-two years old now. Maybe she'd show up tonight from wherever she'd had to go.

"How long has she been gone?" Will asked unbelievingly.

His mother shrugged, placing a bowl of stew before him. "Almost a year now. She sent a letter a month or so ago, said she was about ready to come back and get Maggie."

Will cast a glance at the child sitting across the table. "How…?" He broke off the question that hovered on the tip of his tongue, thinking better of it. He shook his head. How any mother could leave her little girl and traipse off across the country with a no-good husband was beyond him.

"Will?" Cassie caught his attention, easing a thick china mug of coffee next to his bowl. "I've got to talk to you," she whispered in his ear, her breath warm against his skin.

He turned his head, and his mouth came perilously close to hers. Hers was not smiling, he noted. In fact, Cassie looked as if she were mightily upset about something or another. "Gonna sit by me?" he asked, nudging the chair beside his from the table.

"Cassie said she'd sit by me," Maggie sang out from across the table.

"Guess I didn't ask quick enough," Will grumbled, winking at the child to soften his words as he took up his spoon.

"You hafta wait till we pray before you eat, Uncle

Will," Maggie said primly, folding her hands precisely at the edge of the table.

It had been more years than he wanted to count since Will had observed that ritual and he nodded, replacing his spoon.

Many Fingers stood by the door and Will's mother eyed him grudgingly, her mouth pursed as if she must perform a distasteful deed. Will spoke up, taking the task from her willingly, lifting a hand to signal the Indian. "Why don't you sit at the end of the table?" he asked.

Many Fingers hesitated, his gaze following the older woman as she carried two more bowls of stew from the stove. "You might as well, I guess," she said. "If you're going to be working here like Will says, you'll have to eat your meals in the house. I don't serve supper in the barn."

As a welcome it left something to be desired, but her attempt at jocularity was a good sign, Will decided. She'd apparently accepted the man's presence, and that was all he could expect for now.

The food was blessed and was consumed quickly. "I'd expected that stew to last for a couple of days," Will's mother said. "It's a good thing I cooked up plenty this afternoon." She paused, hands full of crockery, eyeing her son. "I put clean sheets on your bed. You can take your things up and show Cassie where to put her clothes."

"Cassie?" His mind a blank, Will looked across the room to where Cassie was cutting a pie in wedges. He'd had it in his head that Cassie would sleep in Josie's room, and even the appearance of Josie's child had not nudged that thought from his mind. Now he faced the facts. This is what Cassie wanted to talk about.

If Clara Tolliver thought he and Cassie were truly married, she'd certainly expect them to sleep in the same room. In the same bed, as a matter of fact. And how that would go over with Cassie was another thing he'd have to consider.

"I found a bunk in the tack room," Many Fingers offered. "Already put my bedroll on it."

Cassie turned, her hands filled with plates of pie. Her face was flushed, and she refused to meet Will's eye. Carrying four pieces of pie at once took her concentration and she placed them on the table quickly, sliding into her place once more.

"Aren't you having any, Cassie?" Will asked. She looked at him and shook her head. The blush staining her cheeks had not eased, and he attempted a reassuring smile.

"Why's your face all red?" Maggie asked brightly, grinning at Cassie. A forkful of pie went into her mouth and she chewed industriously as she watched the young woman.

"I guess I got a little too much sun today," Cassie managed tightly. A look of pure desperation shot from her blue eyes to where Will watched her misery in silence.

He pushed his chair back from the table. "I reckon I'd better get things settled before it gets to be full dark," he said, motioning at Cassie. "Come on, Cass. We'll carry this stuff upstairs."

"There's candles in the bedroom, Will," his mother called after them. "It'll be dark before you know it."

Their footsteps were loud on the bare stair treads and down the short hallway to the last room. The open door revealed a double bed with two plump pillows perched at the headboard. His old dresser sat against the far wall, between the windows, and his books still stood upright, a wooden bookend at each end. A canning jar filled with an assortment of pebbles and rocks of varied hues caught his eye, and he felt a pang of love for the mother who had saved his boyhood treasures.

"Come on in, Cassie," he said over his shoulder, edging

to one side to give her room. She followed him in and he closed the door. Her eyes flew to the handle and he shook his head. "Don't even think about it, Cass. We need the door closed for a few minutes."

"It's not proper for us to be in a bedroom together, Will," she said in a harsh whisper.

He grinned. "Cass, we've been sleepin' together for almost two weeks already. Unless you want to go down there and tell my ma that we're not the married couple she thinks we are, we're stuck with this until I can figure something out."

"Once we sleep in this room together, we're stuck with the story, no matter how you slice it," she hissed at him.

"Well, I can't come up with any better idea," Will said softly, attempting to placate the angry woman before him. "I'm afraid your reputation is about shot, Cass. It's my fault, I admit it, but I don't know what I can do about it tonight. Do you want me to go downstairs and tell my mother we've traipsed clear from Texas without being married?"

She shook her head. "I don't know what I want, Will. I just know I don't want to sleep in that bed with you tonight."

"Look, Cassie. I'm tired. You're tired. I'm not about to have a fuss over this. I'll sleep on the floor." Ground from between his teeth, the proposal was probably the best she was going to get, he decided. "Take it or leave it, Cass."

"I don't even have a nightgown," she whispered, her eyes widening, her lashes blinking rapidly.

Unless he missed his guess, Cassie was about to become a wailing woman. The tears making their way down her cheeks looked to be a prelude to a veritable waterfall, if he knew anything about it. And Cassie having a bawling fit was not what he wanted to cope with tonight.

He took two long strides and pulled her against his body. His arms wrapped around her firmly, giving her no chance to dispute his possession. "Now, hush," he said sternly against her forehead. "None of that, Cass. We'll settle everything tomorrow. For tonight, you can wear one of my shirts to bed. Tomorrow we'll go to town and get you some clothes, get you dressed up proper."

"What will your mother say when she finds out I don't have any clothes?" It was a subdued wail, and Will tugged her face against his chest to muffle the sound.

"You've got your dress," he reminded her quietly. "Will that do until I can buy you some things in the morning?"

"It's torn and I couldn't get it very clean when I washed it out in the creek," she said, her words mumbled against his shirt. "I've only got the other pants and shirt you bought me, and if I go to town in them, I'll be a laughingstock."

Will's fingers grasped her shoulders, and he shook her once. "No one will laugh at you, Cassie. I promise you."

She looked up at him dubiously, her tearstained cheeks flushed, her eyes swollen. Wisps of dark hair hung on either side of her face, evidence of her failure to keep it properly subdued in its braid. She was a sight to behold, he decided, ragtag and disheveled. Probably the prettiest woman he'd ever laid eyes on, and that was the truth.

Her mouth trembled and he frowned, certain she was about to dampen his shirt once more. There was one way to satisfy his own urges and give Cassie something else to think about. Besides, it was what he'd been wanting to do for the past several days.

Bending to her, his mouth opened as it settled over hers, his lips capturing his prize with unerring precision.

She uttered a muffled protest and then, with a sigh of

defeat, leaned her weight against him and wound her arms around his neck. It was a surrender he had not even hoped for, an embrace he had not imagined he would receive, and it was not in him to deny himself the pleasure of accepting both.

He scooped her against his length, his kiss taking all the sweetness she offered, his tongue careful as he tasted the flavor that was uniquely her own. Her murmurs of assent urged him on and he left her mouth to seek the warmth of her throat. Lifting her in his arms, he made his way to the chair near the bed, settling himself with Cassie on his lap, his arms full of warm and acquiescent woman.

"Will, I'm so tired," she whispered.

He smiled against her warm skin, his mouth leaving a trail of small pecking kisses on her cheek. "Here I thought you were likin' my kissin', and you're just too sleepy to hold your head up," he teased.

"I do like your kissing," she admitted.

"We can get married, Cass," he said carefully.

"Liking your kissing isn't reason enough to marry you," she told him, pushing away from his embrace.

"I think it might be."

"I think we ought to tell your mother the truth," she said, sitting upright on his lap.

"I mean it, Cassie. I don't want you goin' off somewhere else. I said I'd take care of you. If that means marrying you, I'm willing."

Her look was dubious. "That doesn't sound like the kind of proposal I've waited all my life to hear."

"Well, it's the best I've got to offer right now," he said, his words stiff, his manner unyielding as he set her on her feet and rose to face her. Somehow, it hadn't come out the way he'd meant it to.

Cassie's eyes were accusing, her mouth still damp from

his kisses, and unless he missed his guess, she was not in the mood for any more.

Damn it all, anyway. He'd just offered marriage for the first time in his twenty-seven years and been turned down, if he'd heard her right. He ought to let her stew. At least he'd made the offer. It was more then he'd ever done for any other woman in his life.

"I'll get you some warm water from the cookstove so you can wash up," he said, turning to the door. "Maybe you'll think better of it in the morning."

Chapter Seven

She awoke with Will curled around her back, his breath warm against her neck, his big hand flopped across her hip. Cassie sighed and gazed pensively out the window across the room, where the night sky had begun to turn a sort of pinkish gray color at the horizon.

It was too much to expect of him, that he would sleep all night on the hard floor while she occupied his bed. But at the same time she felt an overwhelming guilt as she pictured the two of them nestled in the middle of his bed. What if his mother could see them?

Of course, that wouldn't be any shock to Clara Tolliver, seeing as how she thought they were truly married.

Cassie shoved at Will's warm hand, immediately missing the comfort of his touch as it slid from its place. She sat up and he mumbled, only her name coming through audibly, and then he turned to his back, clearing his throat and stretching his long legs to full length.

"Will? You told me you'd sleep on the floor." Faintly accusing, her whisper brought him bolt upright in bed.

"Don't start, Cassie." He rubbed his head with both hands, scratching at his scalp and then running his fingers through his hair as he brushed it back. "That damn floor was harder than the ground, I swear. You managed to sleep all night with me right behind you. There's no sense in gettin' all riled up this morning.''

Her guilt increased as he spoke. It was true enough. He'd only done what he'd been doing for the past nights, sleeping next to her. He hadn't even kissed her, except for shutting her up last evening, and in her book that didn't really count as a kiss.

"We're in a mess, Will," she said, feeling the tears well up behind her eyelids. "Maybe I'd better just keep going once you take me to town this morning. I can probably find a place to stay. Isn't there a nice family that needs a nurse for their children or something?"

"How would I know, Cass?" he grumbled, rolling back over, tugging her down to the mattress. "I haven't been home in over ten years. Half the people in town wouldn't know me if they saw me face-to-face. And the other half probably don't remember me, anyway." He yawned widely and rubbed his chin against her hair. "There's a nice family right here, honey, and a little girl who needs somebody to tend to her, in the room right next door to us."

"Maggie?" She thought wistfully for a moment of the child she'd found so appealing last night. Round eyed and rosy cheeked, Maggie had won her heart the first time those dimples had flashed her way. The tangled curls needed a good brushing, she'd decided right off, her fingers itching to get hold of the dark ringlets and tie a ribbon in their depths.

"Your mother might not want me to take care of Maggie," Cassie argued mildly. She'd never felt so wishy-washy in her life. Here she was, surrounded by his warmth again, already almost talked out of making her own way, letting him coax her into doing things his way.

"I have a feelin' Ma would pretty much let you do anything you want, Cass. She's tickled pink to have you here. I think she's got the idea that being married guarantees my stickin' around."

Cassie stiffened, pushing herself upright again, and over the side of the bed. Standing on the oval braided rug, she turned back to face the man who occupied half her pillow. "That's the whole problem, Will. You're not married. And neither am I, and probably not likely to be. I want to marry a man who loves me, not somebody who gets stuck with me."

"Oh, I don't know, honey," he drawled. "I don't mind gettin' stuck with you. I've been thinkin' ever since we saw that sheriff the second day out, maybe gettin' married would be a good idea. It's about time I settled down and started thinkin' about makin' a home."

She looked disbelievingly at him. "You've been thinking that for the past couple of weeks? I don't believe you!"

He grinned, his eyes crinkling at the corners, his gaze working its way down the front of her makeshift gown to rest on the length of her bare legs. "Well, I'm sure thinkin' it now, honey. The sight of you in my shirt is causin' all sorts of ideas to creep into my mind."

Cassie looked down at herself in dismay. The shirt covered her wonderfully well, as far as it went, ending just above her knees. From there on, rounded calves curved into slim ankles. She shuffled her feet closer to the bed, as if she would conceal as much as she could from his view.

Will reached out one hand and clutched a handful of his shirt, just below her waist, and tugged her closer. "Sit down here, Cass." He drew her to the edge of the bed and she sank to the mattress. His fingers loosened their grip and fell to rest against her knee, warming her flesh through the material of his shirt as it billowed around her slender form.

Cassie watched him, silent in the dim light of the bedroom, confused and more uncertain of her future than she'd ever been. And that was saying a whole lot, she thought sadly. Through the years traipsing from one place to another with Mama, and then both of them living with Remus Chandler after Cleta had given in to his coaxing and married him, she'd never felt more forlorn than she did right this minute.

She'd always had her mother to look after things, except there at the end, when their positions had been so abruptly reversed. Maybe that night when Cleta had breathed her last had been more confusing than this morning, but the panic welling up in Cassie's throat right now was enough to make her wonder.

"I hear my mother in the kitchen," Will said, his expression somber as his eyes met hers. "Maybe we need to talk about this later, Cassie. For now, let's just get downstairs. I've got chores to do. I'd be willin' to bet my brother Eben is out in the barn already."

He rolled from the other side of the bed, and Cassie's eyes opened wide as she caught sight of his long underwear, one button undone in the rear, a small curving portion of his backside showing in the exposed area. Quickly she averted her eyes. That small, pale slice of skin was about as intimate a sight as she'd ever beheld. She'd had a glimpse of his upper body when he washed up on the trail, furtively noting the curly mat of hair that covered his chest, her gaze taken with the rippling muscles across his back. But that memory didn't hold a candle to seeing a portion of his backside, when it came right down to it.

How she'd managed to get herself into such a pickle was about as worrisome as anything that had ever happened in her life. Will Tolliver made her heart swell within her chest when he held her close to him, made her stomach churn as if it was full of speckled butterflies when he kissed her, and all in all made her yearn for a nameless something she had never held within her grasp.

He'd taken over her life, it seemed, making choices for her and taking her on as if tending to her was sort of a crusade.

Maybe he didn't love her, with all his talk of getting married, but unless she missed her guess, she was well on her way to losing her heart to the man.

Lifting her head, she watched as he buttoned his shirt, then tucked it into his trousers. The bottom of his long underwear was out of sight, his shirtsleeves were fastened snugly and he bent to pick up his boots. Stepping to where the pitcher of water waited on the table by the door, he poured a small amount into the china bowl. Then he lowered his head, splashing the water on his face, his fingers running through his hair to dampen its dark length. He straightened, peering into the mirror, then felt the surface of the table until his fingers touched the brush that lay there. A few quick movements brought a semblance of order to his hair and he turned from the mirror to face Cassie.

"Get dressed and come on down," he told her. "I'll be in for breakfast."

She nodded, thankful for the dim light in the room, aware of the flush that warmed her cheeks. "I'll be right down." This is what it would be like to be married to the man, this intimate sharing of a bedroom, watching him dress and knowing what was beneath the clothes he wore. At least, knowing most of what his clothing concealed. She was only too aware of the parts he'd not exposed to her sight, the long length of his muscled legs, the male strength of his loins.

"Oh, Lordy, what am I going to do?" She sighed as the door shut behind him. "Will Tolliver, you've got me in a pickle, that's for sure."

* * *

The sight of Many Fingers shoved up against the outside wall of the barn greeted Will as he left the back porch. Setting out at a run, he hollered at the broad-shouldered man who held the Indian in a throttling grip.

"Eben, for cryin' out loud!" The words surged forth on separate breaths as Will's long legs covered the dusty earth beneath his boots. "Eben!" He shouted the name as his hands gripped his brother's shoulders, spinning the man about to face him.

Many Fingers slid to the ground, his already ruddy complexion a darker hue as he fought to regain his breath. "I told you..." he gasped, holding up a hand for emphasis as he glared at Eben Tolliver.

"For cryin' out loud, what the hell's goin' on here?" Eben shoved Will from him, his big fists clenching, ready to do business. And then he took a closer look, blinking as he caught sight of the wide grin of the man who'd halted his assault.

With instinctive delight, Eben reached for the brother he hadn't seen in ten years and clutched him firmly, the slap of his palm sounding loudly as he clapped his hand against Will's back.

"Damn, it's good to see you." Will pushed Eben from him, his eyes aglow at the welcome sight of the stocky man his younger brother had become.

"Will? Where'd you come from? Ma said she wrote you, but when she didn't get an answer, we figured you'd headed out again, or got yourself shot or something." Eben's good-natured face lit up with an answering grin as he spoke. And then he turned to Many Fingers. "Where'd the Indian come from? He belong to you?"

Will laughed. "You'll get yourself in trouble talkin' that way, Eben. Many Fingers is my..." He hesitated, eyes fastened on the man who watched in silence. "I guess you could say Many Fingers is my friend. We've been through a lot together."

White teeth flashed against his skin as Many Fingers nodded. "Will Tolliver is a good man. He gave me a job here."

Will's brow lifted. "I did?"

The Indian nodded. "I'm going to take care of your horses."

Eben looked from one to the other. "First time you've heard about this, Will?"

"No, now that I think about it, the idea got chewed over one night around a campfire. Guess I didn't think about havin' to hire him on. He's just part of the package, so to speak."

"What package?" Eben looked confused, as if he had missed an important element in this conversation.

Will grinned. "Let's get the chores done first and then you can get a firsthand look."

"Where you been, Will?" Side by side the two men strode down the wide aisle of the barn, one picking up a pitchfork, the other filling a bucket from the oat bin as they went. From the far end they worked their way back to the door, Will making a trip back to refill his bucket as they talked.

Many Fingers pitched pungent straw and manure from the stalls into a wooden wheelbarrow, wheeling it outside when it was in danger of overflowing. Steadily he worked his way past the brothers, until he'd emptied every stall of its contents.

"Been a while since I've cleaned all the stalls," Eben said apologetically. "It's been about all I could do just to feed and turn the horses out in the pasture, mornings. I'd about decided to leave them out full-time, anyway, what with the weather warming up the way it has lately. But I worried that one of them might get out and Ma wouldn't be able to chase it down. That fence on the north side of the near pasture is pretty well done for."

"I think I've got my work cut out for me," Will answered, putting the oat bucket away and turning to where Many Fingers appeared in the barn door. "About done there?" he asked.

Eben cleared his throat and approached the Indian. "I didn't know you were a friend of Will's. You should have spoke up right off."

Many Fingers nodded. "Maybe so, but you caught me with my pants down."

Eben laughed. "That's what you get for takin' your mornin' leak in a stall."

Will was hard put not to join his brother's hearty laughter, once he caught sight of Many Fingers' chagrin. Then the sound of the bell on the back porch clanging a summons to breakfast caught his ear, and he motioned to the other men.

"Ma's got the biscuits done." His long strides took him in seconds to where the pump handle awaited his grip. He grasped it, pumped twice and then wet his hands beneath its flow. A dish of soap on the edge of the trough caught his eye, and he chuckled.

"Ma left a reminder for us. What was it she used to say, Eben? Clean hands were a sign of an empty belly?" He scrubbed vigorously at his fingers, washing up to the cuffs of his shirt, then waited as Eben pumped more water.

"Yeah, she still says it," Eben said with a sigh. "Ma hasn't changed a whit, still treats me like a kid sometimes." He bent low to splash water on his face and then washed his hands vigorously, Many Fingers following suit. Then, waving their hands to dry them in the morning air, they headed for the house.

The back door closed behind them, and Cassie turned from the stove. Her face flushed from the heat, her hair curling in defiance of her best efforts to slick it back earlier, she was a temptation to behold.

From behind Will a low voice murmured an echo to his thoughts. "If this is the rest of the package, you've got yourself a mighty fine-lookin' female, brother."

Will frowned. He'd gotten used to Cassie's round bottom encased in pants, and to give him credit, Many Fingers had seemed to ignore her womanly charms. Having Eben take note so bluntly wasn't what he wanted to hear. The sooner he got her into dresses again, the better he was going to like it.

They took the wagon to town, Clara Tolliver having decided to ride along. She'd introduce Cassie around, she told Will, although he secretly wondered if she wasn't just worried about the younger woman's reception. Wearing male attire and showing up with Will, unannounced, Cassie might be the focus of gossip, Will's mother told him quietly. And that would never do.

Maggie rode in the back of the wagon, swinging her legs in time with the song she sang beneath her breath. That the child was a constant reminder of Josie was a nagging ache somewhere in the vicinity of Will's heart. His mother had been silent on the subject, and he'd hesitated to bring it up until they were alone. But the absence of his sister was like a sore spot he could not help but dwell on.

As if she read his thoughts, his mother peered past Cassie, who rode in the middle of the wide seat, and spoke in a low tone, so as not to allow Maggie to hear.

"Josie's not a bad mother, Will, no matter what you might be thinkin'." Her mouth pinched and her forehead furrowed as she watched his reaction.

"Why isn't she here, then, takin' care of her little girl?" he asked bluntly, his voice a grumbling undertone. "She couldn't have a better home, Ma, and that's a fact, but the child needs her mother."

Clara nodded. "I know, but there's more to it than that." Looking over her shoulder to where Maggie sang on, she smiled, a gentle upturning of her mouth that softened her features and took years from her face. "That gambler she took up with isn't fit to wipe my girl's shoes, much less be a father to this child. He coaxed Josie to go off with him, said his way of living didn't include a baby taggin' along."

"And Josie went along with that?" Will asked, unbelievingly. "She just left Maggie and walked away?"

"Don't be too hard on her, Will. I think she was trying to make a last stab at keeping her man happy." Clara's face sobered as if she thought Josie's action to be a futile effort.

Cassie's voice was soft as she spoke into the silence. "I'm sure Josie knew you'd take good care of her child, Mrs. Tolliver. And I'll be glad to help, if you'll let me."

Will looked down at Cassie, a cautious elation gripping him. It sounded to him as if his little runaway was about to settle in and take hold at the farm. So much for her veiled threats to leave. Stay with a family in town, indeed. As if he'd let her run any farther. As far as he was concerned, her days of being on her own were done for.

He slid an arm around her waist and tugged her against his side. "I'll bet Ma will take you up on that offer, Cass. And Maggie's already taken a shine to you."

"I didn't shine nothing, Uncle Will," the child piped up from the back of the wagon, her ears attuned to the sound of her name being spoken.

Cassie laughed aloud, and Maggie turned to crawl on hands and knees the length of the wagon until she could pull herself upright to stand behind the seat. Her small face appeared between Cassie and Will, her chin resting on Will's shoulder.

"Were you jokin' at me, Uncle Will?" she asked.

"No, I just said you'd taken a liking to Cassie, here. I said you'd taken a shine to her."

"She's pretty, isn't she?" the child said, almost whispering, as if she told a secret against his ear.

Will turned, a crooked smile twisting his mouth. "Yeah, you could say that, Maggie. 'Course, sometimes she's pretty picky, too, givin' me a hard time."

Cassie flushed, obviously not comfortable with being the focus of Will's attention in front of others. "I'm not pretty. My mother always said looks aren't everything. A person has to be beautiful inside, where it really counts."

"Your mother sounds like a smart lady," Clara said quietly. "But I suspect you've got your share of beauty, both inside and out, Cassie. Will would never pick a girl to marry who wasn't worth a bundle."

Cassie shrank in Will's loose embrace. Her head drooped, her shoulders slumping, and she cleared her throat uneasily.

"Well, I've picked Cassie, sure enough," he said, leaning across her slender form to deliver the firm statement in his mother's direction. Something was going to have to be done, and soon, he decided. He might have to do some fast talking, but Cassie was going to agree to be his wife before the week was out, if he had his way.

Cassie's new dresses hung in the wardrobe Will had dragged down the hall from Maggie's room, the child's belongings fitting easily into her mother's old chest of drawers. Three dresses hung side by side, one fit for Sunday wear, the other two designed as everyday apparel. She stood before the wooden cupboard taking stock, her fingers touching first one dress, then another as she considered the riches of having a choice tomorrow morning when she got dressed.

And Will had said there were to be more, that three dresses were not enough. He'd added two petticoats to the collection on the counter, plus two chemises; and her cheeks had turned crimson when Dorinda Bartlett, the storekeeper's wife, had shoved two pairs of drawers beneath the growing pile.

It was a disgrace, Cassie thought as the blush returned, a man buying her personal things. But she'd been the only one in the store to think so, apparently. Certainly the ladies who'd surrounded her had considered it to be his right, if not his duty, to outfit his wife, since her own clothing had been "washed away when they crossed a river, back in Oklahoma."

How Will had come up with such a far-fetched tale on the spur of the moment was beyond her. But manufacture it he had, and with a straight face. She'd been obliged to smile and murmur her thanks as he scouted out the store, calling her to his side to try on a pair of shoes. Protest as she might, he'd bought the soft kid footwear and she'd held the box on her lap all the way home in the wagon.

Now she viewed her riches by candlelight. Will had spent an hour with Samuel, his youngest brother, doing chores and then drinking buttermilk on the back porch as they caught up on all the happenings in their lives over the past ten years. Samuel was kind, quiet and slow talking, a contrast to Will. Warned by Eben that his brother was at the farm, Samuel had turned up early for chores, and then had been persuaded to stay for supper.

Only the arrival of his eldest son, riding bareback on a plowhorse, prodded him into leaving for home. His promise to return, bringing his wife, Elizabeth, along with all three of their brood, rang in Cassie's ears.

It was bad enough that the whole family thought she was married to Will. Now they were planning a party to celebrate the wedding. Eben and Louise were to come tomorrow to visit.

Cassie's groan of despair was loud in the silence of the bedroom. Burying her face in the bend of her elbow, she leaned against the wardrobe, eyes closed, panic rising like a giant fist in her throat.

To the man standing outside the door, holding his boots in one hand, it was a cry for help. Turning the knob, he opened the door, his stocking feet quiet against the polished wood flooring. His eyes softened as he beheld Cassie's dark hair, brushed from its braid to fall in a tangle of waves past her waist. And then he spied the trembling of her shoulders beneath the gleaming mass, heard the soft sound she muffled against her hand.

Silently he closed the door behind himself, depositing his boots by the door, then crossed the room to where she stood, oblivious to his presence. His hands enclosed her shoulders and he turned her around, her arm dropping to reveal a face that echoed the perplexities of her very being. Her mouth trembling, she reached out to him, hands clutching at his shirtfront.

"Will, everyone thinks we're married. I feel like such a fraud." As if she were fearful of being overheard, she whispered her thoughts for his ears alone.

"It's gonna be all right, Cassie," he said quietly, pulling her into his embrace. She leaned against him, seemingly grateful for his support, her face buried against his chest.

"What are we going to do?" she wailed, the sound thankfully subdued, her words muffled.

"I already told you my solution to the problem, honey.

As soon as we can make it, we'll head for Mill Creek. There were a couple of churches there if I remember right. Might even be more by now, and I'll guarantee there're preachers to spare. I'm sure one or the other will marry us and keep our secret.''

She lifted her face from the front of his shirt, rubbing her nose with her knuckles. "I need a hankie," she whispered, sniffing and blinking away tears that begged to be shed.

Will reached into his pocket. "This is a clean one, Cass. Hasn't been blown in since last time Ma washed it. I reckon it'll do the job."

"Thank you," she said politely, taking it and swiping at her nose and eyes. "Will, I won't marry you when I know this isn't what you would choose for yourself." Her eyes were sorrowful as she met his gaze, and he hurt for the sadness there.

"How do you know what I want, Cassie?" And even as he spoke the words his body responded to the soft appeal of her breasts against his chest, the movement of her hips as she shifted from one foot to the other. He slid his hands down her back and pressed her against the proof of his desire.

"Know what that is, Cass?" He lifted her against his body, moving his hips, the evidence of his need for her wedging itself into the place nature had designed for its safekeeping. He moved again, his breathing harsh as he pressed more fully against her softness.

"Will?" Her plea was whispered, her eyes widening as she recognized the primitive urgency of his desire. "Please, Will."

"Do you think it'll be any great hardship for me to make

love to you, honey?'' His words were hoarse in her ear, and then he lifted her higher still, until their faces were level. His lips touched hers and his groan was spent in the depths of her mouth as she opened to his silent plea.

Chapter Eight

"Make love to me?" Her eyes closed as she considered her position.

Her feet dangling inches from the floor, she was about as helpless as she'd ever been, and not all of that was due to the fact that Will had her clamped against him with an iron grip. His mouth was nuzzling in her neck now, under her ear, where there was a spot that had never seemed to be of any great interest to her before. Right now it was sending sparks down the length of her, centering in the lowest depths of her belly and causing her to wiggle against Will's hard body.

"Are you making love to me, Will Tolliver?" she asked breathlessly. "Because if that's what this is, I don't think we'd ought to do it."

He came up for air, his warm breath sending chills down her spine, causing her to shiver. How any one person could affect her so was a puzzlement, that was for sure. Between the sparks and the chills, Will had her body in a frenzy, as if it needed to twist and turn and grind up against him in order to put an end to the way her heart was beating in all her major parts.

"I guess that's what you call it, honey. It's sort of early

lovemakin', like leadin' up to the event.'' His whisper was back at her ear and he blew gently in a circular motion, cooling the spot he'd so recently dampened with his tongue.

Her toes touched the denim fabric of his trousers and she rubbed them against the rough surface, sliding her foot up and down his shinbone. With a lithe movement she hooked her heel behind his knee and drew his leg closer, till he laughed against her shoulder.

"Damn, Cassie! You're playin' a rough game with me. I'm gonna drop you on the floor if you're not careful, girl.''

As if he feared that very thing to happen, he limped to the bed, her foot and leg all tangled up with his, off balance and hanging on to her with a grip that felt as though she'd be bruised by morning.

Together they fell across the mattress, and the headboard thumped up against the wall. Cassie looked up at him, wide-eyed and breathless, aware of the weight of his body shoving her into the mattress. His knees had somehow gotten planted one on each side of her right leg, and her robe and gown were twisted halfway up her thighs.

She was exposed to him in about the most intimate way she could imagine, and she reached to loosen herself from the grip of the fabric. Will laughed, a throaty, teasing sound. And from the droopy-eyed look of him he was pretty pleased with the whole thing.

"I don't think this is a very good idea,'' she managed to whisper, gasping for a lung-filling breath.

Lifting himself from her, he crouched on hands and knees, surrounding her with his male strength. He watched closely as she pulled one breath after another into her, releasing each in a series of silent puffs, feeling as if her head was filling with crackling sparks, like lightning across a summer sky.

"You all right, honey?'' he asked, his brows pulling together over dark eyes that roamed her body as if they searched for an unseen malady.

"You make me breathe funny," she said accusingly. "I can't seem to think straight when you start this kind of fooling around."

With a wry chuckle he toppled to the bed beside her, pulling her into his embrace and burying his face in her hair. It was all pooled around them both, the dark strands clinging to his shirt, curling beneath her and across the bed above her head. She'd never felt so disheveled and exposed in all her life, sprawled out on a bed with a man, and for the most part enjoying it. Except for the part of her that felt guilty about being in his bedroom and his mother thinking they were husband and wife.

His eyes were searching as he examined her face, and then he drew a deep breath. "I think you've just put a stop to it, honey," he said, rocking her against him, making the bed creak. "Let me just kiss you a little bit and I'll quit before things get out of hand, I promise."

She tilted her head back and blinked at him, the candle on the dresser providing just about enough light to make out his face well. "You already kissed me, Will."

His right hand slid from her back to rest on her ribs and she moved restlessly, aware of those long fingers moving in a slow, seductive dance, sliding the material of her gown against her flesh.

Somehow her robe had gotten pushed aside and only the white gown Will had bought her in the general store this morning was between his hand and her skin. Her throat was dry as she inhaled through her mouth and watched his face.

He was frowning just a bit, as if he must concentrate on the minute movement of his fingers, his palm edging to rest beneath her breast, shifting upward just a bit, until he

cupped the weight of it. His eyes closed and his mouth
tilted again in one corner, that satisfied look appearing as
his nostrils flared with the breath he took.

His hand slid up to cover her breast, his fingers wide-
spread as he measured the soft globe with his whole hand.
Two fingers squeezed the crest between them, gently as if
he feared to hurt the tender flesh. And to her dismay, Cassie
felt that small nubbin harden and tingle against his touch.

"Right here's where I want to kiss you, honey," he told
her, then as if he recognized the futility of that wish, dipped
his head to drop a smattering of damp salutes against her
forehead and across one cheek. His sigh was deep as his
mouth found hers, gentling her with a succession of small,
tender kisses, soothing her and cuddling her with gentle
brushes of his fingers across her cheeks.

"Ah, Cassie." He bowed his head against her shoulder.
"I shouldn't have done that to you."

His mouth silenced her before she could speak, kissing
her lips with tender, small, biting touches, soothing them
as he went with the very tip of his tongue. He whispered
words of comfort, his hand busy tucking her gown around
her legs. He withdrew from her, patting her bottom with a
gentle hand, easing her to his side until he could enfold her
in his embrace.

He turned her, his greater strength holding her until he
could pull down the quilt and sheet, sliding them both beneath the covers. Now, still dressed in his pants and shirt,
his arm around her middle, he tugged her against himself,
easing his thighs under hers.

"You all right, honey?" he asked against her ear, lifting
his head just a bit to brush his mouth against the tender
lobe. He caught her hair in his hand, gathering it from beneath her and himself, twisting the length of it around his
hand and then placing the heavy, curling weight of it be-

tween them, against his chest. Brushing his chin over the silken strands, he inhaled the scent of her that rose from the rich, dark tresses.

"Sweetheart?" She nodded a silent reply. He squeezed her just a bit, aware that his lapse had probably frightened her. He'd never needed a woman so badly in his life, not even that first time in the hayloft when he was sixteen and Sally Ann Forbes had offered him his first taste of glory. That Cassie was not a Sally Ann Forbes was obvious. She'd responded, true, but her response had been that of an innocent, her movements governed by a desire she'd obviously never felt before.

He shifted, aware of the discomfort his thoughts were causing. Getting married was the first thing on his list of things to do, that was for sure. Whether or not Cassie was ready for it, with her talk of having a man that loved her, it was going to happen.

Love was something women seemed to take a lot of stock in. Whether or not it was essential to marriage, he didn't know. But whatever he felt for the woman in his arms, it was going to be enough to have him saying his "I do" loud and clear.

In the bright light of morning it seemed his list of things to do was going to have a few additions, right at the top. Three horses had made their way out of the pasture before dawn, Samuel and Will having decided that they'd do just fine out of the barn with two men handy to keep an eye on things.

Many Fingers was riding bareback on a sturdy cow pony, his knees and calves tight against the horse's sides, rounding up the strays. Somewhere he'd learned to handle a rope very well, Will noticed. The loop sailed through the air, landing with a satisfying swish around the neck of one of

Nate Tolliver's prize mares. She halted in her tracks, as if aware that her freedom had come to a screeching halt, bending her head to nibble at the grass beneath her feet.

Many Fingers tugged at the rope and led her back to the barn, sliding from the pony he rode before he led the stray to a stall. In seconds he reappeared and Will lifted a hand against the brilliant sunrise to watch as the Indian leapt gracefully astride the horse. The cow pony broke into a gallop and within minutes the next wanderer had been retrieved.

"Guess he doesn't need me, does he?" he asked, his query an assessment of the Indian's skill.

From within the kitchen, his mother banged the stove lid in place. "I'd say that pasture fence needs you, Will. I knew you were going to have a problem, lettin' those horses out last night."

"There's new grass out there, Ma. We're wastin' money feedin' those animals the last of the hay when they can be fillin' up on fresh stuff."

"You'd better see if there's any new posts out in the woodshed. I think your pa had some cut to length last year and just never got around to starting the job." The frying pan rattled against the stove top and Will caught a scent of coffee.

"How long before breakfast?" he asked, undoing his pants and tucking his shirt inside. He smoothed it down over his rear and then straightened the front against his belly. He was wrinkled from sleeping all night in his clothes, but by the time he finished putting up fence, he'd look a lot worse than he did now.

"I'm putting the bacon in the pan now," Clara said from the kitchen. "The biscuits will be done in ten minutes."

Will slid stocking feet into his boots and stomped them in place, then dropped to the ground and strode off in the direction of the barn. A few minutes later, hammer in hand, nails stuffed in both front pockets, he headed for the near pasture fence. Many Fingers was there ahead of him, carrying several long boards to replace those the horses had broken down when they made their escape. The rest of the mares were huddled beneath a cluster of trees, noses to the ground, ignoring the two men who were making sure of their captivity.

"I think just a few nails will hold them in for now," Will said, nodding as Many Fingers held a board in place. "Ma has breakfast almost ready."

"We're just lucky they didn't all take a notion to run off." Reaching for another board, the Indian moved a few feet down the fence, holding the wood in place so that Will could nail it to the upright post.

"They probably think they're in hog heaven out there where they are," Will said, nodding at the dozen or so mares. "Think we're gonna have some new mamas pretty soon?" he asked.

"Your pa must have bred them pretty late last spring," Many Fingers said. "They should be dropping their foals already. I think a couple of them are about due. They're restless, and one of them looked like she was startin' to drip milk last night."

Will sighed, contemplating the length of pasture fencing he was duty bound to replace. It couldn't wait, that was for sure. There was no way on God's green earth he could haul Cassie off to Mill Creek today—or tomorrow, for that matter.

Caring for Maggie was a delight, Cassie decided. She'd washed and dried the child's dark hair, sitting in the sun on the back steps as she brushed the damp from the curling strands. It had been the first real lazy fun she'd had in

longer than she could remember. Just making silly talk with
a child, playing with her curls and lifting them to the top
of her head to be bound by a blue ribbon.

A feeling akin to contentment washed over her as she
soaked up the warm sunshine, listening to the sound of a
mockingbird in a tree by the corner of the house. The
rooster in the henhouse crowed again, belatedly, considering the sun had been up for over two hours and breakfast
was already settled in Cassie's stomach.

Undeserved bliss. With a sigh she rubbed her hands together, her imagination providing the bloodstains she'd
long since washed away. And yet her soul remained colored
by the horror of her guilt, and her heart ached for the deceit
she had practiced against Will Tolliver. He'd done nothing
but good, regarding her as a helpless woman, believing her
lies, while she wallowed in black despair. If only...such
words of futility they were. So undeserving was she of the
joy he'd brought into her life.

Behind her, Will's mother came out of the kitchen, her
movement drawing Cassie from the darkness of her
thoughts. The egg basket swung in Clara's hand as she
moved down the steps, and Cassie jumped from her perch.
"Let me gather the eggs for you, ma'am. I haven't been in
a chicken coop for years, but I'm sure I remember how."

Clara turned to the young woman. "I reckon I could use
the help," she allowed, giving over possession of the basket
readily. "There's a couple of clutches just to the right when
you go in the coop. I got some old biddies settin' on them.
They won't budge anyway, but it'll go better for you if you
steer clear of them. They get right possessive of their
eggs."

"I'll show her the ones, Grandma," Maggie offered eagerly.

Clara's gaze softened on the child, one hand reaching

out to touch the blue ribbon, then allowing a curl to twine itself around the rough skin on her finger. "You sure look pretty, little girl," she said tenderly, then drew back quickly, as if she had betrayed tender feelings better left unexposed.

Cassie sighed, aware of the love that surrounded the child, even bereft of parents, here on this lonesome farm. "She's a lucky little girl, Miz Tolliver." Her eyes met those of Will's mother and she glimpsed a shadow of sadness in the dark depths.

"She'd be luckier if she had her mama here to take care of her. It's not right for a child to be dependent on an old lady to see to her needs."

Cassie shook her head in mute denial of the woman's words. "I'd have given my eyeteeth to have what she has when I was a little girl. My mama loved me, but we went from pillar to post, one place to another. I never had a real home to speak of, and sometimes I felt like I was the one doing the caring, and my mama was the one needing the care."

She'd spoken out of turn, Cassie thought, spilling out all that about her mother. Her face flushed and she backed from the porch. "I'm sorry. I shouldn't have said all that. You don't need to hear—"

Clara Tolliver held up her hand, halting Cassie's words. "Don't apologize. You're right. The child has more than a lot of young'uns do in this world. I guess when it's one of your own, you just want everything to be right and proper. When you and Will have your babies, you'll know what I mean. Being married and making a home...all that's important, doing the right thing."

Right and proper. The right thing. Cassie heard the words, flinching as they burned into her mind. She'd almost belonged to Will last night. And the night before, too. And here his mama thought they were married and things were right and proper beneath her roof. And they were about as wrong as two deceitful people could make it.

If it was up to her, she'd tell Clara Tolliver right now how things were, but she wasn't sure she could hold up under the shame of sleeping in Will's bed for two nights already without being married to the man...and his mother knowing about it.

And if she knew anything at all, it seemed Will had other things on his mind this morning. He'd apparently put their wedding on the back burner, him out there pulling up rotten fence posts and putting in new ones as fast as Many Fingers could set them in place. Between the two of them they were shoveling dirt and banging nails and boards together to beat the band.

"You all right, girl?" Will's mother voiced words of concern as she peered at Cassie. "I suspect talking about your mama got you all upset, didn't it?"

Cassie mumbled a reply and took the egg basket, willing to grasp at the older woman's explanation. "I reckon so, ma'am."

She made her way to the chicken coop, Maggie skipping ahead. The child chattered on about the rooster, then told Cassie to watch where she walked so as not to carry hen poop into the house. By the time they'd steered clear of the setting hens and gathered up a full basket of eggs, Cassie found herself in a better frame of mind, smiling at Maggie's instructions.

Will might have decided to put off the wedding for a while. Maybe, as her mother had told her a couple of years back, if a man got what he wanted up front, he wasn't in any hurry to tie the knot. Like a farmer who wasn't about to buy the cow if he could get the milk free.

She closed her eyes, remembering the look on Will's

face as he'd hovered over her on the bed. Her cheeks were warm as she recalled his mouth, open and hot against her throat, his hands filling themselves with her breasts.

And if that wasn't making love, she sure didn't know what it was.

The shoring up of the pasture fence took longer than Will had estimated. For three long days he and Many Fingers worked at the task. Evenings found them sitting at the kitchen table, the overhead kerosene lamp burning brightly as they inspected their hands for any sign of wood that might have become embedded in their fingers during the day.

Will's daddy had always said that infection followed if wounds weren't cleaned right off. Will knew that if he hadn't been so cussed stubborn he'd have worn gloves all day long. But the chore of taking them off every time he needed to hold a nail in place or use his hammer was a time-waster. And time was a thing he was running short of.

Cassie sat next to him, chewing on her lip as she took on the chore of inspecting Will's fingers the third evening. Sewing needle in hand, she carefully pierced his tough skin, seeking the elusive bit of wood he'd pointed out. Carefully she washed it with carbolic soap, drying it before she rubbed a bit of salve into the small wound.

His eyes were intent on her, admiring her nimble fingers, her deft handling of his injuries. In the glow of the lantern her hair gleamed, the heavy braid she had pinned atop her head alive with varied hues, from darkest honey to the rich brown of a mink's pelt. Her forehead was smooth, her cheeks flushed with some unknown emotion as she worked, holding his hand within her own.

He bent his fingers, capturing hers for a moment, and

she looked up in surprise. "Don't smear that salve, Will. I want it to soak into your skin."

"Your hand is like a little bird in mine," he said quietly, noting the contrast between her narrow fingers with their smoothly rounded nails and his own rough, callused skin. "I've captured it, Cassie." His fingers enclosed her hand easily, and she allowed it, her fist almost hidden in the depths of his grasp.

"Like you've captured me, Will?" she whispered, her eyes on his tanned fingers and his wide hand with a tracing of dark hair over its back.

He chuckled. "Have I? Captured you, I mean?"

Her gaze rose to meet his. "I'm here, aren't I? I'm living in your home, sleeping in your bed. I'm wearing the clothes you bought me, and every day I live here is a lie."

His smile vanished, and his grip on her hand tightened. "Come along, Cassie." Tugging her from her chair, he circled her waist with his other arm and headed for the hallway where the stairs climbed to the second floor.

In silence they walked up the bare treads and down the hall to where Will's bedroom door stood open. Reluctantly she allowed him to steer her ahead of him into the room, and waited as he closed the door behind them.

Then he turned her to face him. It was getting dark rapidly outdoors, only enough light remaining in the room to outline the furniture. Her features were softened by the dim light and he bent to peer into her face.

"Do you think I've forgotten what I told you?"

She shook her head.

"I've been taking care of the fence for three days, Cass. Keeping those mares in the pasture is about the most important thing there is to do right now. We have a new colt in the barn tonight and three more mares look like they're about ready to drop any minute." His hands on her waist were firm and he tightened his grip, as if he would get her attention.

She looked up, her chin set stubbornly. "All I know is that you haven't talked to me for more than two minutes at any one time for the past three days. If you've decided not to go through with a wedding, I don't mind. I just need to know what's the next most important thing on your list of things to do. After horses, that is."

"Damn, you can get me mad faster than anyone I've ever known," he grumbled, sliding his hands to her back and jerking her against his body. He lowered his head, his lips capturing hers before she could evade him, his low growl of frustration making her shiver with anticipation.

He'd been so careful to leave her alone for the past three nights, sleeping on the edge of the bed, keeping his hands to himself, using every ounce of discipline he could muster. And now she had the nerve to insinuate that he was paying more attention to the horses than he was to her.

The sad part of it was, she was right, he admitted to himself. His sigh was lost in her mouth as he sampled the sweet taste of her. She was acquiescent in his embrace, neither seeking release from his arms nor returning the pressure of his lips against hers. He lifted his head and looked at her, smiling as the tip of her tongue traveled the distance from one side of her mouth to the other.

"You're really mad at me, aren't you?"

"I think you've got that wrong," she told him. "You just told me that I can make you angrier than anyone you've ever known."

"Yeah, but I get over it in a hurry. All I had to do was kiss you and I felt better."

She was silent in his arms and then she pushed at him, seeking release.

For a moment, just a few seconds, he held on, loath to

loose his hold, yearning for the warmth of her body against his. And then he thought better of it. His arms dropped and he watched as she walked across the floor to the wardrobe.

"You goin' somewhere?" he asked, leaning against the door.

She looked at him, one eyebrow raised mockingly. "With you standing in front of the door? Hardly." From within the depths of the wooden cabinet she drew forth a pale garment. Looked to him like her nightgown and its matching flannel robe.

"Going to bed now, Cassie?" If she thought he was going to let her settle down for the night without getting things resolved between them, she was in for a surprise.

"It's getting dark out," she said crisply, waving at the window where the gray of twilight had turned to the gloom of night.

"Let me light the lamp," he said, moving to the table next to the bed where a kerosene lantern rested.

"Don't bother. A candle will do. I don't need much light to get undressed." Already behind the screen in the corner of the room, she was out of sight.

The candle on the dresser was almost on its last legs, he decided. About enough light for them to get into bed before it sputtered out. In the hallway, beyond the bedroom door, he heard Maggie's small voice, his mother's deeper tones hushing the child, and then the closing of the door across the hallway.

He sat in a chair to take off his boots, the glowing candle on the dresser beside him. From behind the screen came the soft sounds of Cassie's disrobing. In a matter of seconds she pushed back the folding barrier, carrying her discarded clothing over her arm. A basket in the corner held soiled laundry and she added her armful to the collection, then came to stand by the dresser where he waited, and leaned forward a bit to peer into the dimly lit mirror.

Her arms rose to unpin the circle of braids she'd worn all day and he watched as she began the task of dismantling the thick plaits. Her fingers moved rapidly up the length of each, until a waving mass of dark hair covered her shoulders, spilling past her waist. Her brush worked slowly through the strands, her arms stretching to their utmost.

She bent then, from the waist, tossing her hair to hang in front of her, the ends touching the floor. His eyes were filled with the picture of beauty before him. Something his father had read aloud once from the Bible nudged at his memory. Something about her hair being a woman's crowning glory.

He could readily understand how the writer had come upon such a theory, if the woman he'd been looking at had come anywhere near the vision in this room, he decided. If ever there was a crowning glory to behold, Cassie was its rightful possessor.

And as soon as he managed to get things in order, he'd have the rest of his life to watch her perform this ritual every night.

She finished her task and, with a slanting glance in his direction, blew out the candle. He saw her shadowed form turn toward the bed, one hand outstretched to find the bedpost as she hesitantly made her way through the darkened room. From the window starlight and moonglow combined, and as his eyes adjusted to the darkness, he watched her shed her robe and settle down in the bed.

Rising from the chair, he undressed, padding to the bed in his long underwear. He'd give a bundle to drop those, too, but he'd have to wait a few days for that pleasure. The bed sank beneath his weight and he felt Cassie roll a bit in his direction.

"As soon as those mares drop their foals, we'll take a short trip, Cass," he said quietly, his hands stacked beneath his head. Waiting for a reaction, he closed his eyes, the weariness of his long day's work tugging at him.

"I'm sure you'll let me know your plans when the time comes," she answered. And then turned to face the window.

"Don't give me your back tonight, Cass. I'm too tired to have another fuss with you."

She was still and silent for a few seconds, and then rolled back to face him. He reached out, his fingers clasping a handful of her hair as he touched her shoulder. "Come here," he said tugging at her, his hand easing behind her back.

Cassie shifted in the bed, the mattress his friend as she rolled toward him. Her breasts were soft against his ribs as she lifted her head to rest on his shoulder. Nestling there, she shifted, forming her body to his side. Then she sighed, a whisper of sound that was sadness and acceptance combined, if he knew anything about Cassie Phillips.

"It will all work out, honey," he told her, nudging her closer with the hand that pressed against her back.

"We'll see," she answered, and with that enigmatic reply he had to be content.

Chapter Nine

"You goin' to church, Will?" Clara Tolliver dished up breakfast with a generous hand, and Sunday morning's offering looked to be an exceptional display of her cooking skills.

Will eyed the overflowing plate before him, wondering if he hadn't better eat first and answer later. That his mother would whisk away his meal was dubious, but her tone of voice lent doubt to that theory. Unless he missed his guess, she was expecting an affirmative answer.

The thought of the mare he'd left only minutes ago, obviously in the beginning stages of labor, made up his mind, and he shook his head firmly.

"I don't dare leave with that mare ready to drop this morning, Ma," he said firmly. Fork in hand, he readied himself to make short shrift of the meal before him, lest he dally over his food and not be nearby when the bay he'd penned in a box stall was at the end of her labor.

"You didn't pray yet, Uncle Will," Maggie reminded him.

He placed the fork on the table, aware of Cassie's smothered laugh beside him. Coffeepot in hand, she paused to fill his cup and then made her way around the big table to pour the dark, steaming brew into the oversize mugs Clara Tolliver used in her kitchen.

"Why don't you pray, Maggie," Will suggested.

"We hafta wait for Grandma and Cassie," the child told him primly, folding her hands and pursing her rosy mouth.

"We're ready, Maggie." Sliding into her chair, Clara motioned Cassie to do the same and then nodded at the small child who appeared to be directing the proceedings.

Lowering her head, she spoke the words Will had heard at the table for all the years of his youth. His father had spoken them, and he remembered waiting impatiently for the ritual to be at an end, his appetite always at the ready.

"How about you, Cassie?" The older woman's question had been expected, but Cassie dreaded the answer she must give.

Entering a church would almost be sacrilege, she'd decided, what with the sham marriage she and Will had been living in this house. She'd not be able to hold up her head in God's house, her guilt weighing heavily on her soul.

"I think I'd better not today," she said softly, unwilling to meet the older woman's eyes. She bent over her plate and sawed her fork through a sausage. "By next Sunday, things should be more settled. I'll plan on going then."

As excuses went, it was decidedly weak, but Clara accepted it with a nod, only glancing shortly at Will as if to judge his reaction. He looked up at Cassie, unsmiling, his hesitation brief before he spoke.

"Want to come out in the barn and watch with me, Cass?"

It was the branch she'd sought and she grasped it eagerly. "Yes, I'd like to. Do you think it will bother the mother to have me there?"

He shook his head. "Naw. A mare usually gets in a

world of her own when she's birthing. Like all her energy is on doin' what she has to do and gettin' it over with.''

"Can I come, too?" Maggie asked hopefully.

Will shook his head. "Maybe another time. You need to go with your grandma to church this morning."

The child subsided with grace, eating her breakfast, only a longing look in Cassie's direction revealing her disappointment.

She was a dear child, not only in mood and temperament, but in her manners and cheerful acceptance of her circumstances, Cassie had decided after the first day or so. That any mother could go off and leave such an innocent behind was more than she could comprehend. The hours she had spent with Maggie had only reinforced the bond that had sprung into being that first day.

A wistful yearning for the day when she would have a child of her own was at the forefront of Cassie's mind. To have someone love her with the unstinting devotion she'd felt for her own mother was a temptation she found impossible to resist. That Will cared for her was almost a certainty. That he might come to love her was possible. But a child...ah, that was a promise of heaven here on earth.

Maggie was tugging at her sleeve, her manner impatient with Cassie's daydreaming.

"Will you, Cassie?" she asked, tilting her head to peer into Cassie's face.

"Will I what?"

"You were gonna fix my hair for me this morning. Remember?" the child prodded.

"Yes, of course." Cassie pushed back from the table, suddenly aware that she was the last one to finish the meal. "Get your brush and we'll do it on the porch."

"Go along, Cassie," Clara told her. "I'll clear up here before I get ready to leave if you'll tend to Maggie."

Will's hand on her elbow hustled her out the screen door to the porch. He stepped to the ground and turned to face her. "You all right, honey?"

She nodded, unwilling to share her doubts and fears with him, the brilliant sunlight somehow dissipating her worry.

"I'm fine, Will. I'd rather wait till things get a little more in order before I go to church, though."

His nod was slow. "This week, Cassie. I promise."

She bent forward a bit, her whisper intended only for his hearing. "Only if it's what you truly want." She felt the rush of tears, and closed her eyes against the heated response. Coercing Will into making an honest woman out of her was far from what she had in mind, and tears would be an unfair weapon.

His hands reached to encircle her waist and he lifted her to the ground to stand before him. One long finger pressed beneath her chin and tilted it up. "Look at me, Cassie."

It was an order she could not ignore, and she opened her eyes, allowing a single, salty tear to escape from each one. She blinked, willing the sun to evaporate the moisture swimming before her gaze.

"You're the only woman I've ever wanted to marry, Cass." His words were low, softer than a whisper. "Shall I kiss you right here and now? Then would you believe me?"

"Everyone would see," she whispered quickly, darting a look at the barn, then glancing over her shoulder at the kitchen window.

His smile lit her heart with its radiance. "I don't care who knows how I feel about you, sweetheart," he told her softly, in that same almost soundless undertone.

"Go take care of your mare," she managed to say, her mouth trembling in a smile.

She watched him walk away, her eyes on the slight swag-

ger of his stride, the length of his legs—made to look even
longer with the boots he wore. His hat sitting at a jaunty
angle, his shirt fitting like a glove across his wide shoulders
and his belt riding low on his hips, he was a specimen of
manhood she yearned to have for her very own.

Men, in a general way, had never appealed to Cassie.
Until Will Tolliver had dragged her from a swiftly moving
stream and taken her under his wing. Now she could hardly
envision life without his presence to brighten her days.

"Cassie? I found my brush." Maggie nudged her, leaning from the porch to get her attention.

"How shall we fix your curls this morning?" she asked
the child, turning to settle on the top step, Maggie between
her knees on the stair below.

"It has to be kind of slicked back and plain on Sundays," Maggie said, her nose wrinkling in distaste.
"Grandma says we have to be proper when we go to
church."

"Well, we'll still make you look pretty," Cassie told her
soothingly, knowing that anything else would be an im-
possibility.

Eben and Louise came for dinner, followed closely by
Samuel and Elizabeth. Their three sons rode in the back of
the wagon, tumbling to the ground like three puppies when
their father pulled the team to a halt.

"Grandma, we're here!" the tallest boy called out.

"We came for dinner," the next oldest decreed with a
grin.

The smallest boy was short and sturdy, his legs churning
as he made for the porch, his words an indecipherable bab-
ble in Cassie's ears. She scooped him up and hugged him
to her bosom.

"You must be Cassie," Elizabeth said, her skirts settling

to the ground as Samuel lowered her from the wagon seat. She looked over her brood with what appeared to be a practiced eye, if Cassie was any judge. And then their eyes meshed in an appraisal that left Cassie on tenterhooks.

Elizabeth strode toward her, and her smile scattered Cassie's fears to the four winds. "So you're the woman who brought Will back home." Her arms reached to enclose Cassie in their depths.

"I guess you could say he brought me home with him. He was on his way here when he met me," she said, inhaling Elizabeth's scent, a blend of soap and powder that spoke of clean skin and clothing.

"Well, however it came about, we're glad to have you in the family," Samuel's wife told her crisply. Releasing her, Elizabeth looked around. "Where are those scallywags? Matthew, Mark and Luke?"

From near the barn came two replies, and from within the kitchen Clara answered quickly. "I've got the baby, Elizabeth."

The young mother shook her head. "I swear, it's all I can do to keep up with them. It's a wonder I get anything else done."

Dinner was a memorable event, Cassie the center of attention for most of the meal. Eben and Samuel gave their older brother the benefit of their experience as they traded gibes, causing their wives to alternately blush and scold their husbands. That the three brothers were happy to be together was obvious to Cassie. Clara's delight was thinly veiled, but the gleam in her dark eyes gave away the happiness the woman found in her family.

The house was silent as darkness fell, the wagons having headed for the neighboring farms before the sun set, chores waiting for Eben and Samuel. Elizabeth was older than Samuel's twenty-five years. She'd brought Matthew and

Mark to her marriage with Samuel, Luke, the baby, being a child of their union. And yet all three were accepted into the family by Clara as if they were, in truth, her blood kin, a fact that made Cassie feel more secure than ever in her own position.

Now she stood in the barn, squinting into the dimly lit stall where the newborn filly nudged her mother's udder, her neck stretched at an unbelievable angle in order to nurse.

"She's beautiful," Cassie whispered, as if to speak aloud would somehow shatter the wonder of the scene.

Will's eyes gleamed and he shared a look of mutual delight with Many Fingers. "This makes five, and every one of them healthy," he noted.

"Good stock," Many Fingers said, his words, as usual, short and to the point.

"I'm taking Cassie to town tomorrow," Will told him. "We need to do a little shopping."

The Indian nodded. "I'll be here."

Cassie's heart lifted at Will's words. "In the morning?" For all the attraction of the new foal, the mention of Will's intentions took her full attention.

"Early." His gaze was piercing as Will turned it in her direction, his nostrils flaring as he examined her in the dim light.

Cassie felt a surge of heat wash over her face. She stepped back from the stall. "I think I'll go in and get ready for bed," she told him in a rush of words. "I'll want to help with breakfast and gather the eggs before we go."

His nod was silent agreement and she sensed his attention on her back as she left the barn.

Tomorrow. Will would marry her tomorrow.

As weddings went, it was short and sweet. Although never having been a guest at an actual church ceremony, only listening quietly in a corner as her mother married Remus Chandler several years ago, Cassie didn't consider herself a worthy judge of such events.

She and Will stood before the Methodist minister in Mill Creek. He was a tall, slender young man, whose wife was splendid in dark curls and a ruffled dress, standing up as a witness. Will was handsome in a white shirt, his tie a narrow black string, tied in a bow at his collar.

Cassie wore one of her new dresses, an everyday gingham, but new and crisp and barely wrinkled from the buggy ride. She was short of breath, her vows spoken in a low voice that sounded as if it might belong to someone else, so scant was her ability to utter the words.

"Till death do us part," Will said firmly, his eyes locked with hers, his hands warm as he enclosed both of hers within his grasp. Solemn and looking older than the twenty-seven years he claimed, he slid a plain gold band on her left hand, easing it past her knuckle and twisting it in place.

"I don't plan on you ever takin' it off, Cassie," he whispered as she spread her fingers to admire its fit.

Startled, she lifted her gaze to his and found him offering her a smile that reached the depths of his dark eyes. "This is forever, honey," he told her quietly.

Her nod accepted his decree. A wave of tenderness for the man she had shared her vows with spread over her like the incoming tide. As if it washed away the hurts and fears of her past, leaving only a blank page upon which to write her future.

Will Tolliver had married her. As they made their farewells to the preacher and his wife, as they walked to the Tolliver buggy parked in front of the parsonage and as they rode through the small town of Mill Creek, Missouri, Cassie's mind sang the refrain over and over.

Will Tolliver had married her. She was no longer Cassie Phillips, runaway, but Cassie Tolliver, wife.

Flashing a glance in his direction, she noted the strength of his hands on the reins, the tensed muscles in his thighs as he braced his feet against the front of the buggy, holding the mare to a rollicking trot through the main street of town. The general store on the left, the Golden Garter saloon on her right, the hotel and sheriff's office all passed in a blur of windows and doors.

And then they were on the open road, a vista of trees ahead, a farm off to the right in the distance. The bells Will had attached to the horse's harness jingled in time with her dainty steps, and Cassie's heart rang with the delight of knowing she was beyond the days of being Cassie Phillips.

Only the specter of her past nudged at the edges of her mind, the memory of the scene she'd left behind the night her mother drew her last breath. Perhaps Will would not have married her had he known the truth about that night. If she'd told him that Remus Chandler was dead, that her hand had held the knife, would he still have taken her with him? Or would she even now be sitting in a jail cell, or perhaps dead from a hangman's noose? She shuddered at the thought.

"You all right, Cass?" Will's arm went across her shoulders as he bent in her direction.

Her eyes fluttering open, she shook her head. "I'm fine. Just shivered a little."

He dragged her closer, his hand dropping to her waist for leverage, till she was scooted tightly against his hip. "I'll keep you warm, Mrs. Tolliver," he told her with a grin. And then he sobered. "Feel better, honey, about getting married and everything?"

If she could tell him, if she could be honest with the man who'd given her his name, she wouldn't feel so much as if she was skating on thin ice, she decided. But her smile was determinedly bright as she nodded her agreement.

And if she knew for sure that Will felt more for her than an appreciation of her body and a tender regard for her well-being, she'd be a whole lot happier.

It had been a shopping trip, in fact. The general store in Greenbush, though not stocked with the very latest from Paris, managed to have a reasonably good choice in nightclothes. Once he'd gotten past the flannel, beyond the practical cotton, into the realm of fine batiste and lawn, Will had begun to sweat. The final choice was a filmy delight in pale blue, a color he felt would complement Cassie's eyes, although he wasn't sure she'd allow him to have a light burning by which to compare the two.

If Many Fingers or Clara raised an eyebrow at the lack of purchases when Will carried one small bundle from the buggy upon their return, it was not noticeable. Arriving too late for supper, Will and Cassie sat at the kitchen table beneath the kerosene lantern, eating leftovers.

Food was the very least of Will's priorities tonight. Having taken care of the last of the chores, getting his new bride up the stairs and into his bed headed his list. And from the look on Cassie's face, she would be dragging her feet all the way.

Before they ate she wanted to go to the barn to see the new foal. Then, after checking out the filly, she had to look in on a mare who was pacing the area of her stall, contemplating the imminent birth of her youngster, if Many Fingers was to be believed.

Eating was a time-consuming chore, Cassie spending long minutes on devouring a chicken leg, then poking at her plateful of vegetables, which Clara had left on the back of the stove. The cornbread required butter and syrup, Cassie relishing each bite. Finally she drank down a glass of milk and, pushing her chair from the table, announced it was time to check on Maggie before bedtime.

Will left his seat and circled the table. His arms found their way around her waist, his hands clasping at her back. "Maggie's probably sound asleep." He bent low to whisper the words against her ear, and she shivered at the sensation. His grin was wide, and he nuzzled her neck, pleased at her response. A wedding night was something he'd not spent a lot of time considering in years gone by, but the past week had given him much food for thought.

He'd answered all of her excuses neatly, he thought. The final hurdle was getting past his mother, and she had conveniently sought out her rocker in the parlor, her hands busy with a shawl she was crocheting.

There wasn't one good reason on God's green earth why he couldn't sashay his bride up the stairs and make his wedding night a reality.

That he would no doubt visit pain upon her small body was a fact he could not help but dread. Only the sure knowledge that he could also bring her a great deal of pleasure made him eager to hustle her up the stairs to his bedroom.

"Cassie? Are you frightened of me?"

She shook her head and her lashes fluttered open, her eyes wide as she opened her mouth to speak. "No...not really."

His grin was immediate. "Now, that's a statement of trust if I ever heard one," he told her in a soft whisper.

"I'm not afraid," she protested. "I just don't know what you'll want me to do."

"You'll figure it out as we go along," he assured her with a grin. Then he sobered as he reached over the table to turn down the wick on the lamp.

The light dimmed and the kitchen became a shadowed and quiet place, Will moving to join her near the door. "Ready to go up, honey?"

She nodded her head and he caught the movement in the faint light that glowed from the parlor. She turned from him and paused at the double doors across the hall.

"Good night, Mrs. Tolliver," she said through the doorway.

Clara looked up over the rims of her spectacles. "Going to bed already?" she asked, glancing at the mantel clock.

"It's been a long day, Ma," Will put in quickly. "I've got a man coming tomorrow with a new stallion for us to take a look at."

Clara shrugged and slid her glasses back into place, looking down at her lapful of pink and magenta yarn. "I'll see the both of you in the morning, then."

With one hand at Cassie's waist, he turned her to the stairs and guided her up to the second floor.

The bedroom had never looked so small, with the bed taking up so much room, Cassie thought with a sense of desperation. Will had spread something on the white coverlet and she eyed it with apprehension as she crossed the room. In the light of the candle Will lit and carried to the bedside table, it looked to be a gown, pale blue and edged with fine lace.

"Take a look at it, Cassie. I bought it for you."

She lifted it from the bed. "This is for me?"

He nodded, waving at the screen in the corner. "Want to try it on? See how it fits?" He grinned as she hesitated. "Or if you want to, I'll help you put it on right here."

"No!" She shook her head, a violent motion, clutching the fragile fabric to her chest. She moved quickly to the screen and behind it, her breathing rapid, her cheeks flushed with a blend of excitement and embarrassment. Surely such a garment as this was more suitable to a boudoir than this farmhouse bedroom.

But if Will had paid good money for it, she'd at least try it on. She owed him that much. Her fingers busy with buttons and strings, she stripped from her clothing, then snatched at the gown, pulling it over her head quickly, as if she must don it before she could change her mind. She pulled it down, luxuriating in the soft caress of fine fabric, the whisper of cobweb-soft material falling into place. The hem brushed just above her knees and no amount of gentle tugging was going to make it any longer. Biting at her bottom lip, she peered around the corner of the screen. Will was sitting on the edge of the bed, watching her, his eyes alight with what looked suspiciously like anticipation.

"Will?"

"Yeah, Cassie?" She could stand it should he smile his pleasure, but not if his grin was amusement at her expense.

"It's awfully short, Will."

He rose, taking three long strides in her direction, his eyes gleaming darkly in the candle glow. They traveled slowly over her form, and never had she felt so small and helpless. With a look of pure hunger he allowed his gaze to fasten on the expanse of bare flesh at her throat, then travel in minute increments down the front of her body.

She lifted a hand to the top of the washstand, her fingers pressing against the wood until her nails were white with the pressure. Her breath caught in her throat and she heard a soft whimper escape. Surely not from her? And yet it seemed that it had—that unbidden sound of fear, or perhaps anticipation, had been born in her throat and had escaped her trembling lips.

"It's supposed to fit like that," he told her.

She looked down at herself, at the taut, swelling shape

of her breasts, the shadowed dip where her belly button hid from view and her long, bare legs beneath the abbreviated hem.

And then she glanced up again at Will, at the flushed line of his cheek, the flare of his nostrils and the clenching of his jaw. His eyes glowed with a light she could only describe to herself as avid, his whole being seemingly reined and held in check.

"Please wear it for me, Cassie." It didn't even sound like Will's voice, this husky exhalation of breath that rang harshly in her ears, as if he'd used up all the tenderness he had to spare.

She nodded, caught in the spell he wove, his hands fisted by his sides, his body almost visibly pulsing in a vibrant wave of desire.

As if that small tilting of her head were the signal he had awaited, he moved. His hands rose to touch her and the fists became long, tapering fingers and broad palms, resting against her body with subtle strength as he lifted her into his arms. He swung her easily against his chest and she looked up into his face.

He was solemn, his lips parted in a feral expression, teeth together and jaw rigid, perhaps seized with the same emotion she had only begun to sense within her own body.

Lifting one hand to brush his unyielding jaw, she met his gaze. Then, pulling his head lower, she found herself caught up in the damp wonder of his kiss.

Chapter Ten

William pulled the bedcovers back, leaving them rumpled, half on the floor. The pillows skidded helter-skelter across the bottom sheet, and he barely noticed the disarray as the mattress received the woman he held in his arms. So long as Cassie was within its depths, he didn't give a hang for the condition of the bed or its bedding.

Will's eyes devoured her, then focused on the wonder of her hair, primly wound at the back of her head, only a few strands escaping the pins. His fingers itched to remove the restraints, and he bent over her, one hand on either side of her.

"Are you going to undress, too?" she asked.

His grin came easily, easing the tension. "I reckon that'd make us even, wouldn't it?" Straightening, he began the task of undoing his shirt, allowing it to fall over his trousers. "I need to wash up a little, honey."

She watched him, her scrutiny only adding to his arousal, and he turned his back, stripping the clothing from his body. Standing before the washstand, he bathed quickly, not daring to frighten her with the burgeoning tumescence he could not hope to hide should he turn to face her.

The towel he dried with was the concealment he needed,

and he held it in his hands, allowing it to drape across his belly and below as he returned to the bed.

Her cheeks were rosy, more flushed than before, the candlelight revealing a warmth in her perusal he had only hoped for. Within him, the yearning to see her without the covering of the flimsy gown she wore battled with his sensibilities.

Cassie's innocence won and he leaned to blow out the candle, only then dropping the towel to the floor before he lowered himself to the mattress.

He rolled, lifting himself above her, his forearms receiving his weight as he framed her face with his palms. He bent, burying his face against her, inhaling the glorious scent that was so much a part of her, that faintly seductive fragrance he'd designated in his mind as being Cassie's own.

It resembled the taste of her, that sweet yet spicy tang that met his tongue each time he dared to sample her mouth. His fingers spreading wide, he loosened the twisted coils of her hair, closing his eyes as he buried his hands in its shining length. Dark strands twined about his fingers, and as would corn silk, they clung to his skin. Like the finest spiderwebs, they floated on the air as he drew his fingers from their captivity.

One by one he plucked the pins from their hiding places within the dark strands. They fell from his fingers and he brushed the sheet, sending them to the floor.

Once more he bent to her, his lips against her throat, his hand sweeping the fall of hair back to bare the tender flesh to his caress. Opening his mouth, he tasted her, suckling just a bit, careful lest he mar the perfection of her skin. The temptation to leave his mark on her was almost beyond his ability to resist, and with reluctance he eased from her.

The moon was full, bathing her in its radiance streaming

through the window. He watched as her eyes opened, her hand rising to touch the dampness he left behind, and then she spoke his name. It vibrated in his ears, the soft, subtle sound of her whispered call.

"Will?"

Easing his arms beneath her, he cradled her, his lips seeking hers, a small mating that did little to satisfy his primitive need for the greater merging that was to come. She met him with an eagerness he had not expected, opening to the touch of his teeth and tongue, allowing his ownership.

Moving on, from her brow to the tip of her chin, he plotted his course, ever aware of the delicate flesh he branded with mouth and tongue. Her lashes fluttered against his mouth and he bathed her eyelids with the tip of his tongue.

Cassie laughed, a soft, seductive sound, manna to his hungry soul, and then as he drew back, her eyes opened, a languid revealing of dark pools. She focused on him and smiled. "You didn't kiss me this way before, Will."

"We're married now, Cass," he told her, his voice low, rasping in his throat, as if the words strained to be spoken.

"I feel like my bones are all soft inside my skin," she whispered, her tongue swiping once at her upper lip.

It was almost his undoing, that small pink bit of flesh he'd only begun to include in his love play. "Do that again," he said.

She blinked at him, shaking her head. "Do what? What did I do, Will?"

"Better yet," he told her with a smile, "brush your tongue against my mouth. I want to see how it feels."

It felt wonderful, better than he'd dreamed, and with a groan of passion unleashed he turned to his side, drawing her with him, pulling her leg to rest atop his hip.

His palm flat against her back, he pressed her closer. The softness of her belly received his arousal and he stifled the urge to thrust against her. Cassie's indrawn breath, a measure of her surprise, called for soothing, and soothe her he did, his hand moving in a circular motion between her shoulder blades, then shifting to brush gently against her hips.

She whimpered once, stiffening against him as his hand sought the rounding of her bottom, and he hushed her, whispering nonsense in her ear, his kisses soft and gentle until she relaxed once more beneath his touch.

It was bliss, undeniably a touch of heaven, and his very being sang with the joy she brought him, his hopeful heart finally sensing the beginning of her surrender.

Lifting himself on his elbow, he surveyed the gown she wore. Covering the curves of her breasts, it was a hindrance, and his fingers worked at the buttons. Unfastening his trousers with one hand had never been a problem, yet these small pearl fastenings resisted his attempts, and he shook his head at his own ineptness.

"Undo your gown, Cassie," he whispered, then watched as she lifted her hands to do his bidding. He inhaled sharply, then, rolling her gently to her back, he hovered over her, resting on his forearms.

Her breasts, uncovered, rounded and full, lured him and he watched as his long, tanned and callused fingers brushed against the pale flesh. He smiled as she shivered, and reveled in her soft intake of breath. His palm fit beneath one breast, and it molded to the curve of his hand. Ripe and firm, it was barely contained by his grasp, and he shifted his gentle hold until his index finger and thumb tested the small crumpled bit of flesh he'd yearned to possess. It tightened beneath his touch and he bent to brush the tip of his tongue against the textured crest. Carefully his mouth took it within its depths, and he suckled it gently against his tongue, tugging it deeper.

Cassie looked down at herself, to where that clever mouth loved her with such thorough care. "I can hardly hold still, Will." Her voice was high, whimpering as she lifted her head from the pillow.

"Wiggle if you want to, honey. There's only you and me here, and I suspect I'd enjoy your wiggles more than I can tell you." His words were muffled against her flesh, and then he released her to lift himself higher, his skin sliding across the curves of her breasts.

She let out her breath slowly, her breasts tingling from the rough texture of hair and firm muscle. They felt swollen, pulsing with a need she began to recognize, and she rose against him, craving a closer contact with his body that her gown would not allow.

It was twisted and tangled around her bottom, and he rose to his knees over her, his hands careful lest he tear the fragile stuff as he stripped it from her. "Ah, Cassie..." His gaze traveled her length as he knelt between her thighs. "Don't move," he said, his voice raspy as he sat back on his heels. "Just let me touch you, baby."

She held her breath as his fingers spread to span the width of her belly, his thumb caressing the shallow dip of her belly button. A flash of warmth seared her at his touch and she flinched, then eased back to test the small pleasure of his knowing caress. He smiled down at her, the pad of his thumb moving in a circular fashion, and she shifted, her hips rising.

His hands moved upward, and her flesh tingled at the brush of callused fingers. And then she felt twin sensations of pleasure as he enclosed each breast with a wide hand, brushing the tender peaks with his fingers, squeezing and tugging, watching with a rapt expression on his face.

"You're blooming right in front of my eyes, Cass," he whispered, those dark orbs barely visible beneath his lowered lashes.

She felt a flush of delight warm her flesh as he bent to suckle, first at one breast then the other, the drawing and tugging of his mouth bringing to life a new, curling need in the depths of her belly. Her hips rose, that secret place where her thighs joined brushed against him, and she jolted with the sensation as his body rubbed gently against her.

Rising above her again, he molded her flesh, his hands firm against her breasts, her waist, squeezing the fullness of her hips and then grasping with gentle strength the tops of her legs. He lifted them, draping her over his thighs until she was vulnerable to his touch, his gaze intent on her face, as if he would gauge her willingness.

Then his index finger traced the folds of flesh he had exposed, and she flinched. He hesitated for just a moment until she softened once more, moving, shifting beneath his seeking hand.

That she would allow such intimacies was beyond her wildest imaginings. That her modesty would fall so easily before Will's coaxings was unbelievable. Yet, knowing in her heart of hearts that Will Tolliver would bring her only what was right and good in this marriage bed, she allowed whatever he willed to happen.

The lure of her submission was almost his undoing as, warm and damp, her woman's flesh opened to him, and he swallowed a groan of frustration. And then Cassie's eyelids rose and she smiled, a tempting turn of her mouth, a twitch of her pursed lips, then a glimpse of white teeth as she regarded him in the light shed by the moon outside the window.

"Will... You make me feel..."

"What, Cassie? How do you feel?" The words growled

from his throat and he eased forward just a bit, shivering as hard flesh touched soft woman.

Her eyes widened. "Don't hurt me." Her whisper was breathless and he swallowed, holding himself still, fighting the urge to bury himself within her depths.

"I'm afraid there's not much either of us can do about it, sweetheart," he said sadly, torn between the knowledge that he would surely tear her tender flesh and the terrible need to do that very thing.

"Hold on to me, baby." The admonition was delivered between gritted teeth and he bent over her, waiting until she lifted her arms to surround his shoulders. His body shifted, one hand guiding his arousal as he pressed carefully, invading the untried flesh.

Her hands were frantic as she clutched at him, her head twisting against the pillow, and he held his breath, shuddering as he pushed within her. The fragile barrier gave way and he groaned, fearful of the pain he visited upon her virgin body.

"It burns," she whispered, gasping as her inner muscles clamped against his length.

"I'm so sorry, sweetheart," he muttered, his words broken as he caught deep breaths. Great shudders racked his frame as he resisted the urge to thrust, and he moved with deliberate care as he penetrated that heretofore forbidden place within her.

He flinched at hurting her, and yet she reached for him again, her arms circling his waist, pulling him closer, as though she must comfort him, assure him of her forgiveness.

"Cassie!" He called her name in a sharp, expectant tone, drawing her with him, as if they journeyed a path he hesitated to take alone, and she nodded, her eyes meeting his in the dim light.

For long seconds, while Will moved against her with careful yet eager thrusts, she held him, fingers spread wide across his back, blending their bodies as she would their souls. Her mouth open against his shoulder, her tears hot against his skin, she clung, wrapping herself in the sanctuary his body provided.

Despite her inexperience, she knew that Will had made her his wife. Knew that all of the kissing, the touching, the words of praise he'd whispered against her flesh had only been the beginning. That at this moment, when she held his manhood within her, she'd become a woman, a part of the man she had married.

Will stood at the window, just out of the path of moonlight, his guilt weighing heavily. His glance at the bed did nothing to relieve his tension. The sight of Cassie, tearstains gleaming against her cheeks as she slept, was like a sword in his heart.

He'd tried to hold back, his teeth still aching from the endeavor. And yet he'd hurt her. The towel he'd had the good sense to scoop from the floor held bright splotches of her blood, and he'd found another to spread beneath her, lest the sheets bear stains that would expose the lie he'd lived for the past week.

If Cassie ever let him near her again, it would be a miracle. She'd been so small and he was so dang big, and it had been longer than he could remember since he'd found release in a woman's body. Now there wasn't another female alive in his memory, only the soft cries and whispers of his wife filling those spaces in his mind.

He'd botched it. Worse than that, he'd probably scared her off for good. His groan was heartfelt, audible in the silence of the night.

"Will?" She called him from the bed and he stood erect,

turning a bit to shield her from the sight of his flagrant arousal. Thinking of her had brought him to a full, brazen readiness, and he shook his head at the evidence of his masculine need.

"Will...come here. I feel awfully alone in this bed."

He squinted at her in the moonlight, the tearstains still apparent against her cheeks. Yet there was about her a gleaming radiance that owed little to the glow shed by the moon outside the window. She reached a hand to him and he uttered a low sound, a blend of petition and thanks.

"Cassie." Somehow he'd reached the bed. Someway he'd managed to enclose her in his arms and, wonder of wonders, she was clinging to him and spending rash kisses over his face.

"Will, I woke up and you were gone." Her voice caught in her throat. "I thought you were upset with me...because I cried."

He rocked her, leaning to brush his jaw against her hair, grasping a handful to expose the beautiful woman he'd had the intelligence to marry today. After all the mistakes he'd made in his life, he'd finally done one thing right.

"Oh, baby! I felt so bad when I hurt you. I tried not to, but you're so damn little." He covered her face with kisses, as if he could mend his fences with an abundance of loving. And then felt the smile she could not hide.

"I'm really your wife, aren't I, Will?" she asked wonderingly.

"Yeah, you sure are, Cass," he agreed, his spirits lifting as he absorbed the happiness she made no attempt to hide.

"Will it hurt as much the next time?" She shivered as she awaited his reply, as if the memory of her pain was too fresh to be ignored.

"I'm surprised you're willin' to talk about a next time,

honey," he whispered, pulling back from her as his arousal made itself known against her thigh.

She smiled, lifting her arms to encircle his neck. "I can't help but notice that you're ready to try it again, Will."

"Not tonight, honey. You've done enough bleeding for this time. I'm feelin' like the world's biggest ignoramus as it is."

"Oh, Will, don't feel that way," she whispered, her hands enclosing his face, her forehead wrinkled with worry lines. "I'm glad you're big. It makes me feel safe and secure."

"We're talkin' about different kinds of big here, Cassie," he told her. "The part of me I'm talkin' about is the thing that caused you all the pain."

"Pooh!" Her whispered exclamation was accompanied by a swat of her hand against his shoulder. "It felt good, Will. Before the pain, I mean. If it hurt every time, I'd still want to do it with you." She paused and tilted her head, her eyes narrowing a bit. "Well, maybe if it just hurt a little."

"I don't think it will, honey. Once you heal up for a day or so, it'll be all right."

She snuggled against him and he drew a quick breath. "You'd better not be twitchin' like that, Cass," he warned her darkly. "I'm havin' a hard time here."

She giggled against his chest. "I noticed, Will Tolliver. To tell the truth, I couldn't help but notice."

His thrifty heart rebelled as he burned the bloody towel. He'd stuffed it inside his shirt, wearing his jacket to cover the bulge until he got to the barn. Out back, near the manure pile, he lit the corner of the stained length of cotton and watched as the dried blood evaporated in the flame. No way was he going to let his mother catch sight of this proof of Cassie's innocence.

If ever a virgin had walked this earth, it was his bride. Although this morning she wasn't walking too well. She was stepping pretty gingerly, moving a little more slowly than usual. But the warmth in her eyes and the smile she'd bestowed upon him as he'd left the kitchen soothed his guilt, leaving behind only a glow that smacked of masculine pride.

There was no mistaking the happiness she wore like a Sunday-go-to-meeting dress this morning.

Chapter Eleven

All the things she'd never done in her life—the gardening, the tending to a child like Maggie, the long hours spent with Will's mother learning how to run a house—added up to a perfection Cassie had not dreamed of. If for no other reason than this, this life he had given her, she would give her life for Will Tolliver.

And after all, he did not ask her to give her life, only her body into his keeping. She had done so gladly. The pain of her wedding night put aside, she chose only to remember Will's tenderness.

For the next two nights he held her while he spoke of his plans for the farm, the horses and their life together. Spending countless kisses upon her countenance, his hands deft and cautious against her skin, soothing and caressing, he pampered and caressed her without any comfort for himself that she could see.

The third night found the blue gown once more spread across the bed and she heard Will asking in a low, strained voice if she would please wear it again.

She nodded, scooping it up and slipping behind the dressing screen. It was still too short, but Will didn't seem to mind. Watching her from the depths of their bed, he lifted the covers and she accepted his wordless invitation. Settling next to him, she glanced at the candle he'd left burning on the table beside the bed.

"Are you going to blow it out?" The light shed from the single taper left his face in shadow and she searched his features, wondering at the whimsical smile he wore, while his eyes were strangely watchful and heavy lidded.

"Tonight I want to see you in candlelight, Cassie. I settled for moonlight the last time. But I promised myself that next time I'd—"

"Next time?"

"I thought it was time to try again, Cass. If I have to coax you into this, I will, but I figured you were pretty well healed up by now. If it turns out you're not, we'll wait a while longer."

She nodded. At least he wasn't ready to give up on her. And she blurted out the words even as they came to mind.

His surprise was evident and his eyes softened in the candlelight. "Give up on you? Ah, sweetheart, I'm the one who made a mess of things, hurting you the way I did."

"Most of it was good, except I didn't know for sure what was going to happen," she whispered.

Will tilted his head a bit, his forehead touching hers, and he closed his eyes. "I should have known to explain things to you, Cassie. I'll try to do better this time."

She moved a bit closer, breathing words she could not speak without closing her eyes. "I like the kissing best, Will. And the part when you touched my…"

"When I touched your breast, Cassie?"

"Yes…" she whispered.

"Let's try the kissing first, honey," he whispered, his mouth fitting against hers with care, only the impudent tip of his tongue coaxing her into a more intimate touching. She responded hesitantly, beguiled by the moist temptation.

As if he had only waited for that invitation, as if she had opened to him the riches of a thousand gold mines, he took her with greedy strokes of his tongue. Rising over her, he rolled her to her back, tempering his eagerness as he sampled the taste of her desire.

Her mouth opened to his, her hands clutching at his shoulders as his hand slid to take possession of her breast. One nimble finger circled the pouting, hard crest and she shivered at the thread of delight that pierced her.

"Like this?" His hand beneath the gown, he squeezed gently. Then, with a mutter of impatience, he disposed of her gown, and his head bent to savor the lush curves he'd uncovered, his lips tasting the firm flesh.

It was a whirlwind, this sensation he offered, the tugging of his mouth, the bathing of his tongue, the urgent pressure of his manhood against her thigh. His hands were coaxing her, the gentle caress of his fingers skimming her flesh, molding, urging her compliance and offering an abundance of delight.

She closed her eyes, her head tilting back against the pillow as he wooed her, his big hands gentle against her skin. Her mouth opened, sounds she barely recognized as her own whispering in the silence of the night. And then in a shivering, shuddering burst of pleasure, one whose existence she had never suspected, he banished from her mind the pain she had thought to endure once more. Her body shimmering with an encompassing delight, she lifted her hips, offering herself to him.

His words of praise rang in her ears as she clasped him to her, urging him closer until he fit their bodies together with gentle care. And as he led her to a knowledge of her own passion, she gave herself into his keeping.

"One flesh," he whispered. "That's what this means, Cassie." He lifted himself from her, and in the dim light he looked solemn, his mouth unsmiling, his eyes dark with a desire she had come to recognize. "I'm a part of you, Cassie. This is what makes us man and wife."

He hovered over her and she held him within her embrace, her arms clasping him with a strength fed by the blazing need to cherish this man forever. "I love you, Will," she said, her words fiercely spoken, as if she defied him to deny her claim.

"Ah, Cassie." He bent to her, catching his weight on his forearms, his hands cupping her face. His mouth caressed hers, his lips soft, the urgency held in abeyance as he accepted the words she uttered. He lifted his head, his eyes seeking hers. "Am I hurting you, sweetheart?"

"No..." A sense of surprise colored the single word and she repeated it, more firmly.

His lips tightened, the ruddy color across his cheekbones drawing her gaze as he closed his eyes and moved against her once more. He ducked his head then, his jaw tense, his big frame lifting, withdrawing slowly, and then seeking the shelter of her body again. His movements were measured and deliberate, and she rose to him, meeting his urgent rhythm.

"Cassie!" Her name became a primitive growl of satisfaction as he whispered it twice, then again, finally surging against her in a shuddering burst of pleasure.

The tidy rows of beans and carrots were a testimony to her newfound skill. Corn was better planted in the field west of the near pasture, Clara told her, but the kitchen garden had room for more food than they would want to face, come late summer. Cassie delighted in the daily survey of the fenced-in patch near the back porch.

Even the chore of weeding was a source of contentment. Maggie chattering nearby, the warm sunshine overhead and the feel of garden dirt beneath her fingertips allowed her a sense of usefulness. Will's need of her was a celebration, filling her with the joy of being a wife. Working with Clara in the house and the garden was a different sort of satisfaction. She was doing her share, making a home and carrying part of the burden of running the farm.

The sound of horses from the corral caught her ear and she tilted her head, listening for Will's voice. He'd warned her at breakfast to keep Maggie from the barn today and she'd agreed readily. Perhaps she'd do well to take the child inside the house. Whatever Will had in mind, he'd been pretty specific.

"It's time for a cup of tea, Maggie. Why don't you run in and tell your grandmother we've been out in the sun long enough. Maybe you can find a few cookies for us." Her mind on the commotion beyond the barn, Cassie brushed her hands against the dark apron she wore, anxious to scoot Maggie on her way.

"What's Will and Tall Horse doin' out there, Cassie?" Maggie stood and peered toward the barn, unwilling to head for the back door. "That horse is makin' an awful lot of noise."

"Your uncle Will knows what he's doing, honey," Cassie assured her. "Run on in the house now." Lifting the basket of weeds she had plucked from the fertile ground, she stepped down the row, her eyes alert for stragglers she might have missed. And then the shrill whinny sounded once more, and she cast a glance at the child, who was reluctantly making her way through the screen door into the kitchen.

Cassie dumped her basket on a pile beyond the garden and strode for the barn. Perhaps one of the horses had been hurt. Maybe Will would need her to get salve or bandages from the tack room. Her steps quickened and she ran the last few steps to the barn, blinking as she entered the dim aisle running from one end of the big building to the other.

At the far end, an open doorway led to the corral. A whirl of hooves and swishing tail flashed past the entrance and then Will came into view, leading a horse, one hand on the halter, his shoulders hunched as he gripped the animal's mane with the other.

"Hold her, Will." The disembodied voice of Many Fingers echoed through the barn and as Cassie neared, Will spread his feet, bracing himself as the horse he held tossed its head.

Over his shoulder, the stallion the men had brought home yesterday reared, only to settle atop the mare Will held. The stud whinnied, his forefeet covered with pieces of blanket, tied in place. The mare was quiet now, her nose pressing against Will's chest, spraddle-legged and shivering noticeably.

"Will?" Cassie spoke his name, aghast at the condition of the pretty little sorrel mare. She looked so woebegone, so beleaguered with that enormous stallion leaning on her back.

Will looked over his shoulder and frowned. "Cassie, go on up to the house."

Her jaw twitched and her teeth clenched as he spoke. "What are you doing, Will?" The shadows fell behind her as she stepped through the doorway, and she squinted against the noonday sun. Many Fingers stood back from the stud, obviously aware of the danger of the huge animal's flying feet. Then, with a snort, the stallion slid to stand on all four feet and turned away, hanging his head.

Will's mouth thinned as he looked at his wife. "We're breedin' a mare, Cassie. You don't want to be out here. I told you and Maggie to stay by the house this morning."

Cassie glared at him, an unexplainable anger coating her

words. "You told me to keep Maggie away. I'm a grown woman, Will. I know how horses get bred...sort of."

His eyes softened and he shook his head. "You don't want to see this, honey." Snapping a lead rope on the mare, he led her into the barn, one hand clasping Cassie's elbow as he went. He took the mare to a nearby box stall and turned her inside the enclosure, closing the door carefully.

Then he turned to the woman who watched him. "You've got Many Fingers all embarrassed out there," he said with a smile.

She pulled away from his grip and backed to the center of the aisle. "Why was the mare making so much noise? Was that horse hurting her?" Her eyes filled with tears as she remembered the pitiful stance the mare had taken.

"It's always noisy when the stallion covers the mare, Cass," he began.

"Well, she didn't act like she liked it, not one little bit!" Cassie put in sharply. "You didn't even give her a choice."

Will shook his head. "She didn't care, Cass. She was ready for him. She just wanted to twitch her tail a little first."

"Well, I don't like it that you held her and let him hurt her that way."

"Honey, we even padded his feet so she wouldn't get cut up. Come on, look at her, she's fine now." Will reached for Cassie and tugged her toward the stall, standing behind her, his arms enclosing her as he bade her to examine the mare. He rocked her a bit, his nose nuzzling against her ear.

"See, sweetheart. She's eating already. She's fine." His mouth was damp against her skin and Cassie felt a frisson of delight flare from the site he had chosen to visit with his warm kisses.

Putting aside the reaction he so easily drew from her

eager flesh, she lifted her shoulder, nudging him from place. "It just doesn't seem right," she said petulantly.

"Well, next spring when she drops her foal, you'll be glad we bred her. I'll remind you of it," he said with a chuckle.

"Will." Many Fingers stood in the doorway, holding the halter of the stallion, obviously unwilling to come any closer with Cassie in the aisle. Behind him, the big horse blew and snorted, slowly pawing at the ground with his padded forefoot, his movement languid as if he must make a display of his masculine power for the audience in front of him.

Will turned Cassie from where she stood and steered her toward the big front doors, his arm draped over her shoulder. She glanced back, at odds with the eerie sensations that insisted on curling in her belly as she watched the Indian lead the stud into a stall. That so much energy was required for the act of mating puzzled her. And that the mare had so meekly submitted after putting up such a fuss was another thing that was confusing.

Yet, perhaps it was all worth it, when the result would be a foal in the spring. She turned away from the big horse and caught Will grinning down at her.

"You've never seen the likes of that before, have you, honey?" he asked.

She shook her head. "I've never seen any animals mate, Will. I guess I'm kind of sheltered when it comes to that part of life."

"I've been wanting to talk to you about something, Cassie," he murmured as they entered the sunlight once more, walking more slowly toward the house.

She leaned into his side, drawn by the male scent of him, the leather-and-hay blend that seemed forever attached to his clothes, the musky aroma she inhaled from his skin at night.

"Cassie, you know we're not much different from the horses when it comes right down to it. When a male and female mate, sometimes there's results to consider."

She nodded, wondering at his words. What on earth was he talking about? Results? Her forehead crinkled as she pondered his words for a moment. The mare would drop a foal as a result of today's mating. What did that have to do with her, for goodness sake?

"Cassie? Did you hear me?" He stopped, midway through the yard, halfway to the house, and his hands gripped her shoulders. "Cassie, you really don't know yet, do you? It didn't even occur to you that we're probably gonna have a baby early next year?"

She shook her head. "You really think so?" One hand moved, trembling fingers resting against her belly.

Will nodded, heart beating wildly at the idea that had only now begun to feel like a fact. "I'd say we're gonna have a child, Cass, and my best guess would be in January."

She blinked at him, looking like a downy owl still in the nest, he decided. More than ever it looked as if his suspicions had been correct when Cassie had missed her monthly. She hadn't shown any concern, hadn't mentioned anything, that was true. And he sure enough hadn't seen any signs of such a thing since they'd gotten married, and that had been almost two months already.

"Do you really think I'm in the family way?" she asked politely, her cheeks gone a rosy pink, her mouth quivering as she spoke.

"Yeah, I'd say you probably are, honey." His mouth stretched into a wide grin.

Cassie took a deep breath. "Well, how come I didn't know it? Shouldn't I feel something?"

"Cass, didn't your mother tell you about having babies? About how you don't have monthly times and such?" Here he'd thought she was keeping it for a surprise, and now it turned out she didn't have any idea what was going on. No matter how you looked at it, he was getting in pretty deep here, he decided. And not even too sure of his ground, to tell the truth.

"Maybe my mother better talk to you about this," he suggested, deciding immediately that that idea had a considerable amount of merit. His arm around her waist, he turned her to the house, his steps a little quicker as Clara came out the back door.

"Ma, Cassie wants to talk to you," he said brightly.

She stiffened against his arm, dragging her feet as Clara Tolliver moved to the railing. "It's all right, Will," Cassie said. "I'll take your word for it."

"What's the matter here?" Clara asked sharply. "Were you out in the barn, Cassie? Are you all right, girl?" She cast an accusing look at her son. "She shouldn't be out there when you're breedin' those horses, Will. You'll have her all upset."

Will grinned. "She's upset, all right, Ma. But not about the horses. I think you need to talk to her."

Cassie flushed a brighter hue. "She'll think I'm ignorant!"

Clara's face softened as she looked at her daughter-in-law. "I'd never think that, child," she said kindly. "Come on in here, your tea is gone cold while you were out back."

Will gladly gave her over to his mother. Unless he'd read it wrong, Cassie was well on her way to motherhood, and he couldn't have been more pleased if he'd tried. In fact,

he felt a touch of the same male arrogance that fancy stud
had displayed out in the corral a while ago.

Damn, life was good.

"Mama, I wish you knew!" Cassie tugged the quilt over
her shoulder and spoke to the empty room, wishing with
all her heart that the woman she addressed could somehow
hear her. A bubble of pure joy escaped her lips and she
brushed quickly at a single tear that dampened her cheek.

"I can't be sad, Mama. I miss you so much, but I'm so
full of happy, there isn't room for sorrow inside me today."
She gazed across the room to the window, where the afternoon sunshine had faded to early twilight. The sounds
of voices in the kitchen below were muted, only the low
rumble of Will's tones making her aware of his presence
in the house.

She swung her feet over the side of the bed, rubbing her
eyes with the heels of her hands. Taking a nap had seemed
a foolish waste of time, but Clara's admonition, along with
a sudden wave of weariness, had sent her to her bed over
an hour ago.

Now she recognized the scents of supper, the chicken
Clara had been cooking on the back of the stove earlier, in
preparation for the dumplings she would add later. A grumble in her stomach alerted Cassie that it had been hours
since she'd put any food in her mouth, and she bent to
locate the shoes she'd kicked off earlier.

"Cassie." Will spoke from the open doorway and she
looked over her shoulder. He leaned with negligent ease
against the frame, his eyes tender as he surveyed his wife.

"I'm getting up, Will. I should have been downstairs,
helping your mother." She leaned to slip her shoes on and
suddenly he was there, kneeling before her, his hands on

her feet. He lifted one, then the other, putting her shoes in place, his hands big and warm against her cotton-clad flesh.

"You don't have to wait on me, Will," she told him, reaching to pick a piece of hay from his hair. Her hand lingered there, her fingers tunneling through his dark locks.

He looked up at her. "You'll be getting waited on a lot for the next few months. You're going to have my child, aren't you, Cassie? Didn't my mother agree with what I said?"

She nodded, her teeth settling softly against her bottom lip. "I can't believe it, Will. After she told me all the things that happen, how her body changes when a woman gets in the family way, I knew right off she was right."

"How do you feel about it, honey?" he asked, glancing down at her feet as he fastened her shoes. "You don't mind, do you?"

She shook her head. "No!" Her hands rested on his shoulders and she bent forward, her mouth against his, her head turning a bit to better seal their lips in a caress. Soft as the velvet petals of violets in the spring, their mouths touched, brushing and meshing, a current of wonder flowing to capture them in its midst.

Cassie felt the touch of Will's hands, his fingers enclosing her breasts, cupping her, weighing her tender flesh, and she whispered his name. "Will, I've been lying here wishing my mother could know about the baby."

He nodded, his arms sliding to enclose her in his embrace, easing to scoot between her spread knees, drawing her to rest her head on his shoulder. "I wonder if maybe she doesn't know, honey. Maybe part of the advantage of being in heaven is knowing all the good things that go on with the people we love. Maybe she's already thinkin' about a guardian angel for our baby."

"Oh, Will! You're just trying to make me feel better," Cassie said with a soft laugh.

"Don't you believe in angels?" he asked, nudging her to sit erect. He looked long and hard into her eyes and an air of satisfaction touched his countenance.

Cassie shook her head. "Of course I believe in angels. I'm just not sure you do. I think you're joshin' me."

He laughed aloud, then shrugged and rose to his feet, tugging her with him to stand toe-to-toe. "I just know we—"

He broke off abruptly as Maggie shrieked loudly from the kitchen. Clara shouted words Cassie couldn't make out and then Maggie squealed again. One word resonated through the slamming of the screen door and the shouts from the yard.

In a moment of silence, Maggie's voice rose in a cry of pure happiness. "Mama!"

Chapter Twelve

"Josie's here." His chin assuming a stubborn tilt, Will set Cassie aside and stalked to the bedroom door.

"Wait, Will," she called after him. His eyes were no longer soft, and his mouth had lost its tender smile. Will had donned a cloak of anger Cassie had never seen him wear. Not even on the day he'd rescued her from the two cowhands had she found him to be so armed with fury.

He was down the stairs ahead of her, unheeding of her words, and she clattered down the steps, his greater stride leaving her behind. From the yard Maggie's voice rose, shrill excitement coating each word as she greeted her mother.

"I knew you were comin' back! I knew it, Mama! Grandma said I shouldn't be lookin' for you every day, but I knew!"

Then there was the rumble of Will's lower tones, and Cassie burst through the screen door just as he greeted his sister. He'd managed to rein in his anger somewhat, his words not as harsh as Cassie had dreaded hearing. But the scowl he wore was mute testimony to the disapproval he felt.

"It's been a long time, Josie."

Cassie's sigh of relief was echoed by Clara, and their eyes met in a mutual exchange of apprehension. If Maggie noticed any tension, it was blithely ignored as she danced around her mother.

Josie stood by the wagon that had delivered her, uneasy and travel worn, her eyes seeking first one, then another of the trio of adults before her. One hand reached to brush at Maggie's head as the child bounced before her, her glance at the glowing face of her daughter filled with yearning.

The woman's dress was wrinkled and bore signs of having been worn to a frazzle, Cassie thought. Not that she could afford to be critical, considering her own ragtag appearance upon her arrival at this place. Dark hair, almost the identical color as her child's, was pulled into a knot at the nape of Josie's neck, not a wave or curl loose to relieve the simplicity of her appearance.

She was thin, almost to the point of illness, if Cassie was any judge. Her dress hung loosely on her, and unless she had more baggage than the small carpetbag at her feet, she probably didn't own much else to wear. Feeling an affinity for the woman, Cassie stepped forward to stand by Will's side.

"I'm Cassie, your new sister-in-law," she said quietly, offering her hand in greeting.

Eyes of a golden hue met hers, and a mouth that trembled in a smile repeated her name. "Cassie? Will's wife? I guess I didn't know he was married."

"He wasn't until just a while back," Cassie returned, her fingers intent on warming Josie's cold flesh. "Why don't you come in and talk to your mother while I set another place at the table?"

"If we can get Maggie peeled off her long enough, I might even get a hug from my daughter," Clara said gruffly, her eyes moist.

Josie stepped forward, almost stumbling over her carpetbag. "Oh, Mama! I've missed you so." Her words broken with emotion, Josie reached for her mother and was enclosed in welcoming arms.

Will's mouth was drawn into a thin line as he watched the reunion, his shoulders stiff as he regarded his sister.

"Will?" Cassie slid her hand into his and his mouth relaxed as he registered her presence beside him.

"Yeah, Cass." He squeezed her fingers in a silent message. His eyes closed for just a moment, and with visible effort he relaxed his stance. "I'll get Many Fingers from the barn for supper. We'll be in shortly." With a strained smile for her benefit, he turned away.

Josie's gaze followed him sadly and then she turned back to her mother. "Will's mad at me, Ma."

Clara sniffed and raised an eyebrow. "Can't see as he has much to brag about, child. He only managed to make it home himself a while back."

"Mama, Uncle Will's been showin' me how to ride a horse," Maggie bragged. "Him and Many Fingers helped Grandma's mares have a lot of babies."

Josie's face brightened. "You've got new foals, Ma?" And then she looked baffled for a moment. "Many Fingers?"

"He's Will's right-hand man," Cassie offered. "He came with us." Not that she would volunteer the beginning of their strange friendship. No sense in telling more than anyone needed to know.

"An Indian?" Josie asked in surprise.

"He's got lots of names, Mama," Maggie told her eagerly. "His mama called him Tall Horse and I do, too, sometimes."

"He's a good man," Clara said bluntly. "Works alongside Will. Fact is, he's right handy with the horses, like Cassie says.''

"But an Indian, Ma? What do the folks in town say about him being here?" Josie was not so much indignant, so far as Cassie could tell, as she was worried about Many Fingers' presence.

Clara drew herself up, a militant gleam appearing in her eye. "We do as we please here. We're not about to let anyone tell us who can come and go on our place."

Maggie tugged at her mother's hand, reminding her of her presence. "Come in the house, Mama. We're gonna eat supper and you can sit by me." Grasping the carpetbag, the child led the way and the women followed.

"Maggie's about to burst, isn't she?" Cassie stretched and yawned, watching Will's nightly ritual at the washbasin.

His soapy cloth halted its progress and he turned to look at her. "What happens if Josie takes a notion to trot off again, Cass? Do you know what that'll do to that little girl?" He lifted his arm to wash beneath it, his hand taking long strokes, leaving a residue of soapsuds behind. They gleamed in the lamplight and Cassie watched with pleasure as her husband repeated the motion with the other arm.

He'd stripped to the waist, and she marveled anew at the rippling muscles across his back and the solid width of his shoulders. He was strong, his arms heavy and long, his chest powerful, even more developed since their arrival at the farm. Handling the horses took an enormous amount of skill and strength, and Will was good at what he did.

In fact, in all ways Will was good—a good man, kind to Maggie, caring of his mother. But beyond that was the way he took care of her. From within Cassie it bubbled up, this yearning she could not escape. Living with Will, sharing his bed and now carrying his child, she was becoming more and more a part of the man.

Now, as if she needed his touch, the power of his loving to make her whole, she anticipated his movements, hurrying him through his nightly ablutions, anxious for his presence beside her.

Will crossed the room, loosening his trousers as he came, sitting on the side of the bed to shed his boots before he rid himself of the rest of his clothing.

"I don't want Maggie hurt again, or you either, for that matter," he said, tugging the quilt into place. "You've spent a lot of hours with her, Cassie. And yet she can turn to Josie and just ignore you like you were a stranger."

Cassie's throat filled with emotion. "I felt a little jealous, Will," she said meekly. "But I guess it's to be expected. Josie's her mother and you can't deny her that. Maggie loves her, it's that simple. And from what she said at suppertime, she won't be seeing hide nor hair of Maggie's father, anyway."

"Well, Josie's better off without that bast—" He broke off the word he'd almost spoken and hesitated. "I'm sorry, honey. I need to be careful what I say. I can't let Maggie hear that kind of language from me. Bad enough I let slip a cussword every once in a while. She doesn't need to match that kind of word up with her father, such as he is."

"I doubt she knows what it means, Will." Her fingers soothed him, rubbing against the tenseness in his neck, her touch easing to his shoulders to continue the massage more firmly.

"Feels good, Cass," Will rumbled, ducking his head to allow her better access. "Right there, honey." He hunched his shoulder as her fingers changed position.

"Turn over on your stomach," she told him, shifting out of the way as he obeyed her, watching as he settled himself with a groan, before she lifted one leg over him to straddle his behind.

Her hands moved slowly, her fingers curving into his flesh, across his shoulders, down his spine and then back, the heels of her hands dropping to apply pressure as she went. His skin was sleek, the golden hue a result of his shedding his shirt outdoors when it became too sweaty to wear. He'd worked long hours in the sun, mending fences and handling the mares and their foals, not to mention cutting hay and loading it on the hay wagon just this week.

"What will Josie tell Maggie about that man?" Cassie asked Will, wondering aloud as she considered the vast problem facing the young woman.

Will grunted, his shoulders rising in a helpless gesture. "Pretty hard to tell a little girl that her pa never got around to marrying her mother, isn't it?"

"Well, Josie thought they were married, didn't she?"

"I guess so. He probably knew he couldn't get her in bed with him unless he made it legal. Must be he faked the whole thing."

Cassie's hands slowed their movement. "Was that..."

Will reared up with a snarl, Cassie almost falling from the bed at his abrupt movement. "Hell, no! Don't even think that, Cassie. I already had you in my bed, and if I'd wanted to, I could have been makin' love with you before we got here."

She slid from his back, kneeling beside him as he rolled over in a smooth movement. "I wouldn't have!" It was a firm denial of his claim.

"I could have coaxed you into it," he maintained, lifting himself on one elbow as if to survey her anger. His own appeared to have dissipated, and he smiled. "But I didn't, Cass, and that's the whole issue. I thought more of you than to take advantage. And the longer we were together, the easier it was to see us gettin' married, especially after we arrived here and we got thrown together the way we did.''

"Did you ever tell Many Fingers?" she asked, reaching to touch his face, her burst of fury shattered by his words.

"I have a notion he's sorta figured things out on his own, since we went to Mill Creek. He doesn't say much, though.''

"I think he likes Josie," Cassie said slowly, remembering the Indian's watchful gaze during supper.

"He's only part white man, Cass. There's not a chance of anything happening there.''

"I thought you weren't all caught up on the Indian thing, Will," she said slowly.

He moved a little closer, as if he were intrigued by the movement of her hand against the angle of his jaw. "I'm not. I just know how things are, and a white woman stands to lose a lot if she gets tangled up with a half-breed.''

Cassie bent to press the warmth of her mouth on his cheek, her lips tingling from the faint stubble of his beard as she moved against his skin. "I don't care right now about them, Will," she whispered, her lips moving to brush the curve of his ear. "I'd rather talk about us.''

His arm moved quickly, gathering her to his side, then rolling her beneath him. His arousal was immediate, a thick ridge against her leg, and she smiled at his response to her invitation. "I don't think I want to talk at all," he told her bluntly.

"I can read your lips," she offered, her own parted and dampened by the tip of her tongue.

"Shoot, Cassie! If you don't take the cake!" he muttered, his mouth curling as he stifled a chuckle. Their lips met, touched and parted, then with a groan he rolled with her again until she was atop him, soft breasts molded to his chest, legs on either side of his, her face within reach.

His hands clasped the back of her head and he drew her closer until their mouths were only a breath apart. He closed his eyes and a shudder rippled through him, his words a whisper against her lips.

"Damn, you taste good, woman."

"Ma says you're going to have a baby."

Cassie smiled, unable to halt the automatic reaction to Josie's words. "Yes," she said. "In fact, I just realized it a couple of days ago myself." *After Will told me.* That she had been oblivious to the fact was some indication of her ignorance, she had decided. Her mother had sadly neglected some parts of her education, that was for sure.

"It took me a while to figure it out when I got that way with Maggie," Josie said with a sad little smile. "I didn't have Ma there to ask, and I don't think Bennett knew much about women, anyway."

"How did you manage, by yourself?" Cassie asked quietly, unable to imagine such a thing.

"We lived in a small town, and a neighbor woman delivered Maggie late one night. Bennett was at the saloon playing cards, and he got mad because she sent her husband to get him. He said he lost out on a winning hand because of me." Josie bent her head, concentrating on wiping the kettle she held. "He gambled for a living," she said finally, and then lifted her head to look at Cassie. "I didn't know that when I married him. Well, when I thought I married him."

Her face flushed with bright color. "Will is so angry with me, Cassie. And I guess I don't blame him. I was pretty stupid to believe everything Bennett Percival told me."

"He's not angry anymore, Josie. He was just worried

about Maggie. Besides, I'd guess he thought of you as his little sister, like you were supposed to still be a child. And now you're a woman grown, with more worries than you can shake a stick at.''

Josie nodded dejectedly, then slumped into a chair at the kitchen table, kettle and dish towel in her lap. "Will just looks right through me. Maybe he's not angry, but the way he's been acting the past couple of days, I think I'd almost rather have him holler at me than to treat me like I'm not even here.''

Cassie's eyes filled with tears, her hurt for Josie almost equal to that she felt for Will. He loved his sister, she knew that for sure. But somehow he needed to sort things out in his mind, come to trust the woman Josie had become and find it in himself to forgive her for leaving her child behind.

"I think Will's more concerned about you leaving Maggie and going off again," Cassie said firmly. "He just doesn't understand how you could do it the first time.''

"There's no reason to worry about that," Josie said firmly. "I don't know how I'll manage, but Maggie and I will never be apart again. I thought if I went away with Bennett last year, maybe we could work things out and…''

Josie's mouth quivered and she bit hard against the surface of her bottom lip. "When he told me we weren't even married and I left him, he didn't even offer to send me home. Just laughed and told me I'd been a fool. I had to sell my clothes for train fare, and I still owe Mr. Hogan's boy, down at the livery stable, for bringing me out to the farm like he did.''

"Oh, Josie! What a time you've had." Cassie shook her head, her heart aching for the young woman. "You know your mother wants you here, don't you, Josie? This is your home.''

"I always felt kind of left out, even when I was young,"

Josie said quietly. ''With three brothers around, my father didn't pay me much mind, and Ma was always so busy keeping things up....'' She shrugged, a lifting of her shoulders that spoke of the futility of her existence here as a young girl.

''Well, now's your chance to make it right with your mother,'' Cassie told her firmly. ''And Will is going to be fine, you'll see. He loves you, Josie. Would you like to see the moccasins he brought you?''

''He brought me something?'' Her voice was hopeful, and Cassie stifled a surge of disappointment. She'd give the beaded moccasins to their rightful owner, even though she'd cherished them as the first gift Will had ever given her.

''Moccasins. I think he said he got them in Texas. I'll run upstairs and find them as soon as we finish cleaning up the kitchen,'' Cassie offered. ''I had to wear them for a couple of days, so they're not brand-new,'' she cautioned. ''But just wait until you see them. They're so pretty.''

''I gave her the moccasins.'' In the silence of repletion her words were soft, barely disturbing the air, whispering across his chest like a spring breeze. She shifted, her leg easing its way across his belly, the inside of her calf rubbing lightly against the dark patch of hair that guarded his manhood. It stirred a bit beneath her touch, and she sighed.

''I thought you said you couldn't possibly move until morning.'' The whisper was seductive this time, but the stiffening of his body, combined with the impotent snarl he uttered, warned her she had not succeeded in warming him to her purpose.

''I gave the moccasins to you.'' His hand moved quickly, snatching her ankle, long fingers circling it without the faintest hint of a caress, and sliding her left leg to rest beside the right one. "When I want you to give Josie a gift, I'll let you know."

She snaked an arm across his chest, tucking her fingers in his armpit. "You bought them for her," she reminded him gently.

"I don't know why Ma never said anything in her letter about Josie leavin' Maggie here and runnin' off with her gamblin' man."

Cassie blew a small breath against his chest, stretching up just a bit to brush her lips across his flat male nipple. "Probably because she knew you'd put up a fuss, just like you have ever since Josie came home."

"I haven't said a damn thing to her!" His hand against her forehead applied just enough force to move her from the spot she had chosen to tease with her tongue.

"That's the whole problem, Will. You act like she's not even here, except for when you growl and give her one of your dirty looks." Her fingers tangled in the hair beneath his arm and she tugged a bit.

The muscles in his arm tightened, squeezing her fingers in place. "Just cut that out, Cassie. You're not gonna get around me with your shenanigans. I'm willing to let Josie stay here, so long as she takes care of Maggie and does her share around the place. I'll probably feel better about it when I see she's plannin' on stickin' around."

"I didn't know you could be so hard-hearted, Will."

His voice growled in her ear, vibrating against the wall of his chest. "I just believe in bein' up front about things. I guess I was raised to tell the truth, and that's what I'm doin' right now. I still feel guilty as hell over tellin' that sheriff you were my wife. I feel some better knowin' I've made it right, but lyin' is about the worst sin I can think of. If I can't trust the people I love, who can I depend on?"

He turned a bit, enclosing her in his embrace and whispering with an intensity that vibrated throughout her being. "I'll never be dishonest with you, Cassie, and I expect the same from you."

Cassie was silent, the almost forgotten specter of death shattering her cocoon of comfort. She'd lied from the first, telling Will she'd run off from Remus Chandler, threatening him with a knife. She'd let him claim her as his wife. She'd allowed him to speak marriage vows with her, and even put a baby in her belly. All with the horror of that night unspoken between them.

Perhaps now was the time to speak the words that might take him from her forever. What would he say if she were to blurt out the facts of that night? *I killed a man. I stabbed him in the back and washed his blood from my hands in the stream.*

How could she explain her fear? How could Will forgive the deception she'd tangled them in from the first? He didn't even love her—why would he be inclined to keep her with him, should she admit to such a crime? Perhaps because of their child?

Cassie's hand slipped to rest against the soft flesh of her belly where not even the slightest bulge announced the presence of the baby they'd made in this bed. She'd protect that small bit of flesh with her life, if need be. Rotting in a jail cell or dangling from a rope might be a fitting end for a murderer; but her child deserved a life, and if deceit on her part could provide it, she would be forever silent.

"Cassie? You sleepin' down there?" Will's deep, rumbling tones stirred her from the frantic thoughts that beset her and she shook her head, wincing as the locks tangled beneath his arm pulled at her scalp.

"Let me loose, Will," she mumbled. "You're lying on my hair." Gone was the playful mood she'd worked hard to create between them earlier. Only a deep sadness remained to wrap her in its depths. She turned from him, gathering up the length of her hair, quickly plaiting it in a rough braid.

Will waited while she settled herself, then curled his long body behind her, his knees pushing up beneath her bottom, his arm tugging her in place. "You don't think it's bad for the baby, me lovin' you every night, do you, Cass?"

She shook her head. If he took away the joy she found in their hours alone beneath these covers, she'd be bereft of comfort. The love she felt for the man she'd married could be expressed only by the giving of her self into his keeping. She'd told him once aloud, and he'd accepted her declaration without comment.

She closed her eyes, soaking in the warmth of his big body, luxuriating in the feel of his hand cupping her breast. It was all right, she decided with firm resolve. If he never told her he loved her, she'd survive. And the fact was, he'd managed to convince her pretty thoroughly that he enjoyed the warmth of her body and the pleasure he found in her arms.

For now, that would be enough.

Chapter Thirteen

Eben and Louise came right from church, their spanking-new two-seated surrey gleaming in the sunshine. With a great flourish of prancing hooves and bells jingling on the harness, the vehicle halted near the back door and Eben scanned the yard.

"It's Eben," Josie whispered from behind the kitchen curtain.

"Well, go on out and tell your brother hello," Clara told her, standing in front of the open oven door, sliding a pan of biscuits from sight.

"Does he know I'm here?"

"Well, if he doesn't, he will in a minute, won't he?" her mother asked practically.

"Hello in there!" Eben called, sliding from the surrey and lifting his arms to Louise. Swinging her to the ground in a flurry of skirts, he gave her a quick kiss, then looked around.

"I saw that, Eben," came Will's mocking call from the door of the barn. "Kissin' in broad daylight, like a newlywed."

Louise blushed, ducking her head in obvious embarrassment, and Eben laughed, wrapping an arm around her waist and ushering her to the porch.

"You come over to give me a hand in the barn?" Will asked, his long strides bringing him to the pump.

"Naw, we just thought Ma might have enough dinner cooked for two more," Eben said with a laugh. "Louise here is always hungry."

The water splashed into the trough and Will ducked his head beneath the flow, scrubbing at his face, then washing his hands quickly with a bit of soap. He stood up, long fingers combing through his dark hair, and headed for the house.

"How come no one came to church this morning?" Eben asked him quietly, eyeing the screen door. "Is Ma all right? Where's Maggie?"

"Ma's fine and Maggie's out back, lookin' at the mares and their babies. We ended up with seventeen foals, did you know that?"

"No, haven't had time to come by lately, what with spring planting." Eben shuffled his feet. "Uh, look, Will. I heard tell in church that Josie came home. Mr. Hogan's boy said he brought her out here in a wagon. Said she didn't have any baggage, and she looked pretty poorly."

"She's here, Eben." Will glanced at the kitchen window. "Probably watchin' us from behind the curtain."

"Well, why in hell didn't somebody tell us? I'll bet Samuel doesn't know either, does he?" He took the steps with his long-legged stride, leaving Louise wide-eyed and abandoned.

"Josie?" He was in the kitchen as he called his sister's name and then there was silence, except for the soft sound of a woman's tears.

"Josie never did cry very quietly," Will told Louise,

snatching his hat from his head and swatting it against his leg. "Might's well come on in, Louise."

His hand between her shoulders, he opened the screen door and followed her across the threshold. Eben had his hands full, what with Josie crying on his shoulder and both Clara and Cassie looking on vigilantly.

"I'm sorry, Eben, it's just so good to see you," Josie managed between sobbing and blowing her nose on the white handkerchief her brother offered.

"I sure am glad you're not sad about it, Jo, or we'd both be floating away," Eben said, his voice more cheerful than the somber look in his eyes. He held her away, scanning her slender form. "You need a little fattening up, sis."

"Well, I've been here four days, and between Ma and Cassie, they've been feeding me at least six times a day," she said with a catch in her voice. "I ought to be looking like that fat old sow out in the pigsty any day now."

"Not much chance of that," Clara scoffed. "She's still too spare for Cassie's dresses, and Lord knows there sure ain't much to that young'un."

"Well, it appears Cassie'll soon be needin' new ones," Will said with a knowing look at his wife. "She won't be fitting into hers much longer. Maybe Ma can take them in and pass them along to Josie."

Eben looked at Louise and winked. His arm fell from Josie's waist and he moved to where his wife waited by the doorway. "Would Cassie by chance have the same problem we do?" he asked in a loud whisper, his mouth fully a foot from her ear.

Louise blushed again, her elbow jabbing without a trace of pity into her husband's ribs.

"Oof..." he grunted. "What'd you do that for, Lou?"

"You don't have to tell everybody so soon," she

scolded. "Being in the family way's sort of a private thing."

Eben looked around the kitchen, lifting his brows in feigned surprise. "Well, it sure enough looks like we're surrounded by family here, sweetie. And I didn't hear Cassie fussin' at Will when he told her news right out loud."

"*She's* going to fuss at him later on," Cassie put in, glaring at Will for Eben's benefit. Her mouth wobbled as she frowned her best at him, and then she chuckled, eyeing Louise's waistline. "I don't see where Louise is going to need any new clothes for a while, Eben. If anybody gets new clothes, I think it ought to be Josie. She'll have to eat hearty for a while before she can wear mine."

"I found a couple of things in Maggie's room I left here, and they'll do me," Josie said, her tears a thing of the past. Her eyes darted to Will as if she sought some sign from that direction. "I wouldn't think of taking Cassie's new things."

Will cleared his throat in a noisy fashion, looking at Cassie—as if for approval, if she knew anything about it. "I was just teasin', Jo. I thought we might take a trip to town when we take Ma's eggs in this week and pick up a dress or two for you."

"I don't want to be any trouble," Josie said quietly.

Cassie stepped to her side. "You're not a bit of bother, so don't say that again, you hear?" With a cautioning look at Will, she continued. "Will just hasn't had time to go into town this week. He's been planning on buying you some new clothes since you got here."

And if that was a lie, she'd just go right ahead and commit what Will thought was a mortal sin, for Josie's benefit. But Will apparently was willing to forgive her words of appeasement, and he nodded his agreement.

"Well, at least for a couple of days," he amended, with a glance at Cassie's wary expression.

"When's your baby coming?" Louise asked eagerly, stepping closer to Cassie.

"First of January, Will says," Cassie answered.

"Will says?" Eben repeated, one eyebrow lifting in mocking query. "You the expert around here, big brother?"

"I'm going to beat you by a month or so," Louise said quietly, ignoring her husband. "I figure around Thanksgiving time." Her smile was brilliant as she touched Cassie's arm. "I've been wanting to come over and get to know you better, Cassie. That one day we were here, we didn't have much time to talk, and you were having a hard time just figuring out who everyone was. But Eben's been so busy with the new calves and planting and I've had four clutches of new chicks hatch."

"We'll make time, Louise," Cassie assured her, her spirits soaring as she stood between the two women who had become her sisters the day she married Will. There was a lot to be said for family, she decided. "Did you ever know Josie?" she asked, reaching to pull Will's sister closer.

Louise nodded. "We used to go to school in town together. I was a couple of years behind Josie, but I always thought she was so lucky to live in the same house as Eben."

"Well, you sure got your wish, didn't you, honey?" Eben said, grinning at his wife. He turned to Josie. "You home for good, Jo? Where's that husband of yours?"

Josie looked stricken, her eyes seeking Will's, as if for guidance.

He met her gaze and nodded. "Let's go on out to the barn, Eben. Got a problem with one of the colts, a sore on his leg I can't seem to get healed up."

Eben grinned at the women grouped by the stove. "It's kinda crowded in here, anyway, Will. These ladies need room to get dinner on the table, and we sure wouldn't want to hold them up."

The two men went out the door and across the yard, heads together as they talked, their broad shoulders looking identical, their longs legs eating up the distance to the barn.

"Eben looks good," Josie said, blowing her nose once more on her brother's handkerchief.

"Oh, Josie, it's so wonderful that you're home," Louise said, reaching for her own hug of greeting. "Eben really missed you, you know."

"Where is he?" Eben asked without preamble, his usually cheerful face dark with concern and the beginning of anger as he strode beside his brother.

"Damned if I know," Will answered. "Probably a good thing he's not handy or I'd be tempted to go gunnin' for him."

"That bad?" Eben asked.

"He faked a wedding, conned Josie into believing a friend of his was a judge."

"When did she find out?" Eben stopped in the barn door and looked toward the house.

"About the time he decided he didn't need her hangin' around anymore. Told her to skedaddle and walked away."

"She looks pretty puny."

Will nodded. "I was sore at her, leavin' Maggie here last year and takin' off like she did. But Ma reminded me I didn't have much to brag about myself, and by the time Cassie got done with me, I'd pretty much gotten over fussin' about it. Just had to blow off a little steam, I guess."

"She can come to us if there isn't room here, Will,"

Eben offered with alacrity. ''We've got an extra bedroom and Louise would be glad of the help.''

''No, I doubt Cassie and Ma would let her go. They've been hoverin' over her like a newborn calf this week. And Maggie's at home here. She doesn't even mention Bennett Percival.''

''I'd like to get my hands on that bastard,'' Eben growled.

''I get first crack,'' Will announced. ''You'll have to get in line.''

''Not if I see him first,'' Many Fingers said from the first stall. Backing from its depths, he closed the door behind him and nodded greetings at Eben.

''The man doesn't stand a chance,'' Will muttered. ''Especially once Samuel finds out about the stunt he pulled.''

''Does he know Jo's here?'' Eben asked.

Will shook his head. ''I've been busy. Haven't been off the place all week.''

''I'll stop by on our way home later and tell him,'' Eben offered. ''He'll want to come by and see her.''

The sun was a red ball falling toward the horizon and the house was quiet. Cassie was curled on the sofa with Maggie, reading to her from a storybook, and Will sat at the kitchen table mending a bridle, his mother offering bits and pieces of news as she mixed a batch of bread to rise for morning.

Josie slipped from the front door, walking around the house beneath the tall maple trees that shaded it from the hot sun during the summer months. From where she stood, she could watch the colts frolicking in the pasture, their mothers standing beneath a cluster of trees, noses to the ground as they fed on the new meadow grass.

A movement caught her eye and she glanced past the

barn to where a tall figure leaned on the fence, watching the small creatures at play. "He's about as lonely looking as I feel," she whispered, a sudden impulse tugging her in his direction. His lean strength, his dark, knowing eyes and the innate knowledge that he was drawn to her led her steps.

Many Fingers watched her approach, his eyes hungry as he gazed his fill. "You like the horses?" he asked, his words urging her closer.

She nodded. "They've always been my favorite part of the farm. Ma used to send me out to gather eggs and pull weeds in the garden, but I'd rather have worked with the foals."

"You want to help with them?" he offered, keeping a respectable distance between himself and Will's sister.

She nodded eagerly. "Do you think Will would let me?"

Many Fingers smiled at her. "I take care of the horses. I'll tell Will I need your help."

"What can I do?" Her voice was eager, her eyes sparkling with anticipation as she moved closer to where he stood.

"We'll fasten a lead rope on them and you can get them used to being handled. They don't learn a lot, but they need to know a human touch. Mostly they follow, get used to the rope tugging at them." He watched her closely, his eyes intent on her graceful movements as she moved along the fence.

"Tomorrow morning?" she asked.

"Right after breakfast, if you don't have work to do in the house."

"I'm cooking in the morning, so I can come out as soon as I tend to Maggie. Cassie will clear up." Her mouth lifted in a smile, her face rosy in the rays of the setting sun. "It's so good to be home."

"Your brothers want revenge on the man who hurt you," Many Fingers said quietly. He watched the light fade from her eyes as she looked at him. "I intend to be the one to defend your honor," he told her. "If he comes anywhere near, he will answer to me for what he did to you."

"Why?" It was a barely heard sound, whispered through dry lips, confusion alive on her face as she stepped closer to the man who had befriended her.

"You are the sister of my friend. You are a member of Brave One's family. I would honor him in this way."

"You'd defend me because of Will?"

He hesitated, perhaps a moment longer than the question merited. And then he shook his head. "Partly, Josephine. Partly because of you."

"No one calls me Josephine. I've been Josie all my life," she said. "Did Will tell you that was my name?"

Many Fingers nodded. "He told me. I will call you Josephine."

Her fingertips rose to brush against the heat in her cheeks as Josie watched Many Fingers turn from her.

His hair loose against his shoulders, the Indian walked to where the horses grazed, melting into the shadows beneath the low-hanging branches of the maple trees. With a lithe movement he was astride one of the mares, and without benefit of bridle, with one hand clutching her mane, he rode the sleek animal in a circle, herding the foals and their mothers to the open barn door.

Josie watched in awe as the horses disappeared into the depths of the barn, only an occasional whinny testifying to their presence within its walls. She walked around the big building to the front door and slid it aside, entering the dimly lit interior.

Down the long aisle Many Fingers moved from stall to stall, closing the doors, his low voice murmuring to the occupants of each stall as he went. His chore complete, he came to where she stood. His dark eyes narrowed as he scanned her slight form, then he lifted one hand to touch her face, his fingers gentle as they cupped her chin.

"You will be my woman, Bright Eyes," he said quietly.

"You don't even know me," Josie said. "I've only been here a week."

"I have known you since time began." His fingertips brushed the length of her jaw, then rested on her shoulder for a moment. As if reluctant to release her from his grasp, his hand slid slowly down the length of her arm, their hands touching briefly before he stepped back.

A visible shiver ran through Josie and she caught her breath. "I don't know what to say to you," she whispered.

He shook his head. "Say nothing. The time will come. Go to bed. They will wonder where you are."

"You're missing having Maggie trail around after you, aren't you, girl?" Clara's words jolted Cassie from her reverie and she spun to face Will's mother.

"Heavens, no!" she said blithely. "She was just lonesome for her mother and I was handy. She needs to catch up on things with Josie."

Clara looked out the kitchen window to where her daughter and grandchild worked in the garden. Rather, Josie worked and Maggie squatted between the rows of plants and chattered. "You've been good for her, Cassie. She'll come around, once Josie's been here a while and the newness wears off. It's like she was starved for her mama's attention and she's soakin' it up as fast as she can."

"She's lucky her mama pays her mind the way she does. My mother was always so tired when I was comin' up. There wasn't much time for fun and foolishness."

Clara looked around. "It sounds like she had a hard time making ends meet."

Cassie nodded, dropping her gaze.

"Where was your pa?"

"I don't remember him. He died when I was little. I never had a father till she married Remus Chandler. I was almost grown by that time, fourteen years old, I guess."

"How did you live, Cassie?" Clara's eyes looked worried as she pressed the issue.

Cassie hesitated, brought face-to-face with the knowledge of her beginnings. All the years of her childhood she'd felt an outcast in the small Texas town where they lived. The children in school ignored her, and even the teacher barely tolerated her presence in the classroom.

The only bright spots in her memory were of the times she'd spent watching Cleta sew throughout the early evening hours after supper, making dresses for the women who worked at the saloon in town. And then, late at night, an occasional visitor would knock at the back door, and from her bedroom Cassie would hear voices, the low tones of a man, her mother's soft responses.

Until she was fourteen, when Remus Chandler had offered marriage, and Cleta had grasped at the chance for respectability and a better life for her child. That the man was basically a cruel, demanding tyrant had been brought home to mother and daughter very quickly.

"My mother worked at home," Cassie said finally. She turned to look from the window, aware of Clara's presence behind her.

"We can't change things in our past," Clara said quietly. "But we can choose our future, Cassie. The way Josie is right now. She made some mistakes, foolish mistakes. But she's doin' her best to make amends now. I reckon that's all we can expect from anybody. I suspect your mama just did the best she could, don't you?''

Cassie nodded, her memories of Cleta dying all mixed together with the early days, when Mama had been young and pretty, before those years with Remus had dulled her beauty and dimmed her laughter.

"There's worse things than being without a husband, Miz Tolliver," she said after a moment. "There's being with the wrong man. I'm glad Josie came home."

"Don't you suppose you could call me Clara?" Will's mother asked.

Cassie turned to her, her heart aching with the memories she had called forth from the deepest recesses of her soul. "Can I call you Mother instead?" she asked hesitantly. "I don't want to be forward, but I think I'd like…"

"Of course you can, child." Clara's voice was firm, her nod a silent affirmation of Cassie's position in the house. "You're Will's wife—that makes you my daughter. Now, why don't you go take a look and see if we have any early carrots out in the garden. They'd be good in the soup we're having for dinner."

"I really like Louise." Cassie smiled at the memory of her new friend. Sharing drew folks together. Sharing their pregnancies was a certain route to friendship with Eben's wife, as far as she was concerned.

Will's feet pressed against the footboard of their bed as he stretched and yawned. Relaxing, he smiled as he turned to her. His hair was rumpled by his pillow, his tanned skin dark against the white sheets, and his lazy grin caused a dimple to form in his cheek. Truly the man was more of a temptation than she could resist, even though she suspected she had tickled his funny bone with her vehement approval of Louise.

She rolled to face him, one hand rising to smooth the rumpled locks of hair that fell across his forehead. "Don't laugh at me, Will Tolliver," she warned, lifting one eyebrow as she tugged his hair.

"Ouch! Dang, Cassie! You're a mean woman." He moved suddenly, catching her unaware, rolling her beneath him with one heavy leg pinning hers to the mattress. "You're supposed to like your relatives. You just announced it like it was some big surprise."

She subsided, allowing his dominance, her smile acknowledging her pleasure in his touch. "You take advantage of me about every chance you get, don't you?"

He dropped a soft kiss against her mouth, demanding nothing, simply brushing the surface of her lips with his own. "You bet I do, sweetie. There's nothin' I enjoy more than rollin' around on this bed with you."

"Will?" She circled his neck with her arms, her fingers buried in the length of his dark hair. "The whole point is that they're not my relations, they're yours. The only reason I can claim them as family is because you married me." Her fingers tensed at the back of his head and she drew him closer, tilting her head to better blend their flesh in a gentle meeting. It was a kiss of longing, a tender yearning forming her lips as she gave him what he sought in the sweetness of her mouth.

"That tasted like more, Cass," he murmured. "Are you feelin' all right, honey?" Even as he spoke, he worked with lazy purpose at the buttons on her white gown. One long finger pressed carefully against the rounded surface of her breast and he edged it toward the center.

"I'm feeling fine," she whispered. She tugged at his hand, lifting it to her mouth where she took the errant finger between her lips. "I've never had family before, Will. I only had my mother, never an aunt or uncle or sister. I always wanted a sister." She suckled gently on his finger, then bit it, her teeth pressing against the callused tip. "Thank you for giving me a whole slew of them, and brothers to boot." Her teeth rubbed against his flesh and his shiver made her smile.

"Hell, if a couple of brothers and some womenfolk can make you this grateful, what are you gonna do when I round up all the aunts and uncles and cousins?"

Her eyes widened in disbelief. "You have more relatives hereabouts?"

"My pa had a mess of brothers down at the other end of the county. We see them come threshing time. Me and Eben and Samuel always used to go with Pa to help for a day. I suspect things haven't changed that much while I was gone."

Cassie shook her head slowly. "I just can't fathom such a big family." Her mouth curved in a sultry smile as she peered at him through her lashes. "I suppose you'll want me to be grateful for each and every one of them."

"I suspect I will," he agreed. "There's Uncle Jake and Aunt..." His teasing rejoinder became muffled as she pulled him closer, and then he was lost in the wonder of their loving.

Chapter Fourteen

The Fourth of July was to be the biggest celebration of the summer. To hear Clara tell it, most everyone in the county would be there. And Elizabeth had promised that Maggie could march with her and the boys in the parade.

Will said they would do the chores early, load the wagon and be in town in time for the main event. It was to be a parade like no other. There were six floats this year, not to mention the Women's League in full regalia.

Cassie's only concern this morning was that Maggie's enthusiasm might wear her out before ten o'clock when the parade was due to begin. Like a whirling dervish, the child danced about impatiently, first hopping on one foot, then the other, twirling in a circle as the notion took her. The center of attention, she preened before her audience.

"Do you like the outfit my mama made me, Cassie?" Resplendent in red, white and blue, Maggie could have been hung from a pole and saluted as the band marched by, Cassie thought privately. Red-and-white-striped muslin made up the skirt of her dress, while star-studded blue fabric of a heavier sort had been sewn into a blousy top. The Women's League had ordered the stuff from St. Louis and some had been left over—left on the shelf, as Dorinda Bartlett had chortled. Josie had delved deeply into her pocket to come up with the money for her daughter's holiday garb, and if Cassie was any judge, it had been well worth the expense.

Maggie spun and danced around the kitchen table, her skirts swirling around her legs, her eyes sparkling, mouth going a mile a minute and impatience adding a flush to her cheeks.

"Matthew, Mark and Luke will think I look *beauteous*," she crooned, her fingers tracing the stars scattered across her chest.

Cassie traded glances with Josie, stifling an urge to chuckle. "Do you think she'll survive until it's time to leave?"

"I'm not sure I will," Josie said, evading Maggie's foray around the breakfast table. "Why don't you go outside and show your uncle Will how beautiful you look, sweetheart?"

Maggie halted midspin. "Oh, can I, Mama? Can I show Tall Horse, too? And can I—"

"Yes, yes and yes!" Josie interrupted, her mouth curving in a smile as she watched her daughter's exuberant display.

"You don't even know what you agreed to," Cassie said, watching as the little girl lifted her skirts above her knees, endeavoring to keep them from the dust of the yard.

"I agreed to go to this parade is what I did," Josie said glumly, dropping into a chair and sagging against the table. "How can I face everyone in town, Cassie? They'll all be looking at me and pointing a finger."

"You can stand next to me and we won't know which of us they're pointing at," Cassie said blithely. "I'm the woman Will dragged home with him. I'd wager the gossips had a field day when we came through town, me in my pants and traveling with two men."

''Well, at least you were married to one of them,'' Josie reminded her.

But I wasn't. The words almost burst from Cassie's lips, held back only by the sure knowledge that Will would never forgive her if she told their secret. On this one subject he was willing to live a lie. And since he was so brutally honest in all of his dealings, she could not fault him for this one aberration.

She had her own secret to hide. If Will could make an exception, so could she, she'd decided during one long, sleepless night, when the specter of her stepfather had invaded her dreams. Remus Chandler was destined to haunt her forevermore, it seemed. Her conscience twinged with regularity these days, her battered soul desperate for a clean slate.

''Cassie? You look like you're a hundred miles away,'' Josie said, rising from her chair.

Cassie forced a smile. ''Just thinking about the parade. Mostly about all the relatives I'm going to meet. It's a little scary, I guess.''

''You met me without any trouble,'' Josie said with a smile, moving to stand by the back door. ''Look out back, Cassie. Maggie's showing off her new outfit.''

Hands fisted on their hips, the two men were watching as the little girl pranced before them. Then with a motion of his hand and a few low words, Will sent her to sit on the wagon seat while Many Fingers brought the team out to the wagon.

''They don't seem to care that she's a...'' As if the word was too painful to be uttered, Josie pressed her lips together.

''There's no blame to lay on either of you, as far as I can see,'' Cassie said bluntly. ''You'll have to get on with your life one of these days, Josie. Most everybody has something they'd just as soon not discuss in public, and before you know it, nobody will even remember that you came home without a husband trailing along behind you."

"She'll never have a father," Josie said quietly.

"She's got Will, and Eben and Samuel."

Josie flashed a quick glance at the two men, working in tandem as they adjusted the leather harness over the broad backs of the mares. "Do you like Many Fingers?" she asked, as if the question were but an idle thought.

Cassie looked at her sharply. "Of course I do. I guess the real crux of the matter is how you feel about him, Jo."

Josie lifted her shoulders, hugging herself as she leaned against the doorjamb. "He's nice to me." She shook her head. "No, more than that. He's good to me. He listens when I talk and he treats me like a lady."

"He's also a half-breed." Cassie's words carried no trace of cruelty, only the simple truth she felt Josie must face. "Folks wouldn't take to a white woman and an Indian together."

"Is that how you feel, Cassie?"

Cassie shook her head. "No. I like him fine, but it isn't me you're going to have to worry about. You'll really have fingers pointing at you if folks think there's something going on between the two of you."

"There's nothing going on," Josie said quietly.

Not yet, Cassie thought sadly. She'd been right to wonder. The tall Indian managed to be at hand when Josie needed anything, his dark eyes never straying far from her at the supper table as she served the food or cared for Maggie. His compliments were simple, usually a thank-you sufficing, unless it was a meal that Josie cooked. It had become a point of humor with Will, trying to outdo his friend, as the stoic Indian praised Josie's efforts with spare words of approval.

Today could bring trouble in the wake of the festivities, what with a certain amount of moonshine being consumed by the men who brought their own tucked away in the backs of their wagons. Cassie frowned at the thought. There would be a fuss to beat the band should Many Fingers appear to pay court to Josie in public.

The picnic lunch was put together with dispatch once Maggie was out of the way, and along with Clara's contribution of a sheet from her linen supply, the three women headed for the wagon. Will spread the sheet over the pile of hay on the back of the wagon for the little girl to sit on.

Clara drove the team, Josie and Cassie beside her on the wide seat, and with Will and Many Fingers as an escort on horseback, they headed for town, Maggie keeping up a running reminder that they dare not be late for the parade.

From beyond the schoolhouse they heard the band practicing, then saw the band members lined up in a haphazard fashion, already sweating beneath the summer sun. The unmistakable sounds of "My Country, 'Tis of Thee" rose into the morning air, and Cassie's spirits lifted. Maggie was suddenly quiet, her eyes wide as she listened to the music.

"Isn't that beautiful?" she whispered loudly as the instruments blared the final note.

Will rode beside her, pacing his stallion's gait to that of the slower-moving wagon. "Wait till you hear the ladies singing along with them," he told her.

"Do we all get to sing?" Maggie asked hopefully.

Will nodded. "Sure 'nough, half-pint."

The road was rapidly becoming a bottleneck in the middle of town, what with wagons and buggies coming in from all directions, and Clara was hard put to find a place to leave their conveyance for the day. The hitching rail outside the community church was only partially filled and offered shade for the animals. It was there she headed.

"I'm gonna see if the livery stable has any room for the horses," Will told the women. "We'll meet you by the general store."

Clara spied some of her lady friends, and with a word of apology, hurried to join them, Cassie waving her on her way.

"I'll meet you back here at noon to get the food for the picnic," Clara called back over her shoulder, her skirts kicking up a dusty trail behind her as she greeted her friends.

Already the band was moving to assemble itself in the road, and a series of wagons decorated with buntings and posters and hung with flags began the trek to line up near the schoolhouse.

"Come on, Mama. I gotta go find Aunt Elizabeth," Maggie said plaintively. "She said I could march with her and the boys."

Josie looked helplessly at Cassie. "I'm not sure I can face all these people," she whispered. "They all know me, Cassie."

"I'll be with you. Let's just find Samuel and Elizabeth first and get Maggie settled," Cassie said practically. Standing on the wagon bed, she scanned the gathering groups of townsfolk and families who had come from outlying farms.

"There!" She pointed at a wagon rolling past the schoolhouse, sending band members to either side of the road. "That's Samuel and his family now. Run, flag them down, Maggie!"

Her short legs pumping, the child hurried to the edge of the road and Samuel drew his team to a halt. Matthew and Mark gave her a hand, and hauled her to sit beside them, legs dangling over the back of the wagon. Cassie waved them on and then slid from the wagon bed to the ground.

"Come on, Josie. We don't want to miss the parade. The men will be waiting for us."

Both sides of the street were lined with people, dogs ran amuck and small flags fluttered from children's hands as the band led the parade down the middle of the road. A grand assortment of marching music set the tempo, and with much clapping and cheering, the crowd greeted each wagonload of participants.

The choir of the community church sang with gusto. The Women's League carried flags, dipping them in unison, twirling them in time to the music and, in general, displaying the results of hours of practice.

Last came the marchers, the Sunshine Club from the church, Elizabeth's Young Farmers group, with Maggie resplendent in their midst, and the men's baseball team, newly equipped with genuine Spalding caps and gloves. Tossing a baseball back and forth among themselves, they cut up, fending off the catcalls of the crowd, offering to meet all comers at a game to be played after the picnic at noon.

"Well, that's the end of it," Will said, his hands resting on Cassie's shoulders as they stood on the wooden sidewalk in front of the general store.

"I've never seen a finer parade," Cassie announced.

Will laughed. "You sure haven't been around the world, have you, sweetheart? You ought to see what goes on in St. Louis on July the fourth."

Cassie's smile was wistful. "I'd love to go there some day."

Josie shuddered. "I've been there."

Cassie turned to her eagerly. "Did you see the parade?"

Josie shook her head, her mouth pinched. "Just a parade of cockroaches climbing down the wall of the room I was living in."

"Well, you're not livin' there anymore," Will told her firmly. "You're with family now, Josie."

Her face brightened as she looked at her brother, and Josie reached up to kiss his cheek. "I love you, Will."

"Mama! Did you see me march?" Maggie's shrill greeting caught Josie's attention and she bent to hug her child.

"We sure did, honey." The small body sagged against her, and Josie smiled. "I think you're about ready to sit down and take a rest, aren't you?"

The picnic ground was situated just outside of town and it was there they headed, gathering up their baskets of food on the way. A quilt was spread beneath a tree and Clara joined them as Cassie and Josie began setting out the food.

"I think Maggie's full stomach is pullin' her eyes shut," Clara said, watching as her granddaughter yawned for the third time.

"I'm going to stay here with her for a while," Josie announced. "Why don't the rest of you go watch the ball game. I can see it from here."

"I will watch with you," Many Fingers said. Squatting by the tree, removed from the rest of the group by several feet, he'd finished his dinner quickly.

"You don't have to keep me company," Josie told him quietly. "I'll be fine here."

"I will watch." As a statement of purpose it couldn't have been any more definite, and Will nodded as he accepted his friend's decision.

Maggie's eyes were closed and she swayed where she sat, her plate still half-full in her lap. Josie eased the child to lie on her side and gently smoothed her hair back from her face, placing a folded towel beneath her head for a pillow.

The baseball game was about to begin and the men's

team had graciously split up, each half choosing young men from the assembled group to fill out the numbers, in order to have two teams. The watchers sorted themselves into cheering sections and settled down to watch the fun.

Will and Cassie sat in the shade of a walnut tree and watched as Clara walked away to join a group of townsfolk. "Will Josie be all right?" Cassie asked.

"Many Fingers is lookin' out for her," Will said. "We can see them from here, anyway."

A shout went up from the crowd as the first ball was pitched and Cassie leaned forward eagerly, eyes intent on the game.

"Get moving, chief." The insult was unmistakable, and Josie turned quickly as the familiar voice came from behind her.

"Bennett! What are you doing here?"

The gambler stood just beyond the patch of shade Josie shared with her daughter and the man who guarded them. "I came to see my daughter," he said, his gaze fastened on Many Fingers. "This brave needs to move on while I talk to you, Josie."

"I stay," Many Fingers said firmly, moving to stand before Josie, his dark eyes taking measure of the intruder.

"Get out of here, Bennett," Josie said sharply. "I don't want to see you, and neither does my daughter."

"She's mine, too," Bennett Percival reminded her with a malicious smile.

"Not anymore, she isn't. You lost out when you told me she was in the way. Besides, you have no legal claim, as you well know."

"Ask any judge in the country. I'm wanting to make a home for my fatherless child." His mouth drawn into a smirk, Bennett Percival presented his case.

"Go get Will." Josie's voice was quiet, but her message for help was unmistakable as she spoke to Many Fingers.

His eyes flared with anger as he stepped forward, hands fisted at his sides. Only Josie's touch on his shoulder halted his steps.

"No, don't!" she said quickly. "Just get Will, please!"

Reluctantly the Indian turned to her, his face a stoic mask. He searched her face and nodded. Not for the world would he cause her to be at the center of a blood battle today.

"You'll be wise to listen to me, Josie," Bennett said archly, watching as the other man set off across the field to where the baseball game was in progress. "I might be persuaded to allow you to keep my daughter, with the right inducement. Your brother seems prosperous enough."

Josie's skin blanched at the subtle threat. "In other words, if I ask Will for money to pay you off, you'll leave me alone? That's blackmail."

Bennett inspected his fingernails, a smile of satisfaction curling his lips. "You always were fairly bright, Josie. Except when you thought that barkeep was a preacher." His short burst of laughter mocked her, and Josie's ashen skin turned crimson.

"Get out and leave me alone," she cried, forgetting for a moment that her sleeping daughter was only inches away.

Bennett Percival looked up, his wary gaze on the rapidly approaching men, and nodded his agreement. "Certainly, my dear. But I'll be around, never fear." His horse stood nearby, and with a few quick steps he was mounted and riding toward the middle of town.

"What did he want?" Will asked, watching as the gambler disappeared between two buildings.

"He threatened to take Maggie. Said that no judge would deny his claim." Josie's voice was strained.

Will shook his head. "There's no chance of it, Josie. She's part of my family. No four-flusher is about to cart her away, you can bet on that."

"Next time it will be my way, Josephine," Many Fingers said bluntly. "I will take care of him."

"You can't afford to make threats, my friend," Will told him. "Don't let anybody hear you say that. Folks hereabouts would gather for miles to watch an Indian get lynched."

"Don't do anything," Josie pleaded softly. "I've caused enough trouble as it is. Just go watch the game, both of you. He won't come back now."

"Go, Will. I'll stay here."

Will nodded, and trotted across the field to rejoin Cassie beneath the tree.

"I don't want you to be involved in this." Josie's words were firm, her gaze meeting that of the man who watched her.

"He will not hurt you, I promise it." The pride of his ancestry shone from his dark eyes as Many Fingers vowed his intentions. "One day you will be mine, Josephine. I will guard you well. I want you with me every day until this thing is settled. Bring Maggie with you in the morning when you come to work with the foals."

Her hesitation was brief, as if the decision she made would be of great import. And then she nodded. "All right. I'll bring her along. She can watch from the fence."

"She is big enough to learn about the horses. We will let her ride each day on one of the mares. She can help with the feeding at night."

Josie's eyes grew warm as she watched the man who had chosen her. "Are you practicing to be a father to her?" Her question was whimsical as she allowed her mouth to curve in a smile.

His own lips were thin, his eyes narrowed as he drank in the sight of the woman and child. "She is mine already, as if I had planted the seed. As you are mine already."

"Are you saying you love me?" Josie's cheeks flushed as she whispered the words, as if fearful that they might be overheard.

He shook his head impatiently. "This 'love' is a white man's word. I tell you that my soul speaks to yours, that we will be as one. You make my spirit sing, Bright Eyes."

"What will you do, Will?" Sheet thrown aside, Cassie pulled her gown above her knees, hoping for an errant breeze to enter through the open window.

"I know what I'd like to do. And it involves shootin' off his…" Will halted, casting an apologetic glance in his wife's direction. "That wasn't a thought fit for your ears, honey."

"Can he take Maggie?" The idea had been preying on her mind since early afternoon, and only the sight of Many Fingers on guard had allowed her to enjoy the frantic pace of the ball game.

"Hell, I don't know, sweetheart. I can't imagine he has a leg to stand on, but I think I'd better find out for sure. Guess I'll go into Greenbush and talk to the sheriff, have him check with the judge."

"What if he comes here?"

Will smiled, a feral movement of his lips, his eyes mere slits as he considered that idea. "Might be the best thing that could happen," he said finally. "A man has a right to defend his property. Shootin' an intruder set on causin' trouble is within the law hereabouts. 'Specially if he threatens the well-being of my family."

Cassie's eyes closed, her mouth drawn down as she considered that thought. "I don't know how you could live with killing him, Will. It's a hard thing to do."

He laughed, his somber mood disappearing as he watched her. "As if you knew, honey. About as close as you've gotten to murder was when you threatened that son of a sea cook your mama was married to. I doubt you'd ever have been able to use that knife on him, but apparently he wasn't willing to take odds on it."

"I could have, Will." Now was her chance. She could tell him now, and have it over and done with. Maybe he'd understand, feeling the murderous rage he did toward Bennett Percival.

Before the words she considered could be spoken, Will was there, leaning over the bed, touching her hair with a large, callused hand. "Not you, sweetheart. You're so soft, so pretty, Cass." His eyes warmed her as his gaze possessed her body. Beneath the cotton gown she felt the flesh of her breasts swell, the deep yearning his touch created began to well within her and her smile welcomed him.

"We'll keep an eye on things, Cassie," he told her, leaning to blow out the candle. "Between us, Many Fingers and I can keep close account of Maggie and Josie both. Unless I miss my guess, our next problem will be knowin' what to do about..." He paused, dropping to the side of the bed, his trousers shed in one easy motion.

"About Josie, you mean? Will Many Fingers take her back to his people?"

Will shook his head, turning to enclose Cassie in his arms, settling with her in the middle of the bed. "He's an outcast there, honey. The man he was workin' for took him on because he needed extra hands, and Many Fingers is just naturally good with horses. But his own people don't have much truck with a half-breed. He told me he doesn't fit in anywhere."

"Well, he can fit in here if he wants to," Cassie declared stoutly. The thought of any person not being welcome in the place of his birth was distasteful to her. "Not having family is about as bad as it gets, Will."

"I guess you'd know about that, wouldn't you, Cass?"

She nodded, her hair brushing against his cheek as she stretched to kiss him. "But not anymore, Will. Not anymore."

Chapter Fifteen

There was neither hide nor hair of Bennett Percival to be seen. At least not in Greenbush, according to the sheriff, who had listened with interest as Will told him Josie's story.

"Hard to say, Will, what a judge would decide. But with all of you out there making a home for that little girl and her mother right there with you, I can't see where a perfect stranger could make a case for himself."

"That's about what I figured, Sheriff Mosley," Will said with obvious relief. "But it seemed like a good idea to check with you."

"Well, like I said, Will, I can't speak for the judge, but when he comes to town next week, I'll lay it on the line and get his opinion for you. In the meantime, if that scallywag shows up here, I'll bring him in for questioning. We'll call him a vagrant if we have to." The husky law officer leaned back in his chair and peered across the room at Will Tolliver. "He really pulled a fast one on your sister, didn't he?"

"Yeah, then left her flat, without two cents to her name."

"It's a good thing she brought the little girl back here

last year, or she'd really have been in a pickle,'' the sheriff said, rising to his feet. "Don't worry about it, Will. I'll watch for him. I doubt he's gonna take you on in your own territory, but you never know. You'd better keep a good eye out yourself.''

The two men walked to the door of the jailhouse and out onto the street, Will offering his thanks before he headed for the general store. The bell clanged behind him as he let the door shut, and he looked around the cluttered interior.

Between them, Cassie and Clara seemed to have piled a month's supplies on the wooden counter, sugar and flour in twenty-five-pound bags surrounded by other foodstuffs. "Did you remember the coffee?" Will asked.

"First thing she ordered," Dorinda Bartlett told him pertly, her voice carrying the full length of the store. "I suspect she takes good care of you, Will Tolliver. You're lookin' pretty spry these days. And I heard tell there's to be two new grandbabies for your mother come wintertime.''

Will's face flushed as the news of Cassie's pregnancy became public property. "You been braggin', Ma?" His grin was crooked as Will's arm circled his mother's shoulder.

"Louise already let her cat out of the bag last week, I heard tell. Cassie might as well get her share of congratulations, I figure.'' Clara pointed at a bolt of checkered blue gingham. "We'll need six yards of that, too, Dorinda. Cassie needs a new dress, seeing as how she's taken out the seams in everything she's got.'' The last sentence was spoken in a whisper, but Cassie rolled her eyes as Clara gave up the young woman's secret. "Never saw a gal fill out so quick.''

Cassie made a garbled sound in her throat and turned to Will, her cheeks crimson. That made two of them turning red, he decided, with his mother having the time of her life at their expense.

"Let's you and me take a walk, Cass," he said, choking down his laughter.

"It's not funny, Will Tolliver," Cassie sputtered, walking ahead of him out the door of the store.

"Now, honey. All the ladies in town will be tickled to death that we're havin' a baby, and Ma hasn't had so much fun in years. Fact is, since Pa's gone, and we turned up like a couple of bad pennies, she's lookin' younger than she did when I left home. She's gettin' to be more like her old self every day." Taking her arm and looping it through his, he led her the length of the sidewalk, two blocks in all, to where three steps led to the door of the Greenbush Hotel.

With a flourish he opened the door, ushering her past the ornate front desk to the open archway leading to the dining room. A young woman wearing a black dress covered with a starched white apron greeted them and led them to a table.

"Just bring us some coffee and a plate of those fancy cakes you folks make in that big kitchen out back," Will said with a dazzling grin.

The waitress scribbled on her pad and smiled coyly at Will.

Cassie watched her stroll from their table, then turned to Will, her expression worried. "What are you doing, Will?" she asked in an undertone. "Can we afford to come in here?"

His laugh was low, his look tender as he leaned across the table to brush at her cheek with his fingertips. "We can afford to do most anything we want to, sweetheart. I had my money wired here from Texas, and even allowing for what I spent on repairs and new equipment for the farm, I've got plenty left. More than enough to buy us a new stallion and fix up the old bunkhouse into a place for Many Fingers to live in."

Her mouth opened quickly, then closed again. Leaning across the table, she whispered her question. "Is he planning on having Josie move in with him? Do Indians get married the way everyone else does?"

Will's glance encompassed the surrounding tables before he answered. "If he's feeling for Josie what I think he is, he'd better plan on marrying her, Cass. As to how they'll manage it, I don't know, but Ma sure won't be happy with anything less than a preacher and a ring."

"Josie deserves a man who'll take good care of her."

Will nodded. "He'll do that, all right, but whether or not people will accept them being married is another story."

"Has he talked to you about it?"

"No. He doesn't do much talkin', you might have noticed. But where Josie's concerned, he does a lot of lookin', and lookin' after. The man's had her in sight about every minute of every day since before the Fourth of July. And since then he's done everything but sleep outside her bedroom door."

Will paused, looking up as the waitress delivered two cups and a plate of small frosted cakes to their table. Pouring from a silver coffeepot, she filled their cups and added a silver sugar bowl and cream pitcher to the array before them.

"Will that be all, sir?"

Will nodded, lifting the cup to his lips.

"What does your mother think?" Cassie asked, helping herself to one of the fancy treats.

"She'll go along pretty much with whatever makes Josie happy and keeps her safe. And if that's marrying an Indian, my mother will take it pretty much in her stride."

"I think she's taken to Many Fingers lately," Cassie

said, licking the icing from her index finger. And then her
eyes widened in dismay. "Your mother! Oh, Will! Your
mother is probably wondering where we are! We just
walked off from the store and left her."

He shook his head. "She'll stand around with the ladies
for an hour or so, catchin' up on things, tellin' them all
about your gettin' fat and how good I am to you." His grin
was teasing as he spoke, a bit of frosting clinging to his lip
from the pastry he'd just managed to consume in two bites.

Cassie leaned across the table, a finger reaching to swipe
at that small bit of sugar, and Will's eyes sparkled at her
action. "Now, what are you gonna do with that?" he asked
smugly.

Silently she took the tip of her finger between her lips,
her movements precise, her tongue coming into play as she
cleaned the evidence from her skin. Her eyes on his, she
ran the edge of her tongue across her lip, returning her hand
to the plate before her.

"Come on, sweetheart, that isn't fair," he said in a low
voice. "You're playin' games with me, right out here in
public. You'd better watch out before I take you over my
shoulder and tote you right up those stairs into one of Miss
Hilda's fancy suites."

"They have suites?" Cassie asked, surprise coating her
words. "In Greenbush?"

"Greenbush is the county seat," Will told her. "When
the judge sets up court here, he has the best room in the
house. Miss Hilda even has a honeymoon suite up there."

Cassie's smile was wistful. "I've always wondered what
a honeymoon would be like. My mama used to sing a song
about honeymoons, but I can't remember it. I just thought
it was a pretty word to say when I was a little girl."

"You don't need to wonder about honeymoons, sweetheart," Will said softly, leaning toward her. "I figure we've

been on one since that trip we took to Mill Creek a few months back. Matter of fact, I'd say our bedroom is about as full of good memories as the best honeymoon suite around."

Cassie flushed, her fingers caught midway into her mouth as she took another bite of the frosted cake. Carefully she deposited the remainder of the sweet on her plate and wiped her mouth with her napkin. "You're embarrassing me, Will."

"Drink up, Cass. We're gonna take these little goodies home with us, and tonight I'm gonna show you a fancy way of eatin' them, right smack in the middle of our honeymoon bed." With a wave of his hand he called the waitress to their table and instructed her to box up the leftovers, his eyes never leaving Cassie's face as he gave his instructions.

When the box of cakes was delivered to their table, Cassie swallowed the last of her coffee and rose, aware only of the man who followed her out of the dining room, across the lobby and into the sunshine. His hand on her back was warm, sending a quiver of delight the length of her spine. His breath against her cheek, as he bent to speak her name, was a blending of sweetness and mint, a faint reminder of the powder he used to brush his teeth every morning. He walked with her down the length of the sidewalk, the small white box from the hotel dining room dangling by a string from his index finger, and she was fascinated by the sight.

If Maggie didn't get hold of the box first, chances were pretty good that Will would make good his promise. Cassie's heart thumped with a new knowledge. Will couldn't talk so sweetly if he didn't feel strongly about her. Maybe even love her a little. Maybe even enough to forgive her should she find the courage to confess the lie she had been living since the day they met.

* * *

"We can't find Maggie."

Will's roar of disbelief was enough to startle the horses into rearing, as he heard the words Josie spoke. Running from the house, she had met the wagon in the middle of the yard, her eyes streaming tears, her hands twisting at her handkerchief in mute anguish.

Sliding from the wagon, Will strode to the head of his team and quieted them with deft touches of his hands and low sounds of comfort. "What happened?" His eyes on Josie, he waited for an explanation.

She lifted her shoulders and hiccuped, shaking her head. "I called her in for dinner at noon. I thought she was in the barn with Many Fingers, and he thought she was in the house with me." Her words ended on a cry of distress and she buried her face in her hands, sobbing loudly.

"Where'd he go?" Will cast a look in the direction of the barn.

"He's gone after her," Josie wailed. "He was lookin' down at the ground and heading out beyond the pasture the last I saw of him."

"How long do you think she's been gone?" Clara asked, her hands on Josie's shoulders as she clutched her daughter close for comfort.

"I don't know. I just don't know." Shaking her head as if she could not think clearly, Josie seemed on the verge of collapse.

Grasping the reins of his team, Will led them toward the barn, calling Cassie to follow him. Hurriedly she gathered her skirts above her ankles and ran behind him, barely able to keep up as he led the horses just inside the big double doors.

His hands were deft as he removed the harnesses and led the animals to their stalls, his instructions to Cassie terse. She was to stay inside the house with Josie and his mother, locking all the doors and watching for any sign of Bennett Percival.

"I can shoot pretty well," she told him, following at his heels as he brought his stallion from his stall and saddled him quickly.

"Then get my shotgun from the cabinet in my office and load it up. I'm takin' my rifle with me. Run up to the house and get it out for me, Cass. There's extra bullets in my bottom desk drawer. I'll be there in a minute."

"Will?" It was a desperate sound and she inhaled quickly, not wanting to cause him distress. "Please be careful," she said quietly, her hand reaching to touch his shoulder. She wanted so badly to hold him, just for a moment, just to let him know her love would be with him.

As though he sensed her thoughts, he turned to her, sweeping her almost from her feet as he enclosed her in a firm embrace. His mouth touched hers softly at first, then in a possessive, passionate blending of their lips that took her breath. He lifted her, and she clung to him, her arms tight around his neck, her lips opening to the full splendor of his kiss.

"I'll be fine, sweetheart. Just don't make me worry about you. Promise you'll do as I asked." His voice rasped in her ear as he held her against his hard body, as closely as their layers of clothing would allow.

"I promise, Will." She leaned back to meet his eyes, their depths dark with purpose. He looked almost a stranger to her, his jaw hard, the flesh tight across the bones of his face, as if a primitive force had been loosed within him.

He looked like a warrior. If he'd borne a spear and carried a knife, he'd have been an image from the past, she decided, watching as he slid a bridle into place on his horse.

"I'll get your rifle," she said, hurrying from the barn to do his bidding, sensing that he was already far removed from this place in his mind, already planning for the return of his niece.

He rode to the porch as she came out the door with his gun and a supply of ammunition. Quickly he slid the rifle into his scabbard and the bullets into a pouch. "Did you load it?" he asked, thanking her with a brief smile as she nodded in reply. "Get in the house, Cassie. I'm depending on you."

The trail was fresh, the unshod Indian pony's hoofprints blending in spots with the horse he followed. At first there had been prints of a man, then at the edge of the far pasture a horse had been waiting, the ground marked with impatient hoofprints. From that point on, it had been two horses.

There weren't many places the man could have taken Maggie, Will thought, looking ahead to where the hills were covered with maple and walnut trees. In several of those areas small caves existed, some shallow, scooped-out sections of rock, others deeper and capable of concealing the quarry Many Fingers was tracking.

The thought of Maggie being held captive by the scoundrel who had sired her was abhorrent to Will, his stomach lurching as he considered the harm that might befall the child. She'd no doubt put up a fight when he took her, and the thought that he might have hurt her physically lent fury to Will's determination that Maggie be rescued without delay.

A rocky section of ground slowed his pace as he lost the trail, riding back and forth over the area. He scanned the surroundings until once more the double set of prints, partially hidden by scattered areas of shale, caught his eye.

Nudging his horse forward, he rode into a grove of maples and up the gentle rise of a hill that was almost covered by the shade of taller trees. The rustle of a small animal in the grass was loud in the silence, and his head turned quickly at the sound. From a nearby tree a robin sang and then was still once more.

Then from somewhere ahead of him the low sound of a whippoorwill caught his ear and, with a sixth sense, he recognized the call. He halted, his stallion stamping impatiently. Again the bird call sounded, closer this time, and Will waited. Through the trees ahead, the gliding form of Many Fingers approached, his torso almost naked, leather leggings and moccasins his only covering as he came into sight. A long gun in his hand gleamed dully in the shadows and his eyes glowed with a barely pent anger.

He approached silently and spoke only when he stood at the head of Will's stallion. "The man is in a cave just at the top of the next hill. He has tied Maggie inside."

"Is she hurt?"

Many Fingers shook his head. "Doesn't look like it. I think she's asleep for now. I don't see a way to get to him without…"

Will nodded. "Show me."

The half-breed ran ahead, dodging between trees, and Will followed, bent over the stallion's back to escape low-hanging branches, until they came to where the pony was tied. Sliding from his horse, Will looped the reins over a tree limb and checked his rifle again, before the two men headed over the crest of the hill and down into the small valley below.

Keeping to the shelter of trees, they moved silently ahead. After a few minutes they came to a vantage point from which they could see ahead, to where their quarry had gone to ground. Will peered intently at the place his friend pointed out, and then shook his head, unable to spot their prey. He closed his eyes for a moment, then opened them to slits, looking once more beyond the overhanging trees to where the side of the hill formed small pockets and hollows of rock.

There, where the sun cast a finger of light through a small clearing, he caught a glimpse of a pale garment. Then another movement caught his eye, and he watched as a horse shifted in the shadows within the small aperture. He looked inquiringly at the man beside him.

"We wait." With no trace of indecision, the dark-skinned man issued the command, and Will nodded his agreement.

The sun moved across the sky, the shadows shifted place and the two men remained motionless, intent on the small opening in the rocky wall ahead. Then, just inside the overhang, the small figure on the ground twisted and turned with a sudden movement, and a soft cry echoed through the silence.

"Mama? Mama!" Maggie's whimper carried to their listening ears, and the two watchers exchanged grim looks of apprehension.

"Hush, girl." The rasping voice of the unseen man within the cave scolded the child, and then he appeared, just a flash of color as he pulled a jacket over a pale shirt and bent to speak to the little girl. "Nobody's gonna hurt you. Just behave yourself and you'll be fine."

"Can you get a good hit from here?" Many Fingers asked, his words lower than a whisper.

Will shook his head. The danger of a ricochet was too much of a risk to take, given the rocky confines of the cave. Maggie was in no danger for now. He would not place her in peril with his impatience.

Once more Maggie called out. "Mama! I want you to take me back to my mama!"

"You behave yourself, hear me, girl?" Bennett Percival blustered, his attempt at mollifying the child a thing of the past. "You're gonna see your mama in a little while. You just stay here and be quiet, and when I come back, I'll take you to your mama, you hear?"

Maggie was silent and unmoving as her father rose to stand over her. Leading his horse, he moved from the shelter of the cave and made his way down the rocky side of the hill to where a level spot allowed him to mount.

"Now?" Will asked, lifting his rifle to his shoulder.

Many Fingers shook his head. "He can still see Maggie. Don't give him a reason to shoot."

"I won't miss," Will said quietly.

"Wait."

Will looked at his friend, lowering his gun slowly. "You want to do this yourself, don't you?"

"Josephine is my woman. Maggie will be my child. It is my place."

"If you shoot him in the back, you're a dead man, my friend. You'll face a lynching, sure as shootin'."

Many Fingers shook his head. "I am not a fool."

They watched as Percival rode past them at a distance, skirting the area where they waited, but without a doubt heading back to the farmhouse.

Moving quickly, the two men ran through the trees and climbed to the opening in the hill where Maggie waited. Her eyes alight with relief, she called out to them.

"Uncle Will! Tall Horse! Did you see him? He made me ride on his horse. Do you know my daddy's a bad man?" Even as Will untied her hands and feet, Maggie spouted her anger, her tearstained face flushed with a combination of fear and fury.

"It's all right, half-pint," Will told her softly, hugging her to himself. "We won't let him hurt you."

"Where's Tall Horse going?" Maggie said, peering over her uncle's shoulder. "He's running real fast, Uncle Will."

Silently, black hair flowing over his shoulders, the lithe form made its way through the trees, disappearing from view in moments. Will stood, holding Maggie closely, unwilling to release her. "We'll follow him, honey. He's gone after the man who took you."

"You mean my daddy?"

Will shook his head, his features grim. "He's not fit to be your daddy, honey. Don't call him that anymore."

At a slower pace than he'd climbed the hill, Will made his way back. Maggie's hand in his, he led the way through the trees, finally topping the next rise to where his horse waited below.

"Come on, sweetheart," he told the child, lifting her to his saddle. "We're goin' home."

"You might as well come out, Josie. You're goin' with me or you'll never see hide nor hair of that brat again."

From the rear of the corncrib the voice of the man she'd put her trust in, and who had betrayed her in the worst possible way, called her name. Josie shuddered, standing next to the kitchen window, her eyes red from weeping, her hands clenched tightly.

"I'll have to go with him," she whispered.

"Not on your life," Cassie told her firmly. "He doesn't have Maggie with him, and it doesn't seem to me that his word is worth much."

"You'd better skedaddle, Bennett Percival," Clara called from the window. "My son will be on your trail before you can lay tracks."

The man laughed aloud. "He's probably in town lookin' for me to take the afternoon train out of here. No way he could know where the kid is, Josie. You come with me now, and we'll head out and get her."

"What do you want me for?" Josie asked pleadingly. "You sent me away just a few weeks ago."

"I got plans for us, woman. I decided you can earn me a bundle, one way or another. Come on out here, now."

"I'm afraid for Maggie," Josie whispered. "What if he gets impatient and goes after her?"

At that, Bennett Percival mounted his horse and appeared around the side of the corncrib, riding toward the house. "You'd better get out here, woman, or I'll leave that kid to rot. You'll never find her."

Josie ran to the door and unlatched it, Cassie fast on her heels. "No, don't, Josie! Will said to stay inside, no matter what."

Josie's tears fell in a torrent as she fought to escape Cassie's hold. "I have to! He means it, Cassie! He won't hurt me if I go with him. I'll be all right."

Tugging loose from Cassie's grasp, Josie went out onto the porch. "I'll go with you, Bennett. Let me saddle a horse first."

He rode closer. "Just get on behind me," he said shortly, offering her his hand to lift her. His eyes darted toward the house. "You in there, don't plan on stoppin' me."

"The hell I won't," Clara vowed, stalking to the door. As Josie started down the steps to where Bennett waited, Clara lifted her shotgun. "Get back, Josie," she shouted. Waiting only until her daughter dropped to the ground, Clara pulled the triggers on the double-barreled weapon, her target too close to miss.

The horse's frightened whinny was shrill in the air, in sharp contrast to the utter silence of the man who fell heavily to the ground. A clatter of hoofbeats followed within seconds, and then the riderless animal halted in its tracks, shivering as blood ran from two or three places on his front quarters.

With a cry of despair, Josie covered her face with her hands. Clara stood stock-still, the smoking gun pointing downward, as if the weight of it were too much to bear. Her face was ashen, her eyes closed, as though unable to bear the sight of the damage she had done.

Cassie rushed past her, only casting one small glance at the man who lay crumpled on the ground, bleeding profusely, the ground a crimson pool beneath his head.

"Josie!" She fell to the ground and lifted Josie into her arms. She held her tightly against her breasts, rocking the slight form to and fro. "Josie, it's all right. It's over."

From across the pasture a sound reached Cassie's ears, a primitive wailing note, and then the form of a half-naked man, stretched out over the back of a pony, came into sight. "Look, Josie. Many Fingers is coming."

She forced Josie to an upright position, blocking her view of Bennett's body, and then, lifting her to her feet, urged her again. "Look! Josie!"

He was there. Sliding from the bare back of his pony and with one scornful look at the crumpled body on the ground, he strode to the woman he had vowed to cherish.

Clara spoke from the porch. "Where's my baby? Is she safe?"

The half-breed nodded, his gaze intent on Josie. "Did he hurt you?" Guttural and rasping, his voice ground out the question.

Josie shook her head, her eyes opening as he spoke. "Maggie?" The single word was a question in itself.

"Will is bringing her. She was not harmed."

Josie's slim form slumped against Cassie, her head bowed, her strength seemingly at an end.

"Josephine, come to me." In liquid tones he called her name, and she responded, her head lifting, her face radiant as he reached for her. He offered her his hand, much as

Bennett Percival had only moments before, and her response was immediate. Her slender fingers gripped his and he led her, mounting his horse before reaching with both arms to pull her before him, so that she sat upright across his thighs.

"Tell Will we have gone. Tell Maggie her mother will return to her later today." His horse moved at the urging of his feet and legs and, carrying its double burden, set off toward the west, where meadows and wooded areas spread to the horizon.

The two women on the porch watched, stunned by the departure, by Josie's ready compliance, and then looked at each other.

Clara recovered first, turning to enter the house, gun across her arms, heading for Will's office, where the gun rack sat empty. "I can't believe I pulled those triggers," she said, shuddering as she looked at the weapon she held.

"Better that you did it than one of the men," Cassie told her, following in her wake, unwilling to be alone in the presence of the dead man.

Clara's movements were precise as she put the gun away. She sat down quickly in the chair before the desk, her hands visibly trembling, her mouth quivering. "I killed that man," she whispered.

Cassie went to her and knelt before her, her hands reaching to enclose Clara's, her fingers folding around the chill flesh. "You did what you had to, Mother. He deserved to die." Her words were laced with bitterness—she spoke of Bennett Percival, yet in her heart the face she saw was that of Remus Chandler.

He deserved to die.

Chapter Sixteen

With deep, shuddering breaths, Josie fought the tears her eyes begged to shed, blinking to clear her vision.

"Lean on me, Josephine," the man holding her said quietly, and she obeyed, relaxing against him, absorbing his strength as he enclosed her within the cradle of his arms.

"Where are we going?" she asked, bewilderment alive in her voice. "There's nothing out here except trees and the meadow, until you get to Eben's place. Are you taking me to see Eben and Louise?"

He shook his head. "We have waited long enough for this, Josephine. Today I will make you my bride. There is a place I will take you."

"Your bride?" She shivered as the word passed her lips, and she leaned her head on his shoulder, looking up at his fierce profile. "You're going to marry me? Today?"

"Hush, Bright Eyes. We will be there in just a little while. Then I will tell you the way of it."

They passed the edge of the meadow, riding beneath overhanging branches, the birds scattering as the pony made his way past their places of shelter. With a flash of pale color a white-tailed deer crossed in front of them, and Josephine's eyes were wide with delight.

''Watch for a young one to follow.'' His voice was hushed as he drew his mount to a halt. The underbrush crackled as a fawn broke from concealment and ran pell-mell in pursuit of its mother.

Their eyes met, sharing their pleasure, and Josephine snuggled closer to the warmth of the man who held her.

He rode on, turning his horse into the wooded area, bowing low to protect her from the tree limbs that snatched at their hair. A gradual widening of the path he took led to a clearing in the woods, the sun in the afternoon sky casting shadows on a clear pool of water. Sliding from his pony, he lifted her from the horse's back to stand before him.

She looked around the clearing and breathed deeply of the sweetness of flowers and grass. ''I remember this place from when I was a child. My brothers used to come here sometimes. It seems different somehow.'' The pony at her back, the man only inches from her, Josie was hesitant as Many Fingers remained silent, listening to her rambling words.

Then, taking a deep breath, as if she must recognize whatever purpose he intended, she turned to him. ''Why did we come here? What do you want of me?'' Her eyes wary yet unafraid, she faced him.

His hand lifted her chin and his gaze was dark with passion as he looked at the woman he desired. ''I've already told you, Josephine. This is where you will become my woman.''

As if in a dream, she stepped from him, looking again at the pool surrounded by lush grasses, the scattered sunlight through the tall trees and the wildflowers growing in abundance beneath her feet. ''I didn't remember it being this beautiful here.''

''This is only a place, each part of it here for a purpose. The sky and sun to warm the water and bring the flowers

to bloom, the pool to lure the animals to drink and the grass
to provide them with nourishment.

"This place is natural and right. You are the thing of
beauty here, Bright Eyes. Our coming together here will be
as it should be. A joining between a man and woman, vow-
ing to spend all of their days together."

Josie's face flushed at his words, her smile a beguiling
invitation to the man who had chosen her. The fluid melody
he wove with his rich voice, the words he chose to describe
the act of marriage brought a joy to her expression she
hardly seemed able to contain.

He reached to touch his horse on the hindquarter nearest
him, several words in a dialect Josie did not understand
apparently urging the animal to move from where they
stood. The pony nickered softly, walked to the edge of the
water to drink, then turned to graze.

"Many Fingers..." Josie began, her words halted by his
fingers against her lips.

"No." He shook his head. "I will not be that name to
you any longer. My mother gave me a white man's name
when I went to the white man's school. She called me
Jeremiah. No one else has named me that. I want you to
say it for me. I need to hear it from your lips to see if it is
right."

She nodded and he slid his fingers to cup her face, brushing the hair from where it had fallen in tangled locks
against her skin. His fingers laced through the dark tresses
and he waited.

"Jeremiah." It was a whisper of sound, and she blinked
as she spoke it aloud. Then with a breath that sighed between them, she said it again, with a soft, crooning edge
to her voice that made music of the simple name. "Jeremiah?" Her smile was tender. "I like calling you a name
that your mother gave you. Will it be mine alone to use?"

"If you like," he said. "If you want, I can be known as Jeremiah from now on. We can use my other name to follow it."

"You mean what Maggie calls you? Tall Horse?"

He nodded. "If you like, I will be Jeremiah Tall Horse. It is my white man's name."

"You are still Indian, even if your father was not."

"I will always be Indian, but I will live in the white man's world with you, Josephine. It is my choice."

"It may be a long time before the people in town accept you." Her eyes were sad as she spoke the truth that would cause pain to both of them.

He bowed his head until his forehead touched hers. "I will be whatever I must be to have you, Bright Eyes. In my heart I will be Josephine's warrior, no matter what name I am called."

He turned her around until she faced the pool, his muscular body forming itself to her back. His arms surrounded her and she leaned against his warmth. Long fingers touched her dress, skimming the slender bones of her shoulders; and then, with surety, his hands formed themselves to the proud thrust of her breasts. She shivered at the pressure of his firm touch, her eyes closing as she leaned into his caress.

"These will feed my sons." It was almost an intonation, a chant, his own eyes closing as he uttered the words.

With firm purpose his hands moved to spread across the width of her, reaching from one hipbone to the other, his fingertips brushing against the joining of her thighs.

"Within this space you will carry my sons, and together we will give them life." His fingertips pressed deeper between her legs, a strangely passionless touch, yet filled with intensity. "And here," he said quietly, "our sons will come forth and I will hold them in my hands."

Her head pressed against his shoulder, and from beneath closed lids tears gathered and fell in a shower that only served to add radiance to her glowing countenance.

"Yes!" It was a whisper of affirmation.

Turning her again to face him, he tilted her head and bent to erase her tears, his tongue a gentle touch against her skin. "You cry for joy, my Bright Eyes?"

She nodded. "I know you don't use the same words I do, but in my heart you have just told me of the love you feel for me, Jeremiah."

"You are my heart." His mouth moved to hers, and with whispering touches he kissed the lips he had only dreamed of possessing as his own.

With a fluid movement he lowered her to the carpet of grasses beneath them and his hands were gentle as he took her clothing from her body. His fingers were as water flowing against her skin as he wooed her, his words a strange blend of his native tongue and soft sounds she recognized. She was lulled by the caress of his voice, the endearments he spoke wrapping her within their embrace. He called her his dove, the brightest star of the dawn. He breathed her name, whispered that her scent was sweeter than that of the meadow flowers.

Beneath his touch she called to him, trying the syllables of *Jeremiah* on her tongue. Her hands traced the shape of his head beneath his dark hair as she told him of her yearning to be all he needed, all he would ever desire in a woman.

His kiss gave her assurance, his arms holding her as he told her she was more than he'd ever dreamed of, that her beauty was more than he'd ever expected to hold. He groaned his praises in scattered kisses against her face. "You are the desire of my heart, Josephine," he said, moving against her.

Her tears of joy flowed as he joined them as one, his touch tender, yet powerful. Soothed by his crooning symphony of endearments, she offered herself to the gentle piercing of her body, her woman's flesh opening to him, enclosing him in her depths and giving him the whole measure of her womanhood.

There, against the surface of the earth he revered, beneath the sun and sky he greeted each day with his hymn to the dawn, he made her his own, called her his wife and prayed for blessing on their union.

No matter that tomorrow might bring another form of marriage vows to his lips. It was in this moment that for Jeremiah Tall Horse, Josephine Tolliver became his bride. In his native tongue he vowed to the heavens above that he would cherish her for the days of his life. Upon the memory of his mother he pledged to protect her and give her sons of his loins.

He lifted his body above her as he offered his seed at the mouth of her womb, and his exultant cry was a paean of praise to the beauty of their coming together. Her name was a whisper on his lips as he lowered his body to rest against the slender form beneath him.

They blended, her soft parts giving way to the muscular frame of the man she had taken to herself in these moments. She held him tightly, her arms around his waist, her hands sweeping in slow measure across his flesh, fingers tracing small scars as she memorized the length and breadth of his back.

"Come," he said finally, rising in one smooth movement and drawing her with him to stand in unashamed nakedness in the sunshine. "We will wash in the pool."

"I can't swim," Josie said quickly, nevertheless following him to the edge of the water.

"No need," he told her, his arm secure around her waist. "It is shallow. We only need go far enough to bathe."

The sun was beyond the trees as they returned to where their clothing was scattered. The air was cool against their skin and Josie shivered, dressing quickly. Jeremiah knelt to help with her shoes and stockings, then rose to don his breechcloth. Folding the petticoat she had dried with, she turned to the man who watched her.

"I'm ready." How she would face the family she had walked away from at this man's command was not mentioned. When they would speak their vows before a preacher and where they would live together was not a matter for them to consider today. It was enough that they had done as Jeremiah Tall Horse had decreed. The wedding they must plan would be for others to observe. This time together had been for two people to share. And with that, she was content.

"Are you planning to put me in jail, Sheriff?" Clara sat at the kitchen table, her expression stoic, her shoulders squared as if she was willing to face whatever consequences she must.

"I don't think so, Miz Clara." Carl Mosley stood just inside the kitchen door, hat in hand. He and John Hogan's boy had loaded the body of Bennett Percival onto a wagon from the livery stable and covered it with a canvas Will had found in the barn. "I doubt you're going to run off, are you?"

Clara shook her head. "Been here for thirty years, Carl. I doubt I'll be pullin' up stakes anytime soon." Her mouth tilted in a grim smile, but her hands shook as she knotted her fingers together in her lap.

Carl Mosley's face held compassion as he looked at the

woman who was so obviously holding herself together with tenacious strength.

With a gentleness that appeared contrary to his authoritative demeanor, he explained the procedure he would follow. "We'll have an inquest when the judge comes in tomorrow, ma'am, but I'm thinkin' everything is pretty cut-and-dried. You were protecting your family. There's not a jury in the country that would condemn you for that."

Cassie's hands rested on Clara's shoulders, hoping her warmth would soak into the woman's chill flesh. "Can I get your shawl?" she asked, bending to whisper in Clara's ear.

"No, I'm all right. I'm just worried about Maggie. She hasn't said a word, just curled up on the sofa and went to sleep. 'Tisn't natural, not to talk about what happened to her."

"She'll be all right, Ma," Will said quietly. "Josie will tend to her when she comes in."

"I don't know why that man took her off that way," Clara fretted. "She should have been here for Maggie."

"Maggie had you and me and Cassie, Ma," Will reminded her gently.

With a nod he signaled to the sheriff, and the two men left the kitchen. "Do I need to bring the women to town for the inquest?" He spoke in an undertone as they walked to the wagon.

"Your mother will have to be there, for sure," Carl Mosley said. "Just as a formality, but the judge will want to talk to her. Where do you suppose the Indian took your sister?" He glanced at Will, his curiosity apparent.

"He said he'd be back soon. Wherever they went, Josie won't be long away from her child. She's gonna be anxious to get her hands on her."

The sheriff mounted his horse and nodded at John Hogan's boy. "Let's go, son. It'll be dark before we get to town. We'll need to bury this fella in the morning, I'm thinking. I doubt anybody's gonna be lookin' for him. No sense in puttin' it off."

"When will the judge be coming? I'll bring my mother in whenever you say."

Carl took up his reins, easing deeper into his saddle. "Probably after noon some time. Shouldn't take long, Will. Sure is funny how things happen, ain't it? Josie's husband showin' up and causin' a fuss that way. Seems to me she's better off without him, anyway."

Will kept silent, nodding his agreement.

"There's some good men in these parts who'd give their bottom dollar for a good woman like Josie. She won't be a widow for long, I'd wager."

Will smiled. "No, I don't think she will."

The death of Bennett Percival overshadowed all else, and the quiet wedding of Jeremiah Tall Horse and Josephine Tolliver took place without fanfare. The pastor of the Methodist church in town interrupted his morning's study time to perform the ceremony, barely raising an eyebrow as the Tollivers gathered in his church for the brief ceremony.

The ceremony was simple. With a few words spoken over them, with a certificate the genial preacher signed with a flourish, and with the combined embrace of her family behind her as she spoke her vows, Josie became the legal wife of Jeremiah Tall Horse. That the real ceremony had taken place a day earlier was a secret they shared with no one.

Clara had supplied the ring, removing it from her finger after breakfast to place it in the callused hand of the groom. "Maybe Josie'll have a better time of it if you put this on her finger," she'd said gruffly. "It held up for me for thirty years."

Jeremiah had bowed his head, nodding his thanks. "I know she'll cherish it, ma'am."

"What's this about your name being different from now on? Here I just got used to callin' you Many Fingers and Maggie talkin' about you being Tall Horse. Now Josie tells me you're going by a different name."

Jeremiah's jaw had firmed as he'd met Josie's gaze across the kitchen table. "I am marrying a white woman. I will use the name my mother gave me when I entered the white man's world. It will be easier for Josephine if I do this."

"Am I supposed to be callin' you Jeremiah, then?" Clara had asked.

He'd nodded briefly. "That will be my name."

From the church to the new courthouse was but a short walk. A gauntlet of stares followed the seven figures who formed a small parade from one place to the other. Josie's hand lay on her husband's arm, Cassie and Will following close behind. Hand in hand, leading the way, Maggie gripped her grandmother's fingers, strangely sober, as if she recognized the solemnity of the occasion. Bringing up the rear, the preacher kept step, having told Will he would lend his support should it be needed.

They climbed the three wide steps to the courthouse door, their reflections gleaming from the glass the town had had shipped by way of train from St. Louis. Head high, Josie swept through the door her husband held open for her, then waited inside for him to join her. Together they entered the courtroom, taking seats in the front.

And then, almost before it had begun, it was over. It was the considered opinion of all concerned, including the judge, that the death of Bennett Percival was due to his own behavior.

Clara was absolved of all guilt in the matter, and at the conclusion of the judge's remarks she sagged in her chair with a faint sigh.

"Are you all right, Ma?" Will slid his arm over her shoulder, bending low to whisper in her ear.

"I will be." Her spine resumed its normal state and she lifted her chin, lips compressed but steady. "We just do what we have to, Will. Better me doin' the deed than that half-breed you brought home with you. He'd have ended up swingin' from the end of a rope if he'd gotten there before I pulled the trigger."

"He's Josie's husband now, Ma." Will's voice held rebuke as he led her to stand near the window.

"I'm gettin' used to the idea," she answered. "I reckon he'll take better care of her than the other one did."

"He'll be sleeping in the house tonight," Will reminded her, a warning evident in his tone.

"It's gettin' pretty crowded in there, Will. How soon can you fix up that old bunkhouse for them?"

"I'm going to stop at the lumber mill before I go home today and pick up some wood to use for another partition inside. Then it'll be up to the two of them to tell me what they want done to the place," Will said.

Jeremiah's eyes were veiled as Will met his gaze across the room. As if he knew the gist of the conversation and had overheard the faint censure in Clara's words, he strode to where they stood, bathed in the sunlight streaming through the window.

"We will not stay in the big house. I'll work in the bunkhouse when we get to the farm," he said quietly. "It has already been washed down. I only need to repair the floor and build a couple of walls. I'll move my belongings from the barn and Josephine and I will sleep there tonight.''

Will shook his head. ''You're welcome to stay in the house until we get the bunkhouse in shape.''

''No.'' His denial was firm, his eyes holding a message Will was forced to respect.

''I don't mind helping,'' Will said agreeably. ''I'll give you a hand when we get home.''

''Thank you,'' Jeremiah said solemnly. ''But this is something Josie and I will do.'' Jeremiah turned to his bride. ''Are you ready? Where is Maggie?''

''Here I am, Tall Horse.'' The little girl reached to take his hand. ''Are we gonna live in the bunkhouse now? Mama says I can help move my bed out there.''

''You can help.'' His eyes softened as he beheld the child, and he squatted to her level. ''You are a brave girl, Maggie. You make me proud of you. I'll be your father from now on.''

''Do I still call you Tall Horse if you're my father?'' she asked, her forehead furrowing as she spoke. Placing her tiny fingers against his face, she pressed her lips together firmly. ''I think I'll still call you Tall Horse. It was my name for you first, wasn't it?''

He smiled, a glow lighting his face. ''You saw into my heart, didn't you, small one? You claimed me long before your mother knew she would share my path.''

''I always loved you, Tall Horse, as soon as you gave me your special name.'' She reached for his hand, tugging him to rise. ''Let's go home and fix up our new house.''

Cassie's hands pressed against her belly and she turned sideways to better see herself in the mirror. ''I think I feel a little fatter.''

''Just around the middle, mostly.'' Will stretched and

yawned, his feet pressing against the footboard of the bed. Patting the mattress next to him, he beckoned her. "Come on to bed, Cass. You've had a long day."

"You can't tell yet, Will?" Her tone was disappointed as she turned from the mirror.

He grinned. "I can tell, all right. You're growing out of all of your clothes. You don't like coffee anymore. You're forever suckin' on Ma's dill pickles and you get all out of sorts at the drop of a hat."

She pounced on him, sprawling across him before he could catch her. Her fists pounded on his chest in time with the words she spoke. "I'm not out of sorts! I'm sweet and kind and—"

Her words were cut off by the pressure of his lips, his big hand clasping the back of her head, forcing it close enough for his mouth to capture hers. "I'll let you prove that right here and now," he said solemnly, releasing her after a moment's persuasion.

She gripped the front of his shirt with both hands, her eyes narrowing as she considered his words. "You want me to prove that I'm sweet?"

"And kind," he prompted. "I could use some kindness at your hands right now. I have this terrible problem."

Her mouth twitched. "I noticed." She shifted against him, her hips settling firmly in place against his groin.

"Don't be twitchin' against me there unless you plan on takin' the consequences, girl." He lowered his big hands to rest them possessively on her bottom, pressing her even more firmly in place.

"I think I'm already full of consequences, Will."

With a movement so rapid it took her breath, he rolled her beneath him, sparing her his weight as he rose above her. "It's too late for second thoughts, honey. We're gonna have a baby, like it or not."

She shook her head. "No second thoughts, Will. I just wonder sometimes if I'll be a good mother. It seems like a big responsibility. I don't want to make mistakes."

"You'll be a good mother, Cassie. Our baby will grow up to be just like her mama, good and honest and kind."

She bit at her lip as he recited the qualities he admired. Her voice wavered a bit as she spoke. "You forgot to mention sweet."

"Yeah, I did, didn't I?" He bent his head to taste her mouth, brushing gently across the softness of her lips. "Don't know how I could have left that part out. If I remember right, there's a little speck of sugar right here...." He dipped his head to her throat, then moved down across her collarbone and pressed his mouth against the rise of her breast.

"Yeah...just as I thought. Sweet as honey."

Her fingers tangled in his hair, her eyes closing at the pleasure he brought her. Pleasure marred by the memory of his voice as he'd numbered her virtues. Good, honest and kind. If only she dared to confess, if only she knew for certain what he would say.

She pressed her lips together as she stopped the words that begged to be spoken. Maybe tomorrow, she thought. *Let me have just one more time with him, and tomorrow I'll tell him.*

Chapter Seventeen

From outside the bedroom window Maggie's voice broke the stillness. "Mama! Mama!" There was a moment's silence, then with even more panic punctuating each syllable, she called again. "Uncle Will! Where are you?"

Rolling from the bed, Will stumbled, a muffled curse marking his path as he tripped over his boots. He leaned from the window, eyes straining in the darkness. "Where are you, Maggie?"

"Uncle Will? Where's my mama? Her and Tall Horse wasn't there when I woke up."

Beneath the window the small child huddled on the ground, her face pale in reflected moonglow. "Damn!" The curse was muttered beneath his breath, and then he called down to the girl.

"I'll be right down, Maggie. Get up on the porch. The back door's open."

"What happened, Will?" Cassie sat up in bed, her breath catching in her throat as he loomed over her, a shadow in the moonlight.

"Something's wrong. Maggie says she can't find her mother or Jeremiah."

Cassie swung her feet out of bed and reached for her

robe. Slipping her arms through the sleeves, she was out the bedroom door and halfway down the stairs before she managed to tie it around her waist. Her feet flew as she hurried through the kitchen, opening the back door as Maggie lurched through into her arms.

"I can't find my mama!" Her sobs punctuated each word and her arms tightened in a strangling grip around Cassie's neck.

Cassie stood clutching the child, then backed up to sit on a chair. She held Maggie tightly, rocking her to and fro, whispering against her dark hair. "Hush now, sweetheart! It's all right. It's all right!" And even as she made the promises, her mind staggered at the possibilities.

Will came through the kitchen door, his mother at his heels. Reaching to the lamp over the table, he lit it quickly, then turned to his mother. "Stay in the house. I'll go see what's goin' on."

Clara nodded and followed him to the screen door, watching as he made his way through the moonlight toward the bunkhouse.

"What's happened?" Cassie asked quietly.

Clara shook her head. "Will thinks maybe someone in town might not have liked…" She stopped, her glance cutting to Maggie. She shook her head.

Only the sound of the child's whimpering broke the silence as Cassie watched the door. Clara went to the stove, shook down the ashes and added kindling from the box against the wall. With a quick flare of light, she lit a match and held it inside, waiting till a glow lit her face as the kindling caught fire.

Carefully she added two more chunks of wood and closed the lid into place. "Might as well heat up last night's coffee. Might not be fresh, but no matter what, Will's gonna need a cup in him before long."

"They're not there." From the porch Will's voice spoke the words Cassie had dreaded hearing, and her heart began once more to flutter in her chest. Her eyes closed as she considered the unspoken threat in Clara's words. Why should it matter to anyone in town whom Josie married?

But perhaps it had.

"I'm gonna head for town," Will said, his eyes hard, his voice harsh as he reached behind the door for his leather belt and holster. He fastened it around his waist, and Cassie watched as he moved the gun's cylinder, loading each empty space with a bullet drawn from the pouch he'd hung there only a day ago. Was it only two days since he'd gone after Maggie and brought her back to them?

And now he was readying himself to look for her mother and the man she'd married. He twirled the cylinder again and placed the gun in its holster, emptying a handful of bullets into his pocket before he turned to look at his wife.

"Be careful, Will." *Please don't get hurt! I love you! I'm so afraid!* All the words she dared not speak raced through her mind. As if he read them in the anxious look she wore, he stepped to the table and bent to press his mouth against her temple.

"I'll be fine, Cass. I'm gonna get the sheriff. Don't any of you go out in the yard. I don't want those prints disturbed."

"Coffee will be hot in a few minutes, son," Clara offered.

"Just heat it drinkable and I'll have a quick swallow if it's ready by the time I'm in the saddle," he said, his big hand resting on Maggie's dark hair. Bending, he whispered in her ear. "Hang on there, half-pint. I'll find your mama."

"And Tall Horse, too?" she asked, her voice muffled against Cassie's breast.

His mouth twisted grimly. "Yeah, and Tall Horse, too."

* * *

"Somebody knows where they are," Will said harshly.

"What do you want to do, Will? Go from one house to another, bangin' on doors to find out who's home and who's not?" Sheriff Mosley's look was glum as he tucked his shirt into his trousers.

"Hell! I don't know. I just know that somebody dragged Josie and Jeremiah out of that bunkhouse without waking up Maggie. There's a whole slew of footprints there, but I couldn't tell much of anything for sure in the dark."

Carl heaved a deep sigh. "I knew there was gonna be trouble when you brought that fella home with you, Will. And then when Josie's husband got shot…" He hesitated, reaching for his gun belt. "You're sure Clara pulled the trigger?"

"Did you take a good look at her?" Will asked, feet braced apart, hands on his hips. "What do you think, Carl?"

The sheriff nodded. "Yeah, I saw her. But the rest of the men around here didn't. They were talkin' down at the saloon last evenin' about how Clara probably lied to cover up for that half-breed."

"And you didn't try to set them straight?" Will stomped across the floor to look out the window.

"Keep it down, Will. You'll have my housekeeper down on our necks if you wake her up." Pulling on his boots, Carl nodded at the door. "Let's head for your place. Might as well start from there."

The two men set off for the livery stable, Will leading his stallion. From the sheriff's home it was but a short walk, but any distance was too far, as far as Will was concerned. God only knew where Josie and Jeremiah were by now, or what shape they were in.

"Looks like John Hogan's up and at 'em already," Carl

said. A light blazed within the livery stable, and several men moved about in its glow.

"They seem to be havin' a party," Will said grimly, stepping up his pace. Pulling his stallion up short, he mounted and cleared his foot from the stirrup. "Get up behind me, Carl," he said tersely.

Without hesitation the sheriff hoisted himself up to sit behind Will's saddle, and the stallion moved quickly to the door of the stable. Will ducked his head, Carl following suit, and the horse trotted inside.

Almost in unison they slid from the horse and approached the group of men who were watching them from the far end of the aisle.

"What you boys up to?" Sheriff Mosley asked, his tone deceptively quiet. His hand on the butt of his gun, he moved ahead of Will.

Only one of the men looked familiar to Will. "Aren't you Devlin Bartlett's boy?" At the young man's startled expression, Will frowned. "Does your pa know you're out and about in the middle of the night?"

"It's pret' near morning," the youth blustered. "And who made it any of your business, anyway?"

"I reckon it's my business, Daryl," the sheriff said, halting Will with an upraised hand. "What about the rest of you boys? You been up to makin' trouble for somebody?"

"What makes you ask, Sheriff?" A lanky cowhand leaned negligently against a stall door, his grin cocky, his hands thrust into his pants pockets.

"Seems to me you've been in enough trouble lately, Rocky, without causin' any more," the sheriff told him. "How about the rest of you? Want to tell me what's goin' on?"

"Hell, you're just pussyfootin' around here, Carl!" Will snarled. Striding past the man called Rocky and shoving

Daryl Bartlett from his path, he stopped in front of the tallest and widest of the lot. "You look like a man who'd know how to organize a bunch of troublemakers, if I ever saw one," Will said quietly. "You want to tell me where you've been the past couple of hours?"

"No, can't say that I do." With a sidelong glance at his companions, the man shrugged, his bold glare a challenge.

Will's hand shot out and gripped the man's shirt, lifting him to his toes. "You'd better start talkin' now, and talkin' fast. I'm not in a mood to put up with any foolishness."

"Now, Will. You haven't any proof and neither have I," Carl Mosley said, striding forward to lay a hand on Will's shoulder.

"You got no right to put your hands on me," the man protested, his face a mask of anger.

His eyes narrowing, Will loosened his grasp and turned to Carl. "Maybe you're right at that, Sheriff. Maybe our best bet is to take a ride over to see Devlin Bartlett and ask him what his boy's doin' out in the middle of the night."

"My pa don't care what I do," Daryl said loudly. "You better not be gettin' him out of bed or he'll be mad enough to lay you low."

Will nodded. "Yeah? Maybe we'll just see about that, sonny." Turning from the assembled group, he mounted his stallion and reined the horse around.

"Hang on, Will. I'll go with you. Let me get my horse," Carl said quickly.

"Aw, for cryin' out loud!" Daryl shook his head and walked to where Will waited impatiently. "We just been out havin' a little fun. Ain't no law against that."

"Did that fun include my sister and her new husband?" Will asked, tilting his hat back with one finger. His horse danced beneath him, and Will tightened up on the reins.

"We didn't hurt him much," Daryl said sourly.

"Shut yer damn mouth," one of the other young men shouted.

"I ain't gettin' my pa mixed up in this," Daryl said stoutly.

"Where are they?" Will asked, his dark eyes gleaming with an anger he fought to suppress. "Answer me, boy!"

Daryl looked back at his companions, none of them willing to meet his eye, and shrugged. "They're out at the Ferris place, east of town. Old Ferris is deaf as a post, and we just used his barn for a little while."

"I'll be back to settle up with all of you," Will said, his gaze sweeping over the six men who watched him. "You want to come along, Sheriff?"

Carl snatched up the reins of an already saddled horse and mounted in a lithe movement.

"Hey, that's my horse!" A pale, slender youth burst from the group, intent on the animal Carl Mosley had chosen.

"Well, you just stick around, Clay, and I'll bring it back in one piece." Following Will's lead, Carl rode back into the dawn, hard-pressed to catch up with the long-legged stallion.

The road was deserted, the sun barely touching the horizon, and the two men rode at a breakneck pace. "How far?" Will asked, holding his horse down to accommodate the other man's slower pace.

"Not more than a half mile or so past the edge of town. Right around the bend," Carl said.

"Someone's out in the barnyard," Will announced, turning his horse sharply to ride up the lane to the farmhouse.

"That's old man Ferris. Must be goin' out to feed his stock." Carl trailed behind as his horse valiantly tried to keep up, and he could only watch as Will leapt from his stallion to run past the old farmer toward the barn door.

"Josie? Jeremiah! Are you in there?" With long strides he entered the barn, his voice echoing as he called their names.

A horse neighed and several cows sounded their discomfort, their lowing a mournful sound. Will halted, listening, then repeated his call. "Josie? Jeremiah?"

From the back of the barn a stall door banged open. "Will? Will! Come quick." Josie stood in the doorway of a box stall and Will caught his breath at the sight of her.

Her face was dirty, her hair tangled and snarled around her face, and beneath the hem of her torn robe she was barefoot. She clutched herself, crying silently as shivers racked her body. He caught her up in his arms and she pushed at him frantically.

"Come see to Jeremiah," she cried. "Oh, Will! He's hurt something awful. It's all my fault."

"Damn! I knew it!" Setting Josie aside, he entered the stall, cursing the dim light as he caught sight of the man crumpled on the straw. He bent low, then dropped to his knees.

"Jeremiah! Can you hear me?" Carefully he rolled his friend to his back, wincing as he caught sight of the battered face and torn clothing. A groan sounded from the injured man, and Josie cried out at the sound.

"Help him, Will. Please!" She fell to the floor beside him and Will hugged her tightly against himself.

"We need to get him home, Josie. I can't do much for him here. I don't even know how bad off he is."

"Let me help." Carl Mosley spoke from the doorway of the stall. "Come on, Josie. Get on out here and let your brother and me see to the man."

"I went to the outhouse during the night, Will," she whimpered. "Someone grabbed me, and pretty soon Jeremiah came out looking for me." She rose, backing from the stall, her eyes streaming tears as she watched the two men lift Jeremiah. Carefully they carried him from the barn to where a farm wagon stood beneath the eaves. From the house the old farmer hurried with his arms full of quilts and a pillow.

"I sent him in for a blanket. Guess he took me at my word," Carl said with grim humor.

Hastily the farmer spread his wagon with a quilt and pillow, then stood back as the two men loaded the inert body of Jeremiah Tall Horse onto the flat surface. Josie hoisted herself up to sit next to him, her hands fluttering over his chest and face, as if she feared to touch him lest she add to his injuries.

Mr. Ferris emerged from the barn, leading two big draft horses. He backed them up to the wagon and in moments the three men had the harnesses in place and the reins wound around an upright spoke. From the house a small, spare woman hurried off the porch, a basin in her hands, a towel draped over her shoulder.

"Here." She approached the end of the wagon where Josie sat, crooning and rocking as she leaned over Jeremiah. "This here is warm water, missus. Take the towel and wash him up a little. You'll be better able to tell how bad he's hurt."

Josie reached for the basin, whispering her thanks, and, dipping the towel in the water, she bent to her task. At her touch a moan escaped his swollen lips and she sobbed afresh, turning her head to brush away her tears against the shoulder of her robe.

"You drive the wagon, Carl," Will said. "I'll ride on ahead and see if I can get the doctor out of bed. He still live in the same place?"

"Yeah, across from the parsonage." Carl tied the horse

he had ridden to the back of the wagon and swung up onto the seat.

"I'll be bringin' your wagon back later on today," he shouted, aiming his words at the old man, who nodded his understanding. "I'll be takin' it easy, Miss Josie," he said, speaking to her over his shoulder.

"Just hurry," she croaked, her hands performing their task with tender care, fearful of hurting the torn flesh as she washed the dirt and blood from Jeremiah's face. She bent low to brush her lips against his, and her whisper was caught and held as his lips moved against hers.

"I love you, Jeremiah. Do you hear me? I love you."

The answer was a groan, so deep and so tortured she wept afresh. "Hush, hush, sweetheart," she sobbed, her tears falling to mix with the water, bathing him with the evidence of her distress.

The doctor was out on a call, delivering a baby, his wife told Will, but she would send him out to the farm as soon as he returned. His mouth grim, Will rode from town, the wagon not far behind.

The sun was well above the treetops east of the farmhouse as Cassie, watching from the front door, sighted the big stallion coming down the road. "He's coming back!" she called, running to the kitchen. "Will's coming up the lane right now."

"The bed's ready upstairs," Clara told her quietly. "I've got Maggie sleeping on the couch. Guess we're about as ready as we'll ever be, in case they've found them."

"You're lookin' for the worst, aren't you?" Cassie asked bleakly.

Clara lifted her shoulders in a gesture that spoke of defeat. "Whether they're dead or injured when they get them here, we might as well be ready. We'll either be tending to them or layin' 'em out for the preacher.''

Cassie shuddered as she ran to the porch, watching as Will slid from his horse. ''Will?'' Her cry was pleading as she clung to him. He patted her back and bent to kiss her, then drew her even closer, as if he drew comfort from the softness that warmed him.

''He's alive, Cass. Josie's all right. She wasn't hurt much, just shook up.'' As he led Cassie into the kitchen, his gaze sought that of his mother.

''We'll need hot water and rags to clean him up. Some salve, probably. We'll have to go ahead and do our best. Doc is out on a call. Hard telling when he'll be here.'' At his mother's nod of assent, he headed for the pantry. ''You got any whiskey in here, Ma?''

''Top shelf, way in the back,'' she called. ''You gonna douse him with it or pour it down him?''

Will's voice was muted, coming from the narrow pantry just off the kitchen. ''Probably both. We'll need to strip off his clothes to find out just how bad he's banged up.''

''They're coming now,'' Cassie said from her post at the door. ''Sheriff's driving at a pretty good clip, Will. You want me to look for the whiskey while you go on out and help with Jeremiah?''

His tall figure appeared at the pantry door, his fingers clasped around the neck of a bottle. ''No, I found it.'' He handed it to Cassie as he passed her. ''Take everything on upstairs, Cass. We'll be bringing him up right away.''

Chairs were brought from the dining room as the family gathered for supper. Eben and Samuel were unusually silent, filling their plates with ferocious intent, as if piling the food high and then eating it with gusto would somehow vent their anger.

Elizabeth and Louise were in the sickroom, taking a turn while the family ate together. Josie was a reluctant participant in the meal, unwilling to leave her husband but aware of her need for food. The three little boys preened under their grandmother's attention, and Clara bestowed it.

It was a true gathering of the clan, Cassie thought as she refilled a bowl with mashed potatoes. She'd barely eaten, choosing to wait on the others. Her stomach had been churning all day.

The cruelty dealt to Jeremiah was not to be believed, although the menfolk had brushed aside the bruises and small cuts. Only the sore ribs had caused their eyes to darken with anger, when Josie told how one of the ranch hands had kicked Jeremiah as he lay on the barn floor, unconscious.

Eben waved his fork in the air, punctuating his words. "You sure you know the whole list of them, Will? Has the sheriff got them in jail?"

Will shook his head. "No, can't see that there's any need for that. Devlin Bartlett's boy came clean when we caught the bunch of them red-handed in the livery stable. Can't figure how they thought they'd get away with it."

"Josie said they were wearing masks when they grabbed her," Cassie volunteered, filling Will's cup with steaming hot coffee as she spoke.

"They're too damn young to know when to go to ground." Samuel reached for another piece of chicken as his scornful words labeled the bunch of troublemakers. "Ain't one of them dry behind the ears, and that's the truth."

Will stabbed a chicken leg and delivered it to Matthew's plate. "If they hadn't been standin' around braggin' over at John Hogan's place, we'd likely have had to do a heap of lookin' for them."

"What will happen now?" Cassie asked, sliding into her chair. She tasted the beans on her plate and chewed slowly, thinking of the man upstairs who would not be eating for a couple of days, from the looks of him.

"They'll all appear before the judge. Probably pay a fine." Will's succinct words were tinged with bitterness. "Whatever the judge decides, it won't be enough in my book."

Clara rose, collecting her plate and silverware as she headed for the sink. "Well, we knew the town wouldn't accept this marriage. Folks thought it was bad enough that we'd taken up with a half-breed. When Josie showed up at the church yesterday with him, it ruffled a lot of feathers."

"He's our kin now, Ma." Eben spoke the words with conviction, earning a look of pure gratitude from his sister.

"We'll be doing his chores till he's back on his feet, Will," Samuel said.

"No need. I can handle most of it, and Josie's good with the colts." Will ruffled the hair of Mark, sitting next to him, sending a warning look at his brothers. "Guess we've about talked the whole thing to death, anyway. Time to feed the stock and get the cows milked."

"Uncle Will, can I help?" Matthew asked, gnawing at the last of his chicken leg. Wiping his mouth on his sleeve, he pushed his chair back from the table and stood beside his uncle. "I like Many Fingers. I'll help do his work."

Josie shot the boy a quick smile. "He'd appreciate that, Matthew. And if you like, you can call him Jeremiah from now on. Since the men from town relieved him of the extra finger, the name doesn't fit anymore."

Cassie's stomach rolled and she bolted from the kitchen, her feet fairly flying as she left the porch, heading for the outhouse. Barely had she cleared the small building's doorway when the contents of her stomach came up. She retched, her throat straining as she shuddered. From behind her, Will's hands circled her waist, holding her on her feet till she was finished, and then he offered her his handkerchief.

"That was the last straw," she said hoarsely. "You didn't tell me they'd done that."

"You didn't have to know." Will wiped at her mouth, taking the cloth from her trembling fingers. "It's okay, honey. He even tried to laugh about it. Said no one would be standin' around countin' his fingers anymore."

"I'll bet Josie didn't laugh," Cassie said with a grimace, thinking of Josie's tender feelings. "She really feels responsible."

"Well, she's not. Jeremiah didn't put up a fuss at first, for fear of involving Maggie. They had Josie, and he said he figured he'd take a beating rather than have them hurt her."

"Will his hand be all right?" Cassie asked.

"Yeah, it oughta be. Josie sure shed enough tears over it when she bandaged it. We gobbed a mess of stuff on it. Jeremiah told us what to use and then Josie wrapped it up."

Cassie leaned against her husband, having gained the outside of the privy. "Will he be all right?"

Will circled her waist with his arm and led her toward the house. "Yeah, as all right as we can make him. Doc said we'd done as much as he could have. The ribs are the worst of it. He'll be takin' short breaths for a while. His face might have some interesting-lookin' marks on it, but once the swelling goes down, he'll be all right."

From the house a swell of voices rose as Eben and Samuel joked with the little boys, and Cassie's frown eased. "Family is wonderful, isn't it, Will? They all showed up to let Jeremiah know he isn't alone in this."

"Well, from what Doc said, the town is pretty much in

an uproar, too,'' Will told her. "In fact, we're supposed to be gettin' some visitors before nightfall.''

"Maybe before then,'' Cassie said, pointing at a cloud of dust across the pasture, where the road to town edged the wooden fence.

"Well, I'll be! Looks like Ma better add some coffee grounds to the pot. We got company comin','' Will announced, nudging Cassie into a quickstep as they neared the porch.

"Don't you think I should take a turn sitting with him?'' Cassie moved indecisively, looking toward the door, then back at the bed where Will was propped against the headboard. Her fingers fiddled with the sash of her robe, pleating the ends and twining them around her hand as she thought of the man across the hallway.

"He's got Josie over there and, trust me, sweetheart, you'd only be in the way. I'll bet she's all curled around him and whisperin' in his ear and makin' him wish he didn't hurt so bad.'' Though his words were teasing, Will's eyes held a shadow of sorrow.

It was enough to decide her, and Cassie's fingers were swift as she untied the belt and cast the robe across the foot of their bed. One knee pressing into the mattress next to Will, she leaned to kiss him. "You hurt for him, don't you?'' she asked quietly, her hands resting on his shoulders as she turned to fit herself on his lap.

"I brought him here, honey. I should have known what might happen. Especially after I knew how he felt about Josie.''

"It was Josie's choice,'' she reminded him. "Jeremiah didn't drag her off kicking and screaming, you know.''

"I know. But even with that whole delegation from town

coming out here, there'll still be those that'll look down their noses.''

Cassie nodded. "Maybe. But did you ever see such a sorry sight as those boys trying to apologize with their daddies nudging them along? The preacher's son looked to be walking a bit carefully, didn't you think? I'll bet his daddy laid him low.''

Will grinned. "He wasn't the only one caught hell. I suspect there was some thrashin' goin' on in town today.''

Cassie shivered at the thought. "I don't like anybody getting hurt, Will, but if those boys caught it from their folks, they deserved every lick. I just wish those two cowhands of Mr. Barnwell's hadn't managed to skip out the way they did.''

He smiled down at her, his lips curving in a satisfactory manner. "From what I hear, they got escorted to the county line, and neither one of 'em was in much shape to do more than try to sit upright in a saddle. Sheriff Mosley managed to be busy elsewheres this afternoon, and a whole passel of men formed a vigilante committee of sorts.''

"That isn't legal, is it, Will?''

His shrug was eloquent. "It appears they were eggin' on the town boys, kind of rigged the whole thing. Seems to me they about got what they had comin'.''

His arms full of soft curves, Will eased her gown up her legs as he spoke. "Those young fellas from town aren't all bad. They just got caught up in something and then felt like they had to go along with the crowd. From what the preacher's boy said, those two hands of Barnwell's did the most of the damage.''

"How'd they know to look in the bunkhouse for them, anyway?'' Cassie asked, lifting her body to allow the removal of her gown, her mouth against Will's throat as she spoke.

"The preacher talked about it at the dinner table and his son repeated the story in the saloon later on."

"The preacher's son was in the saloon?" Cassie's eyes widened with surprise.

"Pretty near broke his mama's heart, from what I hear tell," Will said.

"Your mother's pretty lucky, isn't she?"

"Not nearly as lucky as I am." His mouth settled on hers with a damp caress and he groaned his satisfaction as her lips moved to accommodate him.

Within moments the gown she'd barely warmed with the heat of her body was on the floor and Will had managed to deposit her beneath the sheet, next to him. In moments, Cassie was covered by the long, lean form of the man she'd married. Muscles honed by hours of hard work flexed beneath her palms as she slid her hands beneath his shirt.

"I'd like it better if you took this thing off," she whispered against his mouth.

"I 'spect I could manage that," he said agreeably, rising to kneel between her legs, taking the covers with him.

"Will!" Her protest was muffled as she glanced at the door, fearful of being overheard. "I'm cold!"

His grin was wolfish as he shed the offending shirt, lowering himself once more to cover her. "You'll notice I already took off the bottoms," he said against her ear.

"I noticed." Her hips rose against him. "Are you going to turn out the light, Will?"

He shook his head. "Nope. I kinda like watchin' you, Cass."

Her eyes closed. "Don't embarrass me."

"Nothing we do in the name of love is embarrassing, honey," he whispered, his mouth seeking the soft curve of her throat. "I just like the sweet look you get when our bodies join. Sorta like you're welcoming me home."

Such tenderness was more than she could deny. Cassie's hands covered the back of his head as he nuzzled against her. "We're both home, Will. When I'm in your arms, I feel for the first time in my life like I have a home. After all those years..."

He lifted himself to meet her gaze, rising on his elbows. "This is fine, isn't it, Cass? This being married, having a baby. It's almost too good to be true. Even with the trouble...you know, with Josie and Jeremiah, life is just about perfect, isn't it?"

She nodded. "Just about, Will. Just about."

Chapter Eighteen

"I didn't know a body could feel so glum about..." Clara's voice trailed off, her demeanor totally at odds with her usual cheerful self. Shoulders slumped, she sat at the table, nursing a cup of breakfast coffee, one hand at her forehead.

"I think feeling glum over shooting a man dead is pretty much what anyone would expect." Cassie paused in peeling a potato to peer anxiously at her mother-in-law. "I think you need to consider what would have happened if Jeremiah had been the one to put Bennett Percival in a grave. We'd probably be doing without a husband for Josie and a new father for Maggie. Not to mention Will having to run the whole place on his own."

Clara nodded agreeably. "Oh, I've told myself all that. In fact, I've decided I did the whole world a heap of good when I pulled those triggers. But saying it doesn't make me feel any better."

Cassie's heart twisted within her and her sensible self chided her for what she was about to say. Impulsive as she was, she'd probably rue the moment, once she thought it over, but if ever a woman needed some hard truths delivered, Clara was the one.

"Truth to tell, you might never get over it," Cassie said quietly, paying special attention to the eyes on the potato she was hacking away at.

Clara looked up quickly. "Well, that's about guaranteed to make me feel a whole heap better."

"Sometimes we just live with what we've done. At least everyone here knows about Bennett Percival, and nobody blames you one bit."

Clara shoved the cold coffee from her, wrinkling her nose at the sight of it. "You'd think you were speaking from experience, Cassie. I'd be willing to bet you've never even seen a dead man, let alone made one happen."

Cassie looked up quickly, paring knife stilled by the challenge. "Don't bet more than a plugged nickel on that, Mother."

Clara grinned now, her face softening as she watched Cassie from across the table. "I sure do like it when you call me that. Those boys of mine have been callin' me Ma since the day they found out how to say it, and Louise and Elizabeth are still stuck on Miz Tolliver."

"Don't change the subject." Bending over the speckled bowl she held in her lap, Cassie picked up another potato, examining it closely as if unwilling to meet Clara's gaze.

Clara looked surprised, her eyes narrowing as if she were reviewing the last words spoken. "You mean, talking about you seeing a dead man? Besides that scallywag I shot?"

Cassie nodded. "I've seen one, close by." She glanced up furtively, as if she would catch Clara in the midst of a horrified reaction.

Instead, the older woman lifted an eyebrow in question. "Lately?"

Cassie considered for a moment. "About six months ago, back in Texas."

"Wasn't that about the time you met up with Will?"

"Just about."

"Before you met up with Will?" Clara prodded.

Cassie nodded. "The day before, in fact." She drew a shaky breath. Now that the thing was under way, she was beginning to wish she'd kept her mouth shut. But somehow it had to be told to the sheriff in town, and maybe it would be easier to start off with a friendly audience.

She'd decided last night, after Will's announcement that he considered their life to be just about perfect, that it was a good time to clear her conscience. Not to mention the fact that having a baby growing inside her was making her think a lot about honesty and getting the shadows of the past put in their place.

And the biggest shadow she'd ever had to hide was that of Remus Chandler. The possibility that somewhere, someone might be looking for her with a Wanted poster in hand was enough to make her blood run cold. She shivered at the thought, her index finger poking at a long, curling piece of potato skin that had landed over the side of the pan.

"Quit your lollygaggin', Cassie. Speak up. I have a notion you're stewin' over something, and now's a good time to get it off your chest," Clara said sternly. She rose, coffee cup in hand, her eyes holding more sparkle than Cassie had seen there in over a week.

"Will doesn't know about this." Cassie lifted the pan and plopped it on the table. Then, looking down at her lap, she fit both hands carefully over the more than noticeable curve of her belly.

"About that chick you're hatchin' there? He's proud as punch, Cassie. 'Course he knows about it."

"No. About what I'm trying to tell you." Her sigh was deep, her mouth suddenly feeling as if it had been wrapped around a dill pickle, all pinched and puckered up.

Clara deposited her cup in the cold dishwater and walked

slowly and silently back to the table, her face somber, as if she had only this moment realized that Cassie was dead serious about telling her a secret.

"Who was the dead man, Cassie?"

Once more she shivered, as if she saw afresh the blood and the crumpled body at her feet. As if she felt again the bone handle of that sharp knife cradled in her palm. Looking down, she examined the faint scar she'd gained that night.

"Cassie?" Clara's voice was closer, sharper, as if she sensed the horror that had newly visited Cassie's mind in these few moments.

"I killed a man, Mother." Amazed at the calmness of her own voice, the flat tones of her blunt admission, Cassie looked up, dry-eyed, when deep down inside, tears were begging to be shed. "He was my stepfather, and he'd been waiting for my mother to die so he could get his hands on me. And when she did, when she had barely stopped breathing, he came after me."

A muttered sound passed Clara's lips—a curse, muffled by the palm of her hand as she stifled the words. "You were just a young girl! Still are, for that matter," she murmured, kneeling beside her daughter-in-law's chair. Her hands reached to cover Cassie's, warm against the cold fingers that spread as if to protect the child growing beneath the striped apron.

"I grew up in a hurry," Cassie whispered, eyes closing as twin tears squeezed from beneath her lashes. "I ran away that night and walked all night long. In the morning I fell asleep by a stream. And that's where Will found me."

"Well! I'll be! You never told me where you met Will. I didn't ask, either. Figured if he wanted me to know, he'd say so." A look of pure satisfaction drew Clara's mouth into a half smile. "Rescued you, didn't he?"

Cassie nodded. "He took me along with him and bought a horse for me to ride and then brought me here."

Clara's eyes were piercing as her hands gripped Cassie's. "Look at me, girl! When did my boy marry you?" Her mouth tightened. "He did, didn't he?"

Rising from her knees, she drew Cassie to stand before her. Her brow furrowed deeply as her dark gaze met teary blue eyes.

"When did he marry you?" she repeated.

Cassie shook her head. "It doesn't matter. He married me, truly he did! And he never laid a hand on me till then." She blinked and looked toward the window. "Well, he kissed me and kept me warm at night on the trail, but he never…you know, did the other."

"Well, I should hope not." Clara's eyes softened, a faint relief painting her features. "Many Fingers—Jeremiah, rather…can't get used to him changin' his name, I declare. Was he around when you got married?"

Cassie shook her head. "No, it was just Will and me and the preacher and his wife."

"Not here in Greenbush?" At the negative movement of Cassie's head, Clara heaved a deep sigh. "Well, land sakes, I guess I'd better be grateful for small favors. At least he brought you here all legally wed."

"Jeremiah thought we were married on the trail," Cassie said quietly. "But we weren't. We got married in Mill Creek. Will took me there a week after we got here."

"Well, that scamp!" Clara pursed her mouth, and then the sour expression turned to a grin. "He always was a one to keep secrets."

"He's been good to me. And in return, I lied to him."

"How's that?"

"I never told him that my stepfather was dead. I said I just ran off. So when a sheriff came across us the second day out, Will told him a tall tale. He told him we were married.'' Her hands were clutched together in her apron, the material twisted in a knot, and she looked down at the evidence of her distress.

Carefully she straightened her fingers, brushing at the wrinkled fabric with concentration. ''I guess you're wondering what kind of a person I really am, aren't you?''

''For heaven's sake! I know exactly what sort you are, girl. A scared young thing with a secret hangin' over her head, and her not knowin' what to do about it. Well, you might just as well forget the whole thing, as far as I'm concerned. Any man who'd come after a girl, and her mother not even cold yet, deserves whatever he gets.''

''I can't forget it,'' Cassie said quietly. ''I have to find out if there's anyone after me. I don't want my baby born in a prison, and if I don't get this cleared up, that could likely happen.''

''Well, tell Will and he'll take care of it for you,'' Clara said quickly as if that would solve the whole problem.

Cassie's laugh was tinged with sorrow. ''You make that sound so easy...and I can't even find the courage to begin telling him. I've been lying to him for months, just by keeping it a secret. And every once in a while he lets me know that honesty is the most important thing in the world as far as he's concerned. Almost as if he knows...''

''Do you think maybe he does?'' Clara's words were hopeful.

Cassie shook her head. Looking down at her apron, she reached behind her to untie it, lifting it over her head and folding it with great precision before she placed it on the table. ''I'm going to see Sheriff Mosley in town. I'll tell him what happened and see what he thinks I need to do.''

''Now? Today? You're just gonna ride to town and blurt

this mess out and hope to high heaven he doesn't put you in a jail cell?''

Cassie nodded. "Something like that. I hope he'll let me come back here, seeing as I'm not likely to run off.''

"Do you want me to go with you?'' Clara asked stoutly. "I've known Carl Mosley a good long time. He'll listen to me.''

Cassie shook her head. "No, I have to do this myself. Besides, you have to finish fixing dinner.'' She chewed on her lip, stilling its trembling. "Please. I don't want Will to know till I'm ready to tell him.''

The need for silence was implicit, and Clara agreed with a silent nod.

"Where'd she go? It's time for dinner and it's not like Cassie to be late. Hell, it's not like Cassie to be runnin' off in the middle of the morning!'' Will's loud protest rang out boldly, never mind that he'd been out on the farthest pasture all morning, unavailable should Cassie want to talk to him, let him know her destination. Clara, hands full with a stew pot, holding it by the metal handle, looked up at him with steel in her gaze.

"If you don't get out of my way, you're gonna be wearin' this stew right down your front, Will Tolliver! I swear, I've never seen such a fussbudget. Cassie went for a little ride. Maybe she decided to stop at Eben's to see Louise. She was feelin' a bit edgy this morning. Probably thought it would do her good to get some fresh air.'' She plopped the heavy pot on the table. "I doubt she thought she had to ask your permission. She's a big girl.''

"Not very,'' Will grumbled.

Somewhat mollified, he sat down at the table, muttering beneath his breath as Jeremiah and Josie came in the door. Josie was full of excitement over the colts she was helping to train, and her eyes sparkled. Jeremiah walked carefully, his gait stiff, his demeanor subdued as he favored his left side. Bruises covered his face, and one eye was still swollen almost shut, but at his insistence, Josie had allowed him to move them back into the bunkhouse.

For one night he had stayed in the big bedroom upstairs, Josie sitting by his side. Finally, toward morning, Jeremiah had awakened and reached to pat the bed beside him.

"Lie down here," he'd murmured, his one good eye peering at his wife. "I need to touch you and know you're close by."

She'd done as he bid, and after the second day's rest in that big bed he'd told her to help him walk back to the home they had made. She'd begun to argue, but a long look from Will had halted her fretting, and under Clara's watchful eye they'd made the trek down the stairs and out the back door.

This morning Jeremiah had risen and asked for help dressing. Josie had complied with a minimum of fuss, and he'd watched as she worked with the young horses all morning. Now he sat at the dinner table and quietly filled his plate.

"How you doin'?" Will asked in an undertone.

A long glance from dark, enigmatic eyes was his answer. Eyeing his fork, laden with meat and a chunk of carrot, Jeremiah opened his mouth, only to find the bite too large to handle. His swollen lips refused to part more than a small distance and he was finally reduced to mashing the vegetables before he scraped them onto his fork.

Will watched surreptitiously, slowing his own chewing as he kept time with the other man's progress. Watchful of the open door, ever aware of the absence of his wife, he ate with an absentminded air. Only when he was scraping the second helping from his plate did he finally catch sight of Cassie's horse approaching from the town road.

"Here she comes now," he said, shoving back from the table as he wiped his mouth with his napkin. The screen door slammed behind him as he stepped out onto the back porch. "Cass! Wait up!" he called, heading across the yard to where she rode at an easy lope.

She turned, pulling back on the reins as she saw him coming, and her brown mare eased to a walk, straining at the bit as if she scented the oats waiting in her stall.

"You all done eating dinner, Will?" Cassie asked.

"Yeah, mine and your share, too." He stalked to where she sat atop the horse and grasped the bridle beneath the bit. "Where'd you go? I hope you didn't go into town with britches on." His voice was rough and demanding, and he almost winced as he recognized the abrasive tone he'd used.

Cassie hesitated, cocking her head to one side as she looked at him. "What's the problem? Can't I go for a ride without you being upset with me? And how do you expect me to ride in a skirt? Of course I have britches on." She lifted her right leg over and slid to the ground, removing her gloves as she watched her husband.

"I'm not upset," he said shortly.

"You coulda fooled me." Cassie tucked the gloves in her back pocket and stepped to her horse's head, removing the reins from Will's hand. Pacing at a steady gait, she made a wide circle around Will, speaking soothingly to the animal as she walked, barely acknowledging Will's presence.

"I was worried." It was an admission he gave grudgingly, as if he were unwilling to explain his actions.

"I'm old enough to ride down the road without you stewing over me," Cassie answered, her attention focused on the mare, who was obviously more interested in her stall than in the cooling-down process Cassie was instigating.

"I didn't know where you'd gone."

"If I didn't know better, I'd think you were pouting," Cassie said archly, a smile barely touching her lips.

"I missed you at the dinner table."

"I'm a little hungry, now that I think about it," she said cheerfully. "If you want to put my horse up, I'll go on in the house and see if there are any leftovers."

He took the reins from her hand, his callused fingers gripping hers for a moment. "Maybe you'd better take a rest after you eat," he said gruffly, his gaze on the curve of her bottom where the denim stretched to fit. "I don't want you to overdo."

"Everything go all right?" Clara asked in an undertone.

Cassie nodded. "Sheriff Mosley sent you his regards. I told him what I told you and he said he'd wire Loco Junction and ask about it. He said I could come home, and he'd be out to see me as soon as he hears something."

"Are you worried?"

Cassie shook her head. "No, I'm relieved. I feel like a load's been taken from me. I stopped to check on Louise and she was complaining that nothing in her wardrobe fits anymore, and she said she's got feet kicking in every direction. You don't suppose she's going to have twins, do you?"

Clara lifted her shoulders and sighed. "Could be. My mama was a twin, and I had twin brothers. Eben may be getting himself two at a time. I'll bet he's hopin' for boys. One, at least."

Cassie's fork paused midair. "I wonder what Will is looking for. Do you suppose he'll be disappointed if I have a girl?"

A deep voice sounded from behind her, where a tall figure stood just outside the screen door. "All Will wants is a healthy baby. I'm not partial to sons. We'll take whatever we get."

Cassie spun around, rising from her chair as Will came in the door. "I didn't know you were out there," she said, catching her breath. "You startled me."

He leaned to look past her at the plate she'd abandoned. "You need to clean up your dinner. You're eatin' for two, you know."

"Your mother loaded it up, and I'm just about as full as I'm going to get," Cassie said firmly. "Between the two of you, I'm going to be too fat to climb out of bed in the mornings before long."

"Leave her be, Will," his mother said mildly, heading for the back door with damp dish towels, ready to hang them on the short line she kept strung across the porch.

"Can't do that," he said sadly, looking mournfully at his wife. He bent to whisper in Cassie's ear, softly lest his mother overhear. "I need to see you upstairs for a little while. I'll let you get away without cleaning your plate if you'll come quietly."

Cassie nodded. "All right." Carrying her plate to the sink, she followed his lead, through the kitchen door and across the hall to the stairs. He walked up almost soundlessly, turning at the top to hold out his hand. She accepted it and was drawn to his side.

Puzzled, she entered their room and watched as he closed and locked the door. "What is it, Will?" He walked toward her, his eyes dark and narrowed, his gait ambling as he approached her side.

"I missed you, Cass. You weren't here when I came in for dinner, and I got to thinking about what it was like before I found you. I ate my meals alone, for the most part. I slept alone, and I was lonesome as hell most of the time."

"You don't have to be alone anymore," she told him, hoping with all her heart that it was the truth. Sheriff Mosley had been encouraging, but even he wasn't able to make any promises, and she hadn't expected any.

"I plan on sleepin' with you the rest of my life," Will said simply, reaching out to draw her against his long body. "You fit me real good, honey." His sigh was deep and his smile was winsome as he bent his head to her, his kiss soft and gentle against her mouth.

She reached her arms to circle his neck, standing on tiptoe to better reach him. "I thought I was supposed to be resting after my dinner, Will. If I'm not mistaken, you seem to have other ideas. And what do you think your mother is going to make of this?"

"I believe she's gone out to the garden," he said softly. "She's a pretty smart lady, sweetheart. She probably doesn't want to hear me scolding you for being late to dinner."

"Is that what you're doing?" She slipped her hands from his neck, flattening them against his chest until she was able to pay her full attention to the buttons of his shirt. One by one they separated from the handmade buttonholes as she eased her way down toward the wide belt that held his pants in place.

Will's head was bent, his teeth nibbling at her ear, and he nodded, his words a deep-throated admission of his intent. "I'm gonna take a long time to put you in your place, Mrs. Tolliver." His big hands lifted her, one beneath her knees, the other across her shoulder blades, and he carried her across the room.

She twined her fingers in the curly mat of hair she'd exposed with her actions and tugged. "In my place?" One eyebrow arched as she tilted her head.

"Well, it's where I like having you, come sundown every day." His chuckle was smothered against her throat as he bent to lower her to the bed. One knee on the mattress, he cradled her against himself, then allowed her to slide to the big feather pillow. He followed her down, leaning up on one elbow, his other hand already busy with the buttons on the front of her shirt.

"How'd you get those pants done up?" he asked gruffly, his heated gaze warming her through the batiste camisole she wore. The buttons were tiny, close together and more than troublesome, judging by his fumbling attempts. His fingers stilled their manipulations and he cleared his throat.

"I think you'd better do this, honey. I don't want to tear this pretty little thing, and I don't know how much longer I'm gonna be able to wait to see what it's hiding."

She felt a thrill of delight at his words, her woman's heart pleased by the urgency of his need. He was ready for her, his arousal nudging her thigh, ruddy color edging his cheekbones. His fingers warmed her through the fine cotton fabric, coaxing the peaks of her breasts to his bidding, a low growl denoting his satisfaction.

"Why don't we just sit you up and pull the whole kit and caboodle over your head?"

"I've got them all undone," she told him, her words breathless as she slid the last button from its place.

His hands were there, grasping hers, placing them firmly on the quilt, silently bidding them to remain still. Long, agile fingers returned to the swollen firmness of her breasts, heavy with pregnancy, tender to his touch, the firm crests a silent admission of her arousal.

He bent to suckle her and she cried out, a whimpering sound that brought his head erect, his eyes seeking hers. "Did I hurt you, baby? I wouldn't do that. I'm sorry."

She shook her head, seeing him through a blur of tears. "No! It isn't that. It's just that everything is so much more...I feel it way inside of me when you do that. I can hardly stand the pleasure of it, Will." She felt a flush creep up from her throat to cover her face. "You'll think I'm brazen, telling you that," she whispered, her eyes closing against the heat of his gaze.

"Oh, sweetheart, you can tell me anything you want to. I love it when I make you feel good, don't you know that?"

He bent his head to her again, his mouth gentle, his tongue laving her tender flesh, and she shivered. "I love you, Will." She whispered the words, the admission one she was wary of repeating, knowing he would not welcome it.

He stilled, his lips brushing a final salute against her flesh.

"I know you don't feel that way about me, Will. It's all right, really. I wasn't going to tell you again. It just slipped out. Please don't think I'm trying to make you..." Her words whispered between them and her eyes begged his indulgence as he watched her in silent appraisal.

And then he smiled—a pleading, tender message, conveyed by lips that touched her gently. "I made you feel bad the last time, didn't I? I'm sorry, honey. I've never told a woman I loved her." His brow furrowed briefly. "I'm not sure I know what love's supposed to feel like."

"Well, I've never said those words to another person in my life before, except my mother, and I don't think that counts," she said soberly.

"I'm glad you chose me, that I'm the one you love," he told her after a moment, rubbing his cheek against the fullness of her breast, as if unable to meet her gaze any longer.

His hands moved to her waist and he pushed at the denim pants she wore. "You don't even have these things done up, just this belt holdin' them together," he said with a dry chuckle.

"They don't fit anymore. I had to let my shirt hang over the top." She lifted her bottom as he wiggled the pants past the curve of her hips and down the length of her legs. Then, tucking his thumbs in the top of her drawers, he stripped them off in an easy motion.

One big hand stretched across the swell of her belly and he held it still, spanning her from one hipbone to the other. "It's hard to believe that there's really a baby in there," he said quietly, his eyes closing as he tested her resilient flesh, pressing firmly as if he would measure the child within.

"Sometimes I can feel it move," she said, closing her eyes against the pure pleasure of his touch. It was strangely sensual, this exploration of the tiny life they had managed to create. A sensation like that of butterfly wings trembling in a breeze caught her attention, and she reached to press his hand more firmly against the movement.

"Can you feel that?" It came again, stronger this time, nudging her with a minuscule limb, if she could trust her judgment. From beneath Will's fingertips the small being wiggled, perhaps protesting his encroaching presence, as he pressed her flesh more firmly.

"Cassie? Was that the baby? That little thumpy thing that was right there?" He wiggled his index finger against her and she laughed aloud, pleased by the wonder in his voice.

"He's letting you know he's in there," she whispered, her hands covering his as quick tears formed in her eyes. She did that a lot these days, her love for the child she carried spilling over in a happiness that could find release only in tears of joy.

"It stopped," he said after a moment, disappointment rife in the announcement.

"Your mother says that I'll soon be wishing for peace and quiet, when it gets bigger and takes up all the room down there."

"Will there still be room for me? Can we still...you know." His hand crept lower, his fingers sifting through the curls that guarded her woman's flesh. She moved against his touch, her legs allowing him room.

"I don't know why not," she whispered, her voice quivering as his hand pressed deeper. "I'll go see Doc next time I go to town. Maybe I should ask him."

"You're so soft, Cassie. I'm always afraid I'll hurt you, that maybe I'm too big. I've been tryin' not to lay on you too heavy lately." His voice was a soothing whisper, his fingers coaxing her with a slow rhythm, as if he would ease the way for his swollen manhood.

She reached for him, her hands pressing against his head, fingers twining in the heavy fall of his hair, guiding him to suckle the flesh he had abandoned for the moment.

"Please!" Her whisper was urgent and he complied, his groan of satisfaction the response she had hoped to gain. Her breath was quick and shuddering, her eyes closing tightly against the heated pitch of pleasure his fingers created.

And then he was gone, his hands on either side of her as he rose to find his place, urging her to accommodate him with swift yet gentle movements of her limbs. She reached for him, unwilling to lose the heat of his body, crying out softly as she grasped his waist, pulling him down to rest against her.

He leaned on his forearms lest he crush her, his arousal seeking entrance, and she lifted her hips to the nudging presence, opening and shifting as she pressed upward. And then a sigh of satisfaction whispered from her lips as she contained him. A groan of near fulfillment escaped from between his gritted teeth as he measured his length within her.

Their bodies moved together, with a knowledge imprinted over the nights of loving they had known in this bed. He shifted and she moaned. He lifted himself and she grasped him with the force of one denied. His teasing abated and he bent to her, his movements more forceful, far beyond the soothing of her tender flesh.

It was a coming together such as they had never shared, a dominant, urgent, almost primitive possession of her body that brought her to mindless pleasure. He lowered his mouth to accept her cries, muffling the sounds that burst from her in a crooning cadence of sheer delight. And as she subsided, her whimpers fading, her breathing shuddering against his lips, he rose above her.

His mouth twisting in a silent, wordless plea, his throat taut, his head lifted, he sought his own satisfaction, barely able to contain the fierce urgency that drove him. She met his demand with the force of her young body, seeking to pleasure him as if it were a gift she could afford him. Her rapture hardly less than his own, she held him closely as he muffled his words of fulfillment against her shoulder.

"Cassie!" He called her name softly, shuddering against her slender form, still enclosed within the sanctuary of her flesh.

Then, in the trembling aftermath, he rose a bit, holding his full weight from pressing against her, his mouth caressing her with countless kisses across her cheeks and forehead, whispering broken phrases. She twisted her head, seeking the warmth of his mouth and capturing it as he brushed across her lips. Her mouth was demanding as she opened her lips to his urgent caress, and she held him with hands that sought his attention, her fingers gripping tightly.

"I don't care if you want to hear it or not, Will Tolliver," she whispered fiercely. "I love you, and that's that!"

Chapter Nineteen

The leaves had begun to turn color and the corn in the field was in shocks, waiting to be loaded on the wagon. Shucking corn was a blister-breaking job, Will said. No one looked forward to it, so most everyone tried to get it done with a party thrown in to ease the chore.

The word was out. Will Tolliver was throwing a barn dance and corn shuckin', come the third Saturday in October. Eben brought his team early in the morning, Louise perched on the wagon seat next to him. Within minutes, another followed, Elizabeth keeping herd on the three boys riding on the flat wagon bed behind her and Samuel. Baskets of food accompanied them, and Clara was hard put finding places to store things.

Louise waddled. There was no other word to describe her gait, Cassie decided.

"You poor soul!" Clara exclaimed, hugging her daughter-in-law tightly. "It won't be long now, honey. I'll warrant you won't last till December, with that load you're carrying."

"Doc says maybe by Thanksgiving, from the size of me," Louise confided. "He thinks for sure it will be twins."

Cassie patted her own rapidly expanding girth. "For the first time in days I don't feel so fat," she said with a sigh, and then ducked as Louise responded with a fist upraised in feigned anger.

"My only consolation is that I'll be skinny come Christmas, and you'll still be totin' around a lapful," Louise answered smugly.

Clara laughed aloud, and Cassie looked up quickly. That particular sound had been missing from this household for longer than she wanted to remember. Since the day Bennett Percival had died, right out in the yard between the corncrib and the back porch.

"She's doin' better, isn't she?" Will asked quietly from the kitchen doorway.

Cassie nodded. "I thought she'd never laugh again," she whispered. "She's been carrying a load of guilt, Will. Even if the man was bad to the core, it's a blot on a person's soul to take a life."

"Come on, Cassie. Smile for me," Will whispered in her ear. "Don't let it bother you so, honey. You'd think some days that you were the one that fired that shotgun, instead of Ma. She'll be all right."

"You just don't know what it does, Will, to know that you've..." She hesitated, the words she'd held in abeyance on the tip of her tongue.

"To know what, Cass? What are you tryin' to say?" He turned her, one hand firm on her arm, the other grasping her shoulder. His eyes swept over her face, as if he sought an answer in the expression she wore.

"Will you two move out of that doorway?" Clara called from across the room. "Eben's tryin' to get in with an armload of food and you're blockin' his way. Seems to me you could lend a hand, Will, instead of snugglin' up with Cassie there."

Louise laughed from her perch atop a stool near the table. "He'd better snuggle now. She'll be lookin' like me before long and he won't be able to get those long arms around her anymore."

Will's mouth twisted in a wry grin. "Don't you worry, Louise. She'll never get big enough to keep me away." He turned Cassie to the door, allowing Eben to pass them. His hand beneath her chin, he lifted Cassie's face, his eyes watchful, with unanswered questions alive within their depths.

"I want to talk to you later on, you hear?" It was not a request. Even as a whisper, the tone of his voice brought a moment of panic to Cassie's heart.

She nodded her reply, unable for a moment to meet his gaze. "I need to tell you about something, Will." She closed her eyes against his gaze, unable to face him any longer with the burden of her guilt between them.

A wagon drew around the side of the house, harnesses jingling, its occupants shouting greetings, and Will turned to hail the occupants.

"I need to help your mother," Cassie said quickly, waving a hand at the Barnwell family as they began unloading their contributions to the all-day celebration.

Almost reluctantly, Will released her, his long look a silent reminder of their unfinished conversation.

In an almost jubilant mood, Cassie went back into the house. Today she would tell him. It was almost as if he already knew, as if his suspicions were aroused. She smiled to herself. It would be like setting free her spirit, to finally tell Will the truth, to make things right between them.

A long table made of planks set up on sawhorses provided a place for the crowd to eat beneath the trees in the side yard. Beneath the overhanging branches, where autumn leaves had just begun to fall in earnest, several quilts had been spread, providing a place for children to stretch out for naps.

"It's a perfect day, isn't it?" Clara asked wistfully. "Look out there at Jeremiah, working along with the men. Nobody seems to be makin' a fuss over him bein' what he is, do they?"

Cassie watched for a few minutes as the men worked together, unloading corn into the crib by the bushelful, their noisy joshing making fun of an onerous chore.

"There'll always be some who won't want him here," she said quietly, "but most folks are coming to accept him."

"Marrying up with Josie was what caused the most of the trouble. Till then, they didn't mind that he was here."

"They knew it wouldn't be easy," Cassie said bluntly. "And someone will always be around to point a finger and have something to say about them. I guess it's just the price they have to pay for breaking the rules people have lived by for a lot of years."

"Doesn't make it right," Clara said stoutly.

Cassie shot her a look of disbelief. That Clara, who had been the last of the family to accept the marriage with a degree of goodwill, should now be a staunch defender of the union was almost not to be believed.

"He's pret' near half white, after all," Clara added, and then with a sheepish look in Cassie's direction ducked her head. "I was wrong to shun him at first, Cassie. He's a good man. He's made Josie happy, and Maggie loves him."

Throughout the afternoon Cassie worked unceasingly beside Clara and several of the other women, filling and refilling bowls and platters and carrying them out to the tables where the workers ate in shifts. Children ran beneath the trees and down the lane to the cornfield, picking up stray cornstalks and carrying them back, waving like trophies over their heads.

And then, as the sun began to seek the horizon, the activity slowed. The corncrib was almost full to bursting, great piles of cornstalks mute reminders of the work accomplished. A collection of varicolored ears hung along the wall of the barn, souvenirs of the husking, each a precious discovery, guaranteeing its finder a kiss from the person of their choice.

A great hullabaloo had gone up as Eben had waved his trophy in victorious celebration, and he was the butt of many jokes as several men passed his way to comment on the kissing he'd already obviously done.

Louise blushed prettily, aware of her position of honor as Eben's wife and a favorite among the ladies. Elizabeth held her youngest on her lap, Luke sucking his thumb as he fought droopy eyelids. And amidst it all, Cassie basked in the reflected glow of the family she had so long yearned to possess.

In the barn a fiddle began to sound out a quick refrain, and John Hogan was summoned to call a square dance from the small platform they'd hastily constructed. A few of the men sat at the long table, unobtrusively passing a jug of homebrew down the line, pouring it into their empty coffee cups.

"You gonna dance, Cassie?" Clara called out.

Cassie turned from her position near the barn door, where she'd been wistfully watching the couples forming squares. She shook her head. "I don't know where Will is. Besides, I need to help clear the food."

Clara shook her head. "You've done your share, girl. Go find that man of yours and at least watch the fun. They'll be playin' some slow music later on, when Myrtle Hogan gets her accordion out."

Cassie stepped into the barn, sighting Will at the back, near the box stalls. He met her gaze across the distance, his look sober, and then with a nod he began making his way to where she stood. The dancers were in motion now, swirling and circling the floor, their laughter rising in unison with the sound of flying feet against the wooden floor.

From outside the barn a new voice caught Cassie's ear, and she turned to watch as Sheriff Mosley walked toward her, a tall stranger at his side. With a sinking heart she focused on the man, knowing already that her time had run out. With anxious eyes she turned again to locate Will, but he had halted to speak to a neighbor, his own gaze glancing in her direction even as he spoke.

"Miz Tolliver." Sheriff Mosley nodded a greeting as he faced Cassie. "This here is a U.S. marshal from Texas. He's come to talk to you."

"Now?" Cassie managed the single word in a hushed whisper. "Can it wait till tomorrow?"

The marshal shook his head. "I've got business in St. Louis in another day or so, ma'am. If we could get this out of the way this evening, it'd be a big help to me."

"Maybe on your way back from St. Louis?" Cassie asked quietly, her eyes darting to where Will stood. He'd clapped a hand on the neighbor's shoulder and now, even as she watched, he began to make his way past the dancers, idle now as they waited for the music to begin once more.

"I'm sure Will's gonna want to come along," Sheriff Mosley said quietly. "We just need to get a statement down in writing from you, Miz Tolliver."

"He doesn't know." Cassie closed her eyes as she spoke the words. "I was going to tell him tonight."

"Tell me what, Cass?" He was behind her, his warmth a welcome presence, and she turned to face him.

"I need to go to town with the sheriff and this gentleman

for a while, Will. You'd better stay here with the folks and keep things going,'' she said brightly, blinking her eyes lest the tears form.

"Cassie! What's going on?'' Elizabeth approached, her two-year-old sleeping on her shoulder. Brow furrowed, she cast a suspicious look at the lawmen.

"I have to go to town,'' Cassie repeated.

"I'll go along,'' Elizabeth told her firmly. "Just let me lay this child down somewhere.''

"No, it's all right, Elizabeth,'' Cassie said quickly, but the other woman had turned and sought out a quiet corner, tucking Luke in beside another sleeping youngster.

Louise approached slowly, hand on her back as she made her way to the door. "Is something wrong?'' Her gaze sought Cassie's face. "Can I help?''

"No!'' Cassie said sharply. And then at Louise's stunned expression, she moved to hug her. "I'm sorry, sweetie. I didn't mean to shout at you.'' Her eyes seeking Will's, Cassie felt as though the darkness was overtaking her, even within the brightly lit barn.

"I'm going along,'' he said firmly. "I think you need to tell me what this is all about, Sheriff.''

"No, you stay here and sort things out, Will. Elizabeth and I will go with Cassie.'' Louise stood at the barn door, looking strangely majestic, like a ship in full sail, her mouth set, her chin lifted with firm purpose.

"I'll go, too.'' Clara spoke from the shadows. "Cassie needs womenfolk around her.''

"Well, hell, we don't need to make a party of it,'' Sheriff Mosley muttered, looking around the barn as the laughter halted and the neighbors began talking softly among themselves.

"I'll ride my horse,'' Will said. "I'll be right behind you, Cass.''

The covey of women headed from the barn toward the house, where a surrey had been left, the reins tied to the post at the corner of the porch. At the forefront, Sheriff Mosley walked with Clara, followed by the marshal, holding Cassie's arm in a gentle grip.

"What's going on?" Louise asked in an undertone, grasping Elizabeth's elbow as the other woman set a slower pace.

"It seems the lawman wants to talk to Cassie. Whatever it is, she needs to know we're there." Elizabeth looked at the heavily pregnant woman beside her. "Can you make it, Louise? Will you be all right?"

Louise nodded. "We have to stick together, don't we? We're all Tolliver women, after all."

The surrey was filled to overflowing, what with four women and the two men occupying the seats. "I'm glad I didn't bring a buggy," Carl Mosley said in Clara's ear. They were wedged in the front seat, and Clara looked as if she wasn't sure her position was entirely proper, squashed between the two big men.

The vehicle set off down the road at a smart clip, and Will turned to find his brothers and Jeremiah behind him.

"I'm goin' to town. I want the three of you to keep the party goin' till everybody's had enough dancin'," he said tersely.

Eben looked over his shoulder. "Is that Louise and Elizabeth in the back of that surrey?" His eyes squinted as he tried to make out the figures in the back of the fast-disappearing conveyance.

"Where's Elizabeth?" Samuel wanted to know. "I thought she was tending to Luke right over there." He pointed to where a group of women sat, occupied with their children, and his gaze scanned the area quickly, settling finally on the quilt in the corner where his son slept peacefully.

"What's goin' on, Will?" Josie ran up from where she'd been tending the tables, clearing the last of the food away. "Why'd Ma and the others leave that way?"

"I'm about to find out," Will said firmly. Heading for the farthest stall, he reached for a bridle and unlatched the stall door, within moments leading his stallion into the aisle.

Jeremiah carried the heavy saddle from the tack room and watched with the assembled neighbors as Will looked down at Josie. "Take care of things here, sis."

"I'll be back before you know it, folks," Will called out. "Keep the dance floor warm for us." With a show of merriment, he smiled, waving his hat at the group, then rode from the barn.

"We didn't need to make all this fuss, Cassie," Carl Mosley said, shaking his head at the assembled group of women. "We just need to take your statement, and the marshal will take it back to Loco Junction. They'll have a ruling when court comes in session next."

"A ruling on what?" Elizabeth asked with exasperation.

Cassie stepped apart from the group. "I killed my stepfather. Clara knows about it, and Sheriff Mosley, too."

"You? I can't believe it!" Louise exclaimed, moving to Cassie's side as if she would protect her from harm. "And even if you did," she blustered, "you must have had a good reason."

"Sounds like she did," the sheriff said mildly.

"I expect she'll tell you all about it later," Clara interjected. "Right now she needs to talk to the marshal. Let's the rest of us go sit down somewhere."

"No place to sit but in the cell, Clara," Carl told her bluntly. "You girls should have stayed back at the farm."

"Well, we'll just go sit in the cell, then," Louise said firmly. "Long as you don't lock us in."

"Nobody's getting locked up tonight," the marshal told them. "And this won't take long. I'll need a couple of witnesses, one besides you, Carl."

"I'll sign anything you want. Just get moving so we can get back to the party," Clara announced.

The three women sat together on the bed in the cell, watching as Cassie spoke to the marshal, haltingly at first, then more firmly. His pen moved quickly over the paper, his upraised hand stopping her several times as he scribbled to keep up with her words.

Hardly had she told the brief tale when the office door opened and Will crossed the threshold. "What the hell's goin' on here?" He stood before the sheriff with anger and exasperation alive on his face.

Turning to where Cassie stood by the desk, pen in hand as she prepared to affix her signature to the document before her, he shook his head. "Don't you sign anything, hear me, Cass?"

"I have to, Will." Her head bent as she wrote her name, Will snatching the pen from her fingers as the last letter was barely written.

'I'll witness it," Clara said from the jail cell.

"What are you doin' in there?" Will asked with a shout, his gaze swinging from Cassie to his mother, and then his eyes registering disbelief as he saw the three women sharing the edge of the bed. "What the hell…"

"We came along to be with Cassie," Louise said firmly.

"In jail?" Will's roar was enough to raise the roof, Cassie thought as she reached for his hand.

"It's all right," she told him.

"Hell if it is!" He grasped her by the shoulders and shook her, not as gently as he might. "What are you signin', Cass?"

"A confession." Her chin rose, and her eyes met his with more than a trace of fear in their depths.

"More like a statement, I'd say," Carl Mosley said soothingly.

"A confession of what?" His voice a whisper, Will looked at his wife. "Is this what I think it is, Cassie?"

"If you think it's about Remus Chandler, you're right," she answered, her voice shaking just a bit. "I killed him, Will. I didn't just run off like I told you I did. I stabbed him with that knife and left him dead on the floor. He was going to…you know…" Her teeth gritted together as she fought the sobs that would have blurred her words.

"Why didn't you tell me before?" Will's hands eased their grip and he stepped back from her, his eyes flat and lifeless.

"I wanted to. I tried to, a lot of times. This morning, even. I was going to tell you tonight, after everyone was gone."

He shook his head. "Were you?"

Clara bustled out of the cell. "Where do I sign that thing, Carl?" Her gaze was troubled as she glanced at her son. "This girl's had about all she can take for one night. We need to get her home."

Her eyes were piercing as she turned to Cassie, her arms reaching to hug her tightly. "I know you didn't do anything wrong, Cassie. It will all turn out all right."

"You can say that again," Elizabeth said, her arm around Louise's waist as they rose from the cot to join the group. "From what I heard, Cassie was within her rights."

"That'll be up to the judge in Loco Junction to decide," the marshal put in with a warning look. "I can't second-guess him any more than you can, ma'am." He turned to Cassie and his smile was kind. "You'll be hearing from me, young lady. You won't be going anywhere, will you?"

"Just home, I hope," she whispered, her face pale in the lamplight.

"Damn right!" Will took her arm. "Let's go."

"Got room on that horse for the rest of us?" his mother asked smartly.

"You got here on your own. You can get back the same way," he told her, anger alive on the lean contours of his face. He paused to look at Clara for a moment. "You knew, didn't you?"

She nodded, her mouth set in a mutinous line. "She didn't have to hide from me, Will. I didn't make so much fuss about being all open and aboveboard as you did. Honesty's a fine thing, but when harpin' on it makes a woman afraid of spilling her soul out before you, it's gone too far."

His glare spoke volumes as the angry man lifted his wife into his arms. Cassie's arm snaked around his neck and she buried her face in his throat as he stalked through the doorway with her.

"I reckon we can use the surrey for a return trip, ladies," Carl said, his eyes on Clara. "You'll sit up front with me," he told her firmly.

It was a silent ride, the stallion settling into an easy lope as Will let him have his head. He held Cassie across his lap, nestled against his thighs. Even in his anger he was aroused by the movement of her bottom against him, and that fact added flame to the fire. Blasted woman, managing to worm her way into his life, all bedraggled and forlorn.

That he had taken hold of her life, blending it with his own, unheeding of anything but his need of this wonderful woman, was the farthest thought from his mind. Only the fact of her failure to confide in him gripped him now. Gripped him with the tenacious hold of a bulldog, blinding him to all but the one fault he found in her.

"Will, please let me..." Her whispered plea brought only fresh determination to his heart and he subdued her with a firmer grip upon her body.

"Not another word, Cass. I don't want to hear it."

She shivered in his embrace, and he glanced down at her pinched features. She ought to be afraid. Telling everyone in sight the sorry tale she'd kept from him. And after he'd asked her point-blank almost the first thing. Had she ever given him a straight answer?

His mind recalled the sodden heap of female he'd fished from the stream, the fearful look in her eyes, the courageous tilt of her chin as she told him to leave her behind, told him she didn't need tending. And all along he'd wanted nothing more than to care for her, yearned to keep her close, hungered for the warmth of her body.

He blinked against the image. She'd lied. After all the times he'd told her how important honesty was in his book, she'd lied. Perhaps not lied, his memory urged, but she'd hidden the truth.

The farmhouse appeared as a shadow on the horizon, limned against the bright light coming from the barn. The faint sound of the fiddle caught the air, and Will was struck by the irony of the sound. The happy tune was so at odds with the dearth of melody in his heart, he could have wept. And that fact alone was enough to spur his anger to greater heights.

Jeremiah met him at the barn door, taking charge of the big stallion as Cassie was swept from the saddle to be carried toward the house. "Your womenfolk will be here directly," Will called over his shoulder at his assembled brothers. "They'll tell you the whole story."

The dancers had retreated to the sides of the barn, settling down on benches and chairs as the fiddle and accordion tapered off to silence.

"Do you suppose we ought to chase everyone out?" Eben asked Samuel.

"Naw, let's have another dance. The preacher won't care if folks fall asleep during his sermon in the morning. In fact, he looks to me as if he'd like to swing his wife around the floor another time or two." Samuel stepped to the small platform and addressed the neighbors cheerfully.

"Come on, folks, let's form another square. We've got time for another dance or two." Stepping down, he grasped Dorinda Bartlett by the hand and motioned to his brother to find a partner. The fiddle twanged once and the caller began to count out the time.

She was sprawled on the bed where he'd placed her without a trace of care. Her dress caught above her knees, tangled around her so that she could barely move, she lay silent, watching.

Will paced to the window and back, his mind at odds with the need of his body. How any man could be so angry and yet yearn so to touch the object of his anger was a puzzle he didn't seem able to solve. He drew a deep breath, aware of the lure of the woman before him, only too conscious of the fury that still rode him with thorns of pride.

"And there you lie, like I'm supposed to just say 'forget the whole thing.' Like I'm not supposed to be mad about it."

Cassie scooted up against the headboard. "I never said that. I never even thought it. I don't blame you for being mad. I just hope it doesn't last longer than time for the baby to be born."

"The baby." He halted his pacing to stare at her. "The

baby!'' His steps took him to the side of the bed and he sat on the edge. ''I forgot the baby. I was so damn mad, I forgot the baby. Oh, God! Did I hurt you, Cass? Did I do anything to hurt the baby?''

In a tentative move his hand reached for her, resting on the curve of her belly, and his fingers spread, encompassing the swell of the child within. He bent his head and closed his eyes, moving his palm over the hard rise of her pregnancy, his fingers taut against her flesh through the layers of fabric.

''It's all right, Will. I'm not hurt. You wouldn't do anything to hurt me.''

He opened his eyes, and in the stream of pale moonglow he sought her gaze. His voice was strained, his mouth drawn into a narrow line. ''You have a lot of faith in me, Cassie.''

''I know you care for me,'' she said.

''Care for you!'' The mediocrity of the word was like a spur and his voice rose on each syllable. ''Damn it, woman, I love you! I was so worried about you, I could hardly stand it. I watched the sheriff and that damn lawman with him haul you away, and I didn't know what I'd have to do to get you out of that jail when I got there. And there those women were, the three of them sitting in the cell like they were having a tea party, and you there, signing your name to a paper I hadn't even read. You might have signed your life away, and I wasn't even there to stop you.''

Her smile was a welcome he could not resist and he bent to cover her with his body, his head against her breast.

''I'm so sorry, Will.'' It was a whisper, a plea, a cry for forgiveness. ''I didn't want to lose you. I meant to say the words…a hundred times I tried. But I was so afraid you wouldn't care enough about me to forgive me for not telling the truth at first.''

Her hands pressed his head against the firm cushion of her bosom and she ran her fingers through the dark strands of his hair, clenching them against his head. "At first I was afraid you'd turn me over to the nearest sheriff. Then when you told that lawman I was your wife, the second day we were together, I knew you'd hate me for causing you to tell such a story, and I didn't know what to do."

He was silent, inhaling the sweet scent of her body, his arms edging their way beneath her so that he could enclose her in his embrace. For long moments he held her, and then his head rose and he reached to brush a soft kiss across her mouth.

"I never got this mad at another living soul in my whole life, Cassie. You can make me happier and angrier than anyone else in the world. And at the same time. I don't know how you do it!"

"You're still angry?" Her voice was hopeful, as if she ached for a denial of her query.

"Hell, no, I'm not angry. I'm just nursing hurt feelings."

"I'll never keep anything from you again, Will. I promise." With barely a quaver, her words breathed the sound of relief.

"Nothing important, anyway," he prompted. "I suspect there are things that womenfolk talk about that men don't have to hear. But anything that concerns you and me and our children, those things I have to know. You understand me?"

She nodded eagerly. "I promise, Will." Bending forward, she kissed him again, a warm, damp caress that offered much. "Will? Can you tell me again? And say it nicely this time, not just hollering at me."

"Say what?" His voice muffled against her, he searched for the words she would have him speak.

"Will!" It was a plaintive cry, and he sat erect.

"What!"

"You told me you loved me, and you practically shouted it, like you didn't want to say the words."

"I did?" He thought a moment. "Yeah, I guess I did, didn't I?" His grin was spontaneous. "How about that? And I didn't even know I was going to tell you."

She retreated imperceptibly against the pillow. "Did you mean it?"

He swooped over her, his hands cradling her face, and his mouth pressed hot kisses against hers, punctuated with a series of words. "I..." He took her mouth slowly. "Love..." He nudged her lips apart. "You..." His words were lost in the sweetness of her mouth, and she seized him with eager fingers, her nails biting through the cotton material of his shirt.

"I love you, Will Tolliver. I love you. I love you."

"You haven't told me that in a long time," he whispered after a moment.

"You'll get tired of me saying it." She rubbed her nose against his, a slow, sensuous movement.

"Don't count on it, lady," he murmured as he settled himself on the bed, pulling her down to nestle in his arms. "Don't count on it."

Epilogue

Carl Mosley left the town to fend for itself on Thanksgiving Day, arriving bright and early with news for Cassie and Will that made the day perfect from top to bottom. The judge in Loco Junction had decreed that the death of Remus Chandler was a case of self-defense, and since no one in that town gave two hoots and a holler about the dead man, the case was considered closed.

Staying until the moon was high in the sky, Carl made great strides in his courtship of Clara Tolliver, a project that gained the full approval of all her children. All three of her sons were making bets on the wedding date.

Josie had taken on the task of training the foals and yearlings, leaving Jeremiah free to work the farm with Will. Most of the town had turned out for a house-raising for Josie and her husband. Maggie was making noises to whoever would listen, complaining that she was tired of everyone else having new babies and it was about time for her mama to produce one, too.

Eben and Louise's twins were one of each, born right after Thanksgiving. Louise was Johnny-on-the-spot when Cassie went into labor. "Nothing to it," Louise blithely said, sailing into Cassie's bedroom.

"Yours weren't almost ten pounds," Cassie had grumbled later. Born during a snowstorm, Adam Tolliver made his arrival in the same bed in which he was conceived, right after the New Year. He was to be the first of many sons, his father said, once he'd gotten over the agony of bringing a child into the world.

He'd held Cassie, groaning with her throughout each pain, until old Doc threatened to send him from the room. He'd rubbed her back, let her pull on his hands until they were red and scratched to smithereens, and then knelt beside the bed to press his face into her pillow as she cried out at the last.

Two days later, clutching the tightly wrapped bundle to her breast, Cassie received company. Her mouth pressed tender kisses against his wrinkled brow as her son nursed, and in the chair across the room Louise rocked with a babe in each arm.

"They'll be good friends," Cassie predicted, and Louise nodded agreement.

"You'll have to hurry to produce a little girl to keep mine company," she said with a smile.

"Not me," Cassie told her vehemently. "At least not for a year or two. Maybe Elizabeth can do the trick."

"Elizabeth?"

Cassie grinned. "She told me yesterday. It's due late summer." She tipped the baby over her shoulder and patted his back. "Do you think she'll have a girl?"

Louise snorted, an inelegant sound, but permissible since there were no menfolk present. "Don't count on it. Samuel's still determined to have a boy named John."

Cassie shook her head. "He may have to settle for a Joan or Joanna. Who knows?"

"Life's good, isn't it, Cassie? With you and Will and Jeremiah showing up and the both of them working the farm. Clara was so pleased that Will married you." Louise rocked steadily, looking the picture of mother love. "You really love him, don't you?"

Cassie nodded, deep emotion so close to the surface it almost lit her face from within. "More than I can say. When I think back to what might have been, and what Will made of my life, I can hardly believe it."

"When Will did what?" His low voice from the doorway brought Louise to her feet, and she whispered a goodbye as she left the room, grinning widely at Will as she passed him in the doorway.

"Will! Come see your son." Cassie waved him near, and he obliged, sitting on the edge of the bed, bending over his wife and child.

"When Will did what?" he repeated, his mouth brushing against the black downy fuzz that covered his son's head.

Cassie reached for him, her fingers tender against his face, her eyes glowing with a love she could not conceal. "When Will brought me here and learned to love me," she said.

"Will still loves you," he told her. "With all he is, he loves you, Cassie."

"I know," she whispered through happy tears. "I know."

* * * * *

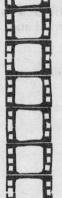

Welcome to *Love Inspired*™

A brand-new series of contemporary inspirational love stories.

Join men and women as they learn valuable lessons about facing the challenges of today's world and about life, love and faith.

Look for the following June 1998 Love Inspired™ titles:

SUDDENLY DADDY
by Loree Lough

IN GOD'S OWN TIME
by Ruth Scofield

NEVER ALONE
by Lyn Cote

Available in retail outlets in May 1998.

LIFT YOUR SPIRITS AND GLADDEN YOUR HEART with *Love Inspired!*™

Steeple Hill™

I698

MEN at WORK

All work and no play? Not these men!

April 1998

KNIGHT SPARKS by Mary Lynn Baxter

Sexy lawman Rance Knight made a career of arresting the bad guys. Somehow, though, he thought policewoman Carly Mitchum was framed. Once they'd uncovered the truth, could Rance let Carly go...or would he make a citizen's arrest?

May 1998

HOODWINKED by Diana Palmer

CEO Jake Edwards donned coveralls and went undercover as a mechanic to find the saboteur in his company. Nothing—or no one—would distract him, not even beautiful secretary Maureen Harris. Jake had to catch the thief—*and* the woman who'd stolen his heart!

June 1998

DEFYING GRAVITY by Rachel Lee

Tim O'Shaughnessy and his business partner, Liz Pennington, had always been close—but never *this* close. As the danger of their assignment escalated, so did their passion. When the job was over, could they ever go back to business as usual?

MEN AT WORK™

Available at your favorite retail outlet!

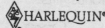 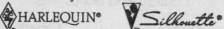

DEBBIE MACOMBER

invites you to the

HEART OF TEXAS

Join Debbie Macomber as she brings you the lives
and loves of the folks in the ranching community
of Promise, Texas.

If you loved Midnight Sons—don't miss
Heart of Texas! A brand-new six-book series
from Debbie Macomber.

Available in February 1998
at your favorite retail store.

Heart of Texas by Debbie Macomber

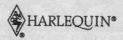
HARLEQUIN®

HARLEQUIN ULTIMATE GUIDES™

A series of how-to books for today's woman.

Act now to order some of these extremely
helpful guides just for you!

*Whatever the situation, Harlequin Ultimate Guides™
has all the answers!*

#80507	HOW TO TALK TO A	$4.99 U.S. ☐	
	NAKED MAN	$5.50 CAN.☐	
#80508	I CAN FIX THAT	$5.99 U.S. ☐	
		$6.99 CAN.☐	
#80510	WHAT YOUR TRAVEL AGENT	$5.99 U.S. ☐	
	KNOWS THAT YOU DON'T	$6.99 CAN.☐	
#80511	RISING TO THE OCCASION		
	More Than Manners: Real Life	$5.99 U.S. ☐	
	Etiquette for Today's Woman	$6.99 CAN.☐	
#80513	WHAT GREAT CHEFS	$5.99 U.S. ☐	
	KNOW THAT YOU DON'T	$6.99 CAN.☐	
#80514	WHAT SAVVY INVESTORS	$5.99 U.S. ☐	
	KNOW THAT YOU DON'T	$6.99 CAN.☐	
#80509	GET WHAT YOU WANT OUT OF	$5.99 U.S. ☐	
	LIFE—AND KEEP IT!	$6.99 CAN.☐	

(quantities may be limited on some titles)

TOTAL AMOUNT	$
POSTAGE & HANDLING	$
($1.00 for one book, 50¢ for each additional)	
APPLICABLE TAXES*	$ _____
TOTAL PAYABLE	$ _____

(check or money order—please do not send cash)

To order, complete this form and send it, along with a check or money
order for the total above, payable to Harlequin Ultimate Guides, to:
In the U.S.: 3010 Walden Avenue, P.O. Box 9047, Buffalo, NY
14269-9047; **In Canada:** P.O. Box 613, Fort Erie, Ontario, L2A 5X3.

Name: _____

Address: _____ City: _____

State/Prov.: _____ Zip/Postal Code: _____

*New York residents remit applicable sales taxes.
Canadian residents remit applicable GST and provincial taxes.

HARLEQUIN®

Look us up on-line at: http://www.romance.net

HNFBL4

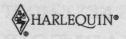

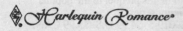

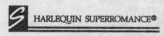